Aquarian Dawn

Aquarian Dawn

a novel

Ebele Chizea

THREE ROOMS PRESS
New York, NY

Aquarian Dawn
A Novel by Ebele Chizea

© 2022 by Three Rooms Press

All rights reserved. No part of this book may be reproduced in any form or by any electronic or mechanical means, including information storage and retrieval systems, without permission in writing from the publisher, except by a reviewer, who may quote brief passages in a review. For permissions, please write to address below or email editor@threeroomspress.com. Any members of educational institutions wishing to photocopy or electronically reproduce part or all of the work for classroom use, or publishers who would like to obtain permission to include the work in an anthology, should send their inquiries to Three Rooms Press, 243 Bleecker Street, #3, New York, NY 10014.

This is a work of fiction. Names, characters, businesses, places, events, and incidents are either the products of the author's imaginations or used in a fictitious manner. Any resemblance to actual persons, living or dead, or actual events is purely coincidental.

ISBN 978-1-953103-25-3 (trade paperback)
ISBN 978-1-953103-26-0 (Epub)
Library of Congress Control Number: 2022935368

TRP-100

Advance Reader Copy—Uncorrected Proof
Pub Date: October 25, 2022

Young Adult Fiction: Ages 14 and up
BISAC Coding:
YAF046120 Young Adult Fiction / People & Places / United States / African American & Black
YAF046020 Young Adult Fiction/ People & Places / Africa
YAF052070 Young Adult Fiction/ Romance / Multicultural & Interracial
YAF011000 Young Adult Fiction/ Coming of Ages

COVER DESIGN:
KG Design International: www.katgeorges.com
with design assistance from Kaitlyn Kinnard

BOOK DESIGN:
KG Design International: www.katgeorges.com

DISTRIBUTED IN THE U.S. AND INTERNATIONALLY BY:
Publishers Group West: www.pgw.com

Three Rooms Press
New York, NY
www.threeroomspress.com
info@threeroomspress.com

Please note: This is an uncorrected proof. Reviewers are reminded that changes may be made in this proof copy before books are printed. If any material from the book is to be quoted in a review, the quotation should be checked against the final bound book or approved by the publisher.

Aquarian Dawn

Part I

Coral High

Chapter One

January 1966

IT WAS THE END AND THE beginning. We had left dry, dusty winds for frigid cold. That previous November, Ma had separated from Ben Iheanachor, an esteemed Diplomat and the only father I knew. All she said was, "Sometimes you stay in there until it is time to move on."

We moved to a small, quaint Pennsylvania town called Greensberg—surrounded by hills and trees and bestowed with majestic seasons that revealed themselves in lush colors. Spring, green. Summer, yellow. Fall, brown, red, and orange. Winter, white. Greensberg differed from the flat lands and the dry and rainy seasons of Southern Nabuka. Ma was driving her dream car from the airport garage, a cerulean blue Cadillac. She was driving on the thick January snow to the radio sounds of *My Girl* by The Temptations, the winding roads and slopes a sign of the twists and turns, the highs, and lows to come, the wide space between us forcefully etched closer by each careful turn, ascent, and descent. As I pressed my brooding face into the side of the passenger side door, all I could see was a stream of white faces, the only black faces being Ma's and mine. Four years ago, we relocated from Ogu, our fishing village in Nabuka, to Lagoon, the country's capital for Ma's new work at a clinic. I was eleven at the time. After globe-trotting with Ben within a three-year span afterwards, I became familiar with the transitory process.

The house has three bedrooms, three bathrooms, two living rooms, a vast kitchen, and a basement with a laundry room, Ma explained to me as she drove, and was previously owned by an Army General whose only concern was selling to the highest bidder. She seemed unperturbed that a house formerly owned by one of the town's finest was now being coveted by a young, black, Afrikan woman with no husband and that this might easily push people the wrong way. In fact, I was certain it made her feel more accomplished.

Ma was a survivor. After I was born in 1951, she completed secondary school, university, and eventually, medical school. Of course, she couldn't have done it all without the sponsorship of The Catholic Missionary Society. At Saint Agnes Secondary school, reverend sisters draped in white and adorned with polished black rosaries were her teachers and mentors. According to Ma, they were extremely strict. She was always quick to add that little tidbit as if her current success was solely attributed to them. And maybe it was; even when Ma had gotten pregnant with me out of wedlock in her final year of secondary school, the reverend sisters had already instilled in her the supposed significance of confession and the sacrament of the Eucharist. As an act of penance, she learned her catechism, went for confession, and received the Blessed Sacrament under the supervision of Nne, my grandaunt, who soon after adopted her as her own upon learning Ma's parents wanted nothing to do with their now disgraced daughter.

Ma left a trail of dust behind in Ogu when she left for Pennsylvania after her secondary school education to pursue her prospects. This was in the fall of 1952. Ten years later, she had attained a medical school certificate (thanks to four years at Bryn Mawr College and another six of medical school and residency at the University of Pennsylvania), a contrived American accent, and several job offers in Lagoon where, in collaboration with The Catholic Missionary Society, a clinic was built. By then her and Ben's whirlwind romance had solidified into a marriage of two years. Ma was a doctor, and my stepfather was a diplomat, so we belonged to the elite class of Lagoon.

By age fifteen, I had traveled to a few countries and was rubbing shoulders with dignitaries. The people I met along the way deemed me to be fortunate. And perhaps I was, but, in reality, I had long settled into a state of detached melancholy.

When we arrived at our new home that New Year's morning, a Mrs. Susan McCormey, who I later discovered was a Bryn Mawr alumna and Ma's former classmate, was there to greet us. She was a nurse at Greensberg Center hospital; the same hospital Ma would be working at. Her much older husband, Mr. James McCormey, was the chairperson of the board of directors, securing Ma's position there—in addition to her credentials. It's fascinating what you can pick up in adult phone conversations.

I studied Mrs. McCormey with her cherry-shaped face, stringy blonde hair, and translucent eyes. She embraced Ma in the driveway with a chirpy greeting: "Happy new year, happy new life!" She embraced me too, commenting on how pretty I looked and how much she liked my "afro plaited ponytail," what we referred to as *shuku* back in Ogu. Ma enlightened Mrs. McCormey saying the correct term was cornrows. She went on to add that it was brains, not appearances, that mattered most, and that young girls needed to know this, especially in their teenage years.

The front door to the house had been left open. Seizing an opportunity to escape, I did a little foot dance, signaling my need to use the restroom, and disappeared inside. I walked into unfurnished spaces and tried to imagine the life of the general, if and how he loved his wife and children. I searched intuitively, and with open eyes, for anything that would reveal the nature of their existence, but there was nothing. It was as if the walls, the ceiling, and the floor had conspired with them to keep their secrets hidden. Or maybe they had made sure to carry their secrets with them. By the end of the tour, I wasn't sure if I even liked the house. Honestly, I was not sure of anything. I was in a dragging haze of uncertainty, which hovered ever so patiently, not eager to dissipate to something like normalcy.

I encountered a hallway on the main floor. There were two doors on the right side. The one closer to me was left ajar. The other, wasn't. I went through the open door to discover a bedroom. Alas, some furniture. So new, I could smell its newness. It was a white chest drawer with a large mirror attached to it. Ma must have purchased it beforehand with Mrs. McCormey's help, I thought. The rug was silver green, the flowery green curtains like Maria's bedroom curtains in *The Sound of Music.* Green, the color of life, the color of the heart, according to a book on colors and their symbolism that I had skimmed through years ago. I settled on the bed, which had a single sheet covering. From there, I could see my reflection in the mirror. I kneeled on the bed and peered out the window. A bed of weeds choked by snow. Beyond the weeds, more houses, like ours. Then I noticed the noise in the background—Ma and Mrs. McCormey were chatting over clacking teacups. "She has to focus on her studies. That should always come first," I heard Ma say, adamantly. In response, there was some protest from Mrs. McCormey, but I couldn't make out the words. I shut the bedroom door. Silence. Then I opened the window, took out a rumpled cigarette pack I had previously buried in my coat pocket, and in moments, I was puffing on a stick, the cold breeze navigating thin clouds away from the house.

I CAN'T EXACTLY SAY CIGARETTES MADE me feel better, at least at the time, but as I got ready for school the following Monday morning, I was going through them like a soap opera binge-watching marathon. I looked at my uniform: a white shirt tucked inside a dark blue skirt, and brown shoes with a knobby look at the tip. I hated them. They made me look studious, but Ma felt they were good because they were expensive. I scratched away one of the multiple skin itches caused by the panty hose against my skin and studied the orange light consuming the tail of my cigarette until it almost scalded my fingers.

I had learned how to smoke in France when I was fourteen. Pauline, a freckled girl with red hair, fluent in English, and the daughter of the French Ambassador to the United States, had taught me how. I remember choking multiple times during the first few lessons, but the process lasted only two days of what Pauline referred to as "intense training." We spent many evenings after catechism classes at a local church in Paris hiding in the woods, complaining about fourteen-year-old things, and puffing away.

My stepfather, Ben, had a habit of dropping me off at the church. Ma had remained in Lagoon to run the clinic, and I was in Paris with Ben as he worked to improve diplomatic relations just a few years after Nabuka threatened to cut ties. Something to do with France testing atomic weapons in the Sahara Desert in the early 60's, and other bullying tactics with regards to former/current Afrikan colonies. Ben hoped the catechism classes would instill in me some moral values as compensation for his absences, official and unofficial—the latter I chose not to bother with after I overhead him making arrangements, via a whisper, for a late-night rendezvous with a big-breasted blonde who had been part of the crew to welcome us at the airport when we arrived in Paris. Whenever he was free, we indulged in ice cream, took strolls, and discussed whatever came to mind. Ben's favorite topic was Afrika. He ascribed to Afrika's so-called "Edenic" past and encouraged me to feed my brain with books about ancient Afrikan Civilizations.

"But what for?" I asked him one evening during one of our strolls in a park.

"What else, but to learn about your past, understand the present, and make preparations for the future," he said in his baritone voice.

"But isn't that what the school system is for?"

"And what has this school system taught you so far?"

I scratched my head. The answer was "very little" and, for the most part, most of it was impractical information. I was always of the opinion that after learning to read and write, school was a waste of time, but I knew better than to express such sentiments to my teachers or Ma.

"Please don't tell your mother that we are having this discussion on the value of education," he half pleaded, as if he had just intercepted my thoughts. "Besides, without a formal education, I wouldn't be a diplomat."

On another stroll in the same park, as he was raving about Egypt, I asked him if any other civilizations had emerged from Afrika. He jumped at the question. "Of course! There was also Benin, Ghana, Afa Ukwu . . . Your own people came from there, one of the most spiritually advanced kingdoms in Afrika. There was also Nubia, Mali, Ethiopia, Kanem Bornu, and many others that rivaled or even surpassed Europe."

"But where is the evidence?" I asked.

"*Ezenwanyi*," he began, using a term denoting royalty, "there is more to civilization than structures, even though we certainly had those. Art, music, philosophy, metaphysics . . . the list goes on. When human ideals are aimed at and achieved, that is true civilization."

I pondered his words, recalling Pauline's concept of Afrika. She believed Afrika was filled with lions and tigers and pygmies, just as she had read in nature magazines. I explained with as much patience as possible that I once lived in the city of Lagoon, a city filled with cars, tall buildings, museums, universities, libraries, and people who wore clothes. She tried to swallow that concept but seemed to struggle with the notion that Afrika could really be as "civilized" as Europe. In those moments, I was tempted to tell her what Ben had revealed to me about the true meaning of civilization but ended up saying nothing. It seemed futile. It was easier to just switch to her favorite topic, boys.

"And you know who was black?" Ben asked, interrupting my thoughts.

Discreetly, I rolled my eyes and mouthed, *there we go again.*

"Cleopatra. Yes, she was black, *onye oji,* even though they are saying she had some Greek Ptolemy blood in her. Hannibal and even Jesus Christ were black too."

"What about Shakespeare? *Kedu maka ya?*" I chuckled.

"Ah, you think this is funny, eh? Okay, oh . . . "

"I've also heard he was black . . . "

"Yes, him also," he smiled sheepishly. "How else could he have depicted Othello so well?"

I burst out laughing. He shook his head, smiling."You don't have to accept everything I say. But question everything, you must." He moved on to his favorite subject, Pan-Afrika.

"A united Afrika is something I wish to see in my lifetime. It is the only way forward. Nnamdi Azikiwe, Kwame Nkrumah, Patrice Lumumba, they all knew what they were talking about."

"Who is Patrice Lumumba?"

"Nwamu, my child, what are they teaching you in school?"

I shrugged.

"First democratically elected Congolese Head of State. Pure revolutionary. But like many revolutionaries, he was killed. In a gruesome way too. They chopped that poor man to pieces . . ."

"Why?"

"Some say it was because he was willing to fight for Congolese interests."

I wanted to ask him to explain but was quickly interrupted.

"My dear, you are only fourteen. Don't fill your head with the mess adults have created. Enjoy your life. For example, your love life. Tell me what is going on there?"

"Pa, I'm only fourteen!" I said in protest, my cheeks flushed with embarrassment. "Ah . . . at your age, my father had already paid for my mother's bride price."

I shook my head and chuckled.

"Anyway, as I've told you, stop calling me Pa. It makes me feel so old," he said.

"What should I call you then?"

"Ben, like I have told you many times before. But not in front of your mom, of course."

"Of course," I said under my breath as I rolled my eyes.

I had shelved many of the things Ben said as overzealous ramblings born from the spirit of the times, but I appreciated his buoyant persona and humor, which contrasted with Ma's serious approach to life.

I could hear Ma's strident voice. She was on the phone, speaking Afa. She was saying it was appropriate for the Afa people to threaten secession since the rest of the country refused to progress. It was only six years ago that we gained independence. I could still remember it vividly: the celebration, the euphoria, the spirit of infinite possibilities that hung in the air, now swallowed up by constant socio-political bickering.

"Ada!"

It came out tense. I wasn't even aware that she had already hung up the telephone. Quickly, I ended my reverie, flung the cigarette out the window, shut the window, and sprayed lavender-scented perfume generously over myself. Of course, I did not neglect the mouth wash, which I would have preferred to spit out but for lack of time swallowed it instead. I felt slight dizziness as it fired my stomach. In minutes, I was facing her with my schoolbag. She let me know that I would be late for school. As I put on my scarf, she preached that a girl my age didn't need to wear perfume. That vanity would destroy me. I pretended not to hear. I wished her a good day and dashed off.

Bishop Coral High was only a quarter mile away. All I had to do was make a right on a steep road, a quick left, and I could see the main building sitting idly on a slope. When we moved into the house, Ma pointed out the school to me. She said it was one of the best in the area. Now, as I strolled towards the entrance, I came across a parking lot with several cars and no human in sight. I checked my watch. I was ten minutes late. I had lost track of time gazing at the white-capped hills, catching my breath at their picturesque appearance.

I found my way to the back of the school and sat on a large stone to indulge myself with a better view of the hills. The hills appeared gray against the morning sky. Even though I was shivering, and the ground was covered with snow, the sun was out in all its brilliance, providing a warm glaze. With stiff fingers, I pulled out my pack of cigarettes and indulged. At first a chain of three. Cold breaths mitigated by a slow buzz. Then it occurred to me that I didn't know the rules around smoking at this school. Was this one of those schools where smoking was banned? Of course, all schools were like that! What would happen if the principal, for example, sniffed it on me, would she send me home on my first day of school? Even worse, would she tell Ma? I took another drag, a deep one, to calm my nerves. I should have brought along my perfume!

She grew brighter, the sunshine. She was warm and friendly and appeared to be dancing towards me. It made me relax, forgetting my rising anxiety. Only then did I observe my surroundings closely. And as I usually did, I saw them—sprites, small, faint, and inconsequential in appearance as a caterpillar. Voices, as familiar as childhood friends, arose from the belly of the earth. I was missing out on something. I yearned to partake of life, of wonder. I closed my eyes to dissolve myself in earth's embrace when a squirrel brushed across my feet as if to warn me of an intrusion. I looked to my left and there she was, a student with long black hair observing me in the distance. I wondered how long she had been there, and if she had been watching me the whole time. What had led her to the back of the school when she was supposed to be in class? I thought I perceived a mischievous grin on her face but didn't scrutinize her long enough to confirm it. I rushed to the front of the building, my heart pounding, my lips tight, furious that an intimate ritual had been interrupted by a wandering student.

It was now 8:40 a.m. and the hall was empty, except for a few uniformed students pacing about. Some did a double take. Some stared, pointed at me, whispered, and scurried on. To my right was a row of blue lockers. A boy with orange hair, who looked about my age, jerked one of them open. I walked up to him and asked for directions to the principal's office. He said nothing, just glowered at me. Someone who had seen and heard me shouted that I make a left and walk straight to the end of the hall. I mumbled a quick 'thank you' at the voice and made my way to the office, too embarrassed to check the identity of the kind stranger.

Minutes later, I found the glass door with the inscription, OFFICE, in gold letters, and knocked hesitantly. "Come in!" said a friendly voice from behind the glass. I hoped they would not get a whiff of cigarette stench as I opened the door to genial faces seated behind wooden desks. Piles of paper and files lay on top of the desks. The room had two offices. Three women occupied three desks in the outer office. They all looked up when they saw me. From the inner office, a woman with large glasses held by strings and wearing her silver hair in a bun peered through the open door.

"You must be Ada Ekene. Goodness dear, did you get lost?!" she asked in a contralto type voice.

"Yes Ma'am, em . . . I had some difficulty locating the right entrance."

My lie seemed acceptable enough to them because the women smiled at me and went back to whatever it was they were doing before I walked in. Also, no one seemed to notice I had just had a smoke. I walked up to the woman with the glasses. The placard on her desk showcased the name: Principal Karen Mason in gold.In her office, there was paper everywhere! The walls, her desk . . . She smiled warmly at me.

"Mrs. Mason, school principal," she said extending her hand.

We locked hands briefly.

"I've been looking forward to meeting you. Please have a seat," she said referring to an office armchair across her desk. I sat down.

"Your mother has told me so much about you."

I wasn't sure if this was true or if it was just one of those small lies people tell for the sake of starting a conversation. She glanced at the sheet of paper in front of her. "Fifteen and a junior? Impressive! Your mom says you are an intelligent child, and from your transcripts, I can see that you won't have any problems here," Principal Mason said, smiling.

Intelligent? Really?? Not used to any form of praise from Ma, my heart pounded with excitement. I wondered what else Ma had said, but Principal Mason did not indulge me. I adjusted my posture (Ma believed slouching was a sign of weakness) while Principal Mason began to speak about school policies, class sizes, and extra-curricular activities. I don't recall much of what she said regarding the first two. As for the third, she insisted that I get involved in as many as possible. She said it would help me make friends and stay out of trouble. I smiled and agreed as any obedient student was expected to.

After our session ended, she led me to a desk in the outer office where I signed some papers. Then I met with an advisor next door, a bald, exuberant man who was excited to see a foreign student at the school. He said other students could learn a lot from me—not true, I would soon learn. With his help, I selected my semester courses—English Literature, Religion (mandatory), Philosophy (I thought it would help satisfy my soul level curiosities), U.S History (Ben would have approved), Biology (picked over Chemistry), Algebra (mandatory), Physical Education (mandatory) Home Economics (thought it might come in handy)—becoming an official student of Bishop Coral High.

Chapter Two

March 1966

As the remainder of winter dragged on, I went along with it as a leaf surrendering to the force of the wind. But there within surrender is where I found my first real friend.

It was in the middle of the week, and I was in the cafeteria, at lunchtime, partaking in the same standing in queue lunch ritual exercised across many high schools in the United States. On this day at Bishop Coral, mashed potatoes, gravy, and peas and a small carton of milk was the menu. With tray in hand, I strolled towards the nearest table and began to eat after being served by the same lunch lady who wore the same white hair caul, blue and white overalls, and aloof smile. It took two uninspiring mouthfuls for me to notice the three girls sitting across from me, at the next table, leering at me. Defensively, I stared back. Two were blonde, one was a brunette. The brunette stood out. She seemed like the leader of the pack and the most hostile. She sat in the middle of the trio, facing me like the rest of them, as her green eyes made fierce contact with mine. Realizing that the battle of the gaze would last infinitum unless one of us conceded, I decided to take the position of the quitter for the moment and focus on my food.

"She's so weird," I heard the brunette say.

This experience was not at all foreign to me. Since primary school in Nabuka, I had encountered girls like these. Often considered a snob because I had a mother who studied overseas, I had been called many things including "*amosu*," witch, or *ogbanje*/spirit child. Ma had encouraged me to dismiss the dreaded *ogbanje* accusations as mere superstition until years later when, like a tidal wave, it came crashing into my life.

As the girls reacted to my personality, that familiar sense of alienation crept back in—the lump in my throat, the building up of a fiery essence in my chest, the wrangled emotions, and the desire to escape.

It was then that I sensed a familiar gaze from an angle behind the girls. I looked up and noticed the dark-haired girl who had intruded on my private rumination on my first day at school. She was a few feet away, sitting on a stage, her feet dangling over the side. She waved me over to join her. I was hesitant at first, but the authority of her gesture compelled me to obey. I stood with my tray as the three girls followed me with their eyes, and walked towards the mystery girl. She was very pretty, with jet black hair, which I suspected was dyed, and dark blue eyes. She had a straight nose and curvy lips painted generously red. There was something wild and free about her face. She looked at me as if she knew me at a level that I had not yet discovered. Instantly, I wanted her to like me.

"No food allowed on stage," she said in a way that revealed she did not care about the rule. I threw the contents of the tray into a nearby trashcan, glad to get rid of the slimy potatoes. Then I set the tray on the stage behind me and sat next to her.

"Do you want to eat or be eaten?" she asked.

"I don't get eaten," I said.

She smiled and introduced herself as Stacey. I told her my name. She wanted to know where I was from. I told her a few details about myself, adding that I was an only child, lived with my mother, and that my stepfather was still in Nabuka. She told me she was from New York, but her family had moved to Pennsylvania the year prior to be closer to her grandparents who felt the sudden need to acquaint themselves with their grandchildren, her and her younger brother, Matt. She frowned.

"The grandparent thing was just a ploy to keep me away from the hippies I was befriending."

I'd learned of hippies from a newspaper article in Nabuka written by a man who had just returned from the United States. He wrote about how they stunk, how they used drugs, how they always wore flowers in their hair and did not believe in going to school. He had concluded the article by stating that if we were to imitate the white man, the hippies should certainly be overlooked as they were degenerates even by the white man's standards.

"You smoke pot?" she asked me.

"No, only cigarettes," I replied.

"Cool, I like cigarettes too. I will show you a better spot later, where you are least likely to get caught," she said and winked.

We sat up on stage for a few minutes, then she blurted out, "Gosh, I hate this school and this town! You would be a liar if you said you didn't hate it here. I mean, you are the only fucking colored girl here!"

We burst into a chuckle, my right hand over my mouth since I was still quite unused to laughing at the time.

"We are stuck here, for now anyway," she said. I nodded in agreement.

After lunch, I headed to the next period, a college course in philosophy. It took me a little longer than expected to find the classroom among the blur of students heading in different directions at the prompting of the bell. When, finally, I arrived at the classroom doorway, I was greeted by three male students, squealing and pounding on their chests. One of them was the boy I had encountered earlier in the hallway. His orange hair and freckles made him look like a carrot-colored *manikin.* I had the strong desire to grab him and teach him a lesson or two about a monkey stranglehold. I nursed such thoughts as I glared at him before finding a seat in the middle of the room.

Minutes later, a gangly, graying man in thick-rimmed glasses strolled in and introduced himself as Mr. White. The noise in the room died down as Mr. White dropped his books on the teachers' table and, like the teachers before him, had me introduce myself to the class. After the awkward introduction, he went straight to the board with his white chalk and wrote *History of Philosophy,* beginning a narration about how philosophy emerged from Greece with Socrates as its founder. As he spoke, it began to happen, the restlessness, my head feeling heavy with something that only my mouth could release. And so it was that, unable to contain it anymore, I raised my hand and stated that philosophy was also taught in Egypt around the same time. The silence that followed was enough to intimidate a cemetery. It slowly consumed my temporary high. I could feel twenty-something glaring eyes burning through my skin. Later, I would imagine them thinking, "There goes this black foreign chick. Who does she think she is?"

Amid the silence, I wondered if I had over-asserted myself. Some of the knowledge Ben instilled in me had influenced me after all. But what if this type of knowledge was only intended for us to know and not to be shared, especially in front of certain groups of people?

Mr. White gave me a steely glare before responding rather staunchly that philosophy, the father of all sciences, began in Greece. In response, I fell silent and dropped my head. Just then, from somewhere just behind me, came a voice incredibly calm and yet assertive.

"But since this is a history course, I would assume accuracy to be an important aspect of it." A silent gasp spread across the room. I felt the room of eyes shift from me to their new target. With zero bashfulness, the voice continued. "It is actually documented that philosophy was taught in Egyptian temple schools that were attended by people from all over the world, especially neighbors like the Greeks, in which Socrates was, perhaps, a student. I bet you in the Orient they already had their form of philosophy as well."

I turned and stared at him in disbelief, along with the twenty-something other pairs of eyes. Mr. White gave him that same steely look for what seemed like an eternity. Eventually, he cleared his throat and retorted, "Okay… and?"

"What you may have intended to say, Mr. White is that Western philosophy began in Greece."

"Salvadore Giacalone, I think it is time to move along," Mr. White said, fuming, and promptly returning to the task of writing on the board.

I could hear whispers in the background as Mr. White had his back turned to the class and furiously continued to write on the board. There were some jeers mixed in, barely audible, but enough to feel it as it passed through the room like a current. Sal's triumphant gaze met mine, and with defiance that appeared illogical, I quickly averted my eyes and faced my notebook instead. I hardly waited for the bell to ring before dashing out of the suddenly congested space.

I arrived at my locker, after the dismissal bell, and started transferring some books from my bag into my locker. That's when I felt him next to me. I looked up at his dark curly hair, tanned skin, and brown eyes as deep as the Pennsylvania woods. He looked more manly than boyish—not because of his age, but because of his countenance, which betrayed a vast awareness that had led him to be tranquil and yet subtly restless. He stood several inches above me.

"Hi, I'm Sal."

I acknowledged his greeting with a nod and a stiff smile. Inside, I yearned to just split.

"It was great the way you spoke out in class earlier, er . . ."

"Ada," I stuttered.

"That's pretty," he said, his eyes lingering on my face.

"Thanks."

What they say about the butterfly sensation is true. It was all over my stomach. I felt weak. I hated it. I mumbled that I had to head home right away to start my homework. Unfortunately, the stacked books in the locker were not in agreement, they all came crashing down at that very moment. I felt hotness bubbling beneath my cheeks. Sal immediately rose to the occasion, gathering textbooks and notebooks and handing them to me as I stashed them in the locker more carefully while muttering my appreciation. When the last book was in the locker, I locked it shut, excused myself, and headed for the nearest exit.

Except for philosophy class, I didn't see much of Sal. And on the few occasions when I encountered him outside of class, I made sure to escape as quick as I possibly could. From that first meeting at my locker, he felt to me like the rented beach house I could never own, or the summer vacation that was destined to end sometime. It was in the dogged way in which he moved, the worldly depth in his gaze, the easy smile that sometimes dissolved into a calm uncertainty. Already he was stirring me up in places very few people could reach. It was for this reason that I did my best possible to keep Salvadore Giacalone at a distance.

Meanwhile, Stacey and I continued to eat lunch together and smoke cigarettes in a wooded area behind the school. Feigning sickness, I skipped a class or two on occasion, just for the sake of making it to our obscure location. Still, I managed a string of As in tests. I would be lying if I said I ever took school seriously; it was Ma's beatings that kept me in line. Ma used a dark cream-colored cane that made a whooshing sound each time it landed on my skin, leaving more than just a residue of discomfort. Then there were the reverend sisters from over the years, who had always been a little more resourceful. They utilized several implements, from sticks to rulers. There was nothing more humiliating than having a symbol of piety hitting you on the head with the edge of a ruler to remind you of how awful you were. "Be grateful you don't have nuns at this school," I once told Stacey. To which she replied, "A little lovin' would loosen those hags up a bit." Outwardly I admonished her for her blasphemy, but inside, I couldn't help but chuckle at the seriousness with which she said what she believed.

After an incident several years ago, excelling at
been physically instilled in me. I was eight at the t
primary school. It was during a mathematics
stormed out of the classroom, to the derision of my classmates and teacher, after I had failed numerous attempts to solve an equation.

I sat outside on the steps and gazed at the sun. She was gliding towards me, radiating so much light. Who needed to wrestle with numbers when you could settle in the moment?

My teacher had not bothered to convince me to return to the classroom. Nor even my classmates. I behaved this way so frequently, they were convinced I was a witch.

Ma, who was then a medical student in the United States and who happened to be visiting Nabuka at the time, came to pick me up from school in a dilapidated Peugeot, her face deepening into a frown as my disgruntled teacher, Miss Okafor, complained to her about my latest antics.

Ma did not say a word to me the entire drive to the house where Nne and I lived, and Ma now visited occasionally. Nne, an expression Ma used for her mother's older sister, her aunt, means mother. Though this made her technically my grandaunt, she was more of a mother to me than Ma. She was the one who taught me how to walk at ten months, how to use the latrine without assistance at age five, how to eat *fufu* (pounded yam) and okra soup with my fingers without soiling myself at age seven. She was the one to comfort me whenever I cried, and the one who would later guide me through my menstrual initiation into "womanhood" at age eleven. Nne's house had a parlor, two bedrooms, a kitchen, and a pit latrine in the backyard. There were cowry shells, wooden figurines of the earth goddess Ani, and paintings of Jesus and Mary scattered around the house.

After Ma dropped me off, I headed to Nne's room, which was also where I slept at night. I sat on her mattress trying to figure out what Ma's silence meant when suddenly the shock of her cane descended heavily on my back. I was so startled that I didn't know whether to cry or scream. I did neither, even as the cane kept landing on my back, my legs, my buttocks, her words ramming through my ear drums: "You are not going to put me to shame, *I na anu*? You hear, snap out of it!" Just as I was about to dissolve into a mysterious black wormhole, she stormed out as wetness coated the roundness of my face.

Nne stood still by the doorway the entire time that Ma had flogged me. It was after Ma's bedroom door had slammed behind her that Nne's feet became unglued, and she joined me on the mattress, holding me against her chest. Rocking me back and forth, she whispered to me that Ma loved and cared for me, but that I needed to stop doing things to get her upset. She said Ma had after all been working hard to give me a good life. It was then that I sobbed. I wanted to explain to her that I was doing the best I could at school, but that for some reason, words, letters, and numbers appeared jumbled before my eyes. But Nne already knew my struggle. I knew she had read my mind when she said to me in her sweet Afa voice, "Treat your classes like your life depends on it, like your destiny depends on it, like the world depends on you to know the lessons you are being taught."

I stopped sobbing. Nne's words, though they made little sense to me at the time, had given me an incentive beyond the fear tactic used by Ma and previous teachers. After that day, I focused more. I taught myself how to memorize and always read a chapter or two ahead of each class so that I was better prepared.

This did not happen overnight. But in time, I went from being at the bottom of the class to being at the top of the class. I was determined to keep it that way not only to avoid another flogging from Ma, but also to make Nne proud as her approach fostered a willingness to learn.

Chapter Three

April 1966

THE SEASONS CHANGED, AND FRIGID WINTER was now swallowed by convivial spring. Robins chirped louder by my bedroom window every morning, lifting my mood. I discovered I was bored. The suburb was a big contrast to the city life I had grown accustomed to living. A city like Lagoon, London, or Paris kept me distracted and engaged with the outside world. A place like Greensberg, on the other hand, only served to make me more of myself.

After school, I'd smoke cigarettes with Stacey then quickly head home so Ma wouldn't start growing suspicions about my whereabouts. Even though she worked long hours as a doctor in the town's largest hospital, she often telephoned the house in the evenings to make sure that I was home.

The few times I had spent with Ma, usually during late evenings and weekends, she seemed agitated. Part of that could be attributed to the house not being fully furnished. She had a taste for expensive furniture and art, making the process drag on, with grumpy men shuffling in and out of the house for weeks on end. But she was more concerned about the events that were occurring in Nabuka. Three months ago, a military coup spearheaded by a Southerner, an Afa person, had disrupted the peace in Nabuka, leaving the Prime Minister, a Northerner, and multiple politicians and army officers dead. Things had already been shaky before the coup, especially since the federal government was dominated by the party representing the Hsoa Muslims of the North, who were contemptuous of the mainly Christian South. The South, made up of the Afa and Uoba, and several other minority groups, resented the domination of the North. If in the early 1900s that useless white man had not had it in his head to conjoin North and South into the collective unit now known as Nabuka, there would be less infighting, Ma complained bitterly over the telephone.

While Ma was busy worrying about Nabuka, I was busy signing up for the drama club alongside Stacey. After I auditioned as one of the wicked witches in *Macbeth,* I was forced to join the costume and stage designers instead. I did not mind. I was more of a backstage girl, while Stacey was more of a center piece. She was passionate about theater and often expressed her desire to relocate to New York City to audition to be on Broadway. She had coveted the role of Lady Macbeth and landed it after a convincing portrayal of the conniving dame. It didn't surprise me, the fact that Stacey could act. She already possessed a flare for the theatrical in her everyday life. But besides her passion for theater, Stacey had a passion for sexual topics.

The first time it came up, it was early Friday evening in early spring, and we were out behind the school smoking cigarettes.

"You mean, you've never had a boyfriend?" she asked, her eyes widening.

"No," I replied, shaking my head slowly from side to side.

"Really? So, you mean you've never, you know, done *it*?"

"Nooo . . . "

"What about kissing a guy?"

"Nope."

She pushed her head back. "Why not, what are you waiting for?"

"I don't know . . ." I said and lowered my head.

My cheeks began to feel inflamed as Stacey stared at me with wide eyes. So, I shifted the attention to her, to her own love life. She said she had a boyfriend, Ted. He was a twenty-something-year-old junior at New York University. She combed through her schoolbag and produced a photograph of him. Ted, like Stacey, had long dark hair that extended to his lower torso. In the photograph, he wore a dyed rainbow-colored shirt. She said he was a hippie too, and that he was against the Vietnam War and helped organize numerous protests all over the city. I found it seditious and imagined becoming a hippie, but the image of Ma's disapproving gaze appeared vividly in my mind, derailing the thought.

As the last remnant of the thought began to fade, I caught sight of Sal walking towards us. As if forced by some invisible mechanism, I flung my cigarette behind me. Moments later, he was right in front of us, his shirt hanging loosely, the straight lines from the iron still visible on his school uniform pants. I could hear my heart pounding.

"Hey there!" Sal greeted Stacey and me while looking directly at me.

Stacey cleared her throat.

"Hi Sal!" she replied, with more enthusiasm than the occasion required.

I was surprised to discover that they knew each other, but then again, the school only held around three hundred students. I later learned that they were also neighbors who had already participated in a neighborly discussion about "the new foreign chick at school" on my first day.

"Hi Stace, how's it been?"

"Groovy. Having a smoke, wanna join?" Stacey said, giving me a knowing look.

I pretended not to notice.

"My lungs are allergic," Sal said, chuckling.

Boom, boom, boom my heart sounded, almost drowning out their words, even as I tried to hide my growing irritation at what was unfolding before me. Stacey stood up from the grass where we had been sitting, stretched, and said she had to rush home to call her boyfriend. Then she quickly turned to me and said she would see me the next day, stroked Sal by the arm, and exited like a star across the night sky. We both watched as Stacey walked away. Then Sal sat beside me as if playing a well-rehearsed role. I gulped and opened my mouth to say something, but Sal beat me to it.

"I like it here," he said.

"Yea, it's alright," I said.

"No, I mean this spot, right here. I can hear the morning doves more clearly."

"I hear them when I wake up every morning," I said timidly. "I used to think they were owls until I caught one doing his coo call right in front of me."

"Oh yeah?" he said with just as much fascination as if I had said I could magically create birds from twigs.

"I like birds," I said, "Especially mockingbirds. Something magical about them."

"I like falcons and eagles," he said. "They remind me of . . . "

He completed his sentence with "possibilities." I ended mine with "freedom." We tittered.

Then silence. Except for my now dwindling heartbeat. I cut through the silence by deciding to play the mature role this time.

"Thanks for defending me in class the other day."

"Well, it was my pleasure to correct Mr. White," he said as if he had hoped I would bring that up. "I take history quite seriously."

I smiled. I asked him about his interest in Afrika, and how it had begun.

He pondered for a few moments. "You know how they say it all started in Afrika, hence Mother Afrika. What do you think about that?"

I scratched my head. I knew what Ben would say about that. He would say, "Heck yes!" So, in following Ben's stance, I said, yes, that I agreed. That it made sense. Then he asked me what I did in my free time. I told him I loved to read and had dabbled a bit in poetry the last few months because there was so much on my chest that needed to be let go of. As soon as I said this, I hoped he wouldn't ask me to reveal them. He didn't. He moved on to my social life and was surprised to learn that I did not go out much. He promised to take me out "one of these days." I informed him of Ma's strict rules and how she would never approve of me spending time with a boy.

"I see . . ." he said, almost too thoughtfully.

He wanted to know more about Afrika. I said she was indefinable, that to know her was to experience her. He thought that was fair. He was able to list a few countries around Nabuka's borders, adding that it was "groovy" that

Afrikan countries were gaining independence at such a rapid pace.

He spoke about himself. He said he lived with his mother and a younger sister. That his father had left them one simmering summer day about seven years ago after a big fight with his mother. He had left carrying a suitcase, a cigar stuck between his lips, and had never returned.

"I am sorry, that must have been terrible," I said.

"No worries. I'm over it."

I knew what it felt like to feel unwanted by a parent. I wasn't over my birth father's disappearance even though I'd never met the man, so I knew Sal couldn't be over his father leaving.

"So, what else you wanna know about me?" he asked in good spirits.

The question of his heritage dangled in my mind, and I couldn't help but express my curiosity. With pride, he revealed that his father, who had worked at a Steel Mill in Pittsburgh for years, was Italian and his mother, a hardworking paralegal at a law firm, was Colombian, but that he was as American as pecan pie. He said he had been to Italy only a couple of times, once when he was three years old and again a couple of years ago with his mother and sister. He had special memories of Florence, which he fondly referred to as Firenze: the exquisite, historical architectures, the museums, walking by the Arno River, and paying random visits to Michelangelo's *David* sculpture to pay homage to the David who was depicted as a Goliath.

"David depicted as a Goliath . . .?" I interjected.

"Don't worry. One day you will know what I am talking about."

I shrugged. Then I asked him about Colombia and if he had ever been there. He said no, but that he would love to visit someday. One day, he said, he would travel around South America on a motorbike, just like Che Guevera. I knew Che was associated with communism—I had skimmed through an article about his book, *The Motorcycle Diaries,* not that long ago.

"Are you a communist?" I asked Sal, like a prying child.

"What exactly is that?" was all he said in response. It may have been rhetorical, but I shook my head to suggest I was not quite sure, even though it was all the media talked about as if it were an affiliation worthy of damnation.

"For everyone in a society to be able to eat and live comfortably. Equality. I think that is what communism in its ideal form is about," he added in a reflective tone. He spoke like such an idealist.

A distant uncle on Ben's side, who had once come to live with us from a nearby village for employment, had been a communist in his brief stint as an activist. His affiliation with the party began in a street market where he had met a white American woman passing out fliers. For several weeks after that, he would receive letters from the so-called labor union. And on a few occasions, he received strange guests in the backyard. Bottoms planted on plastic chairs, twisted faces hovering over a round table retrieved from the kitchen and gobbling beers, they complained about the rise in corruption, unemployment, crime—the usual complaints in any given society—and about Southern agitation against the predominantly Muslim and extremely traditional (in bitterness they had used the expression "backwards") North, and about how capitalism was against the Afrikan way, about how communism and socialism were more aligned to our egalitarian traditions, traditions that emphasized the dignity of all men several centuries before the arrival of the Europeans. Thankfully, in those days, Ma was so entrenched in her work as to fuzz over what was going on in her backyard.

After one such labor union meeting, I walked in on Uncle Ngozi and Ben arguing in the spacious living room. Ben complained that he had been summoned by someone in his inner circle who had warned him about his "brother's" activities, trusting him to solve the issue as soon as possible. Ben told Uncle Ngozi he was taking some risks, risks a man in his position could not afford to take by allowing Uncle Ngozi to continue with his activities. Uncle Ngozi, defensive and red-eyed, felt his rights had been violated. "So now I am being spied on?!" he shouted.

"Just use your head a bit more," Ben responded in a tone that appeared not as demeaning as the words themselves.

Uncle Ngozi vented for a while even though he was at Ben's house and Ben had every right to protest what went on in his backyard. But that would be the last time Uncle Ngozi would receive any strange guests or pamphlets from the mail. He moved out days later. Weeks later, he was found dead. Run over by a police lorry during a protest he and hundreds of others had staged to oppose a housing demolition project taking place in their downtrodden Ikeda neighborhood in favor of a fancy hotel.

"What do your parents do?" Sal asked, bringing me back to the present.

"My mom is a doctor and my stepfather, a diplomat," I told him. I added how that had allowed me to travel abroad before their separation. I also confessed my desire to visit

Italy, a country I had only been to in my imagination. He looked at me, the reddish sunset heightening his chiseled features, and whispered as if making some secret pact, "One day, I will take you to Tuscany."

The sunset exerted itself even more and breathtaking as it was, being swallowed by a cloud, I knew I had to leave in case Ma called. I let Sal know, and he offered to walk me home. I agreed. A few minutes later, we were in front of the house. I glanced across the street and noticed a grey-haired woman spying on us through her blinds. She hid behind her curtains after our eyes made contact.

"Well, it was nice getting to know you," he said.

"See you tomorrow," I replied, and pulled out my key, unlocked the door, and went inside. I leaned my back against the wall by the window to catch my breath, a gripping feeling in my chest, enveloped in heat. Still unable to breathe, I slid open a small portion of the fiberglass platinum gray drapes to catch a glimpse of him. He was at the same spot, staring at the door, as if in a daze. Quickly, he made a motion for the left side of the street, and then as if realizing a mistake, switched footing and headed towards home.

Chapter Four

May 1966

By mid-Spring, we had a living room with a complete set of black leather chairs, a glass center table with a black cylindrical vase filled with yellow plastic chrysanthemums, and a combination of Afrikan and Western paintings that Ma had collected over the years hanging on the walls. The largest painting occupied most of the back wall. It was a wide portrait of a dark-skinned girl, about my age, with two braids dangling from opposite sides of her ample cheeks. What stood out was the dark, moist look in her eyes. It sent shivers down my spine in unsuspecting moments

In my free time, I often locked myself in my room listening to the latest hits on the radio or reading a book while Ma spent hers roaming the house, muttering about furniture, or talking on the phone with her relatives and friends in Nabuka or to Mrs. McCormey down the street.

In the evening of the second Saturday in May, after a meal of rice and tomato stew that Ma and I had cooked together, I found myself lying in bed. I had a copy of Gustave Flaubert's *Madam Bovary*, which I had borrowed from the school library, sitting on my lap. I was about to delve into Madame Bovary's apathy and boredom within her marriage in Provincial

France, when I thought about Stacey but quickly remembered that she had made plans to visit Ted in New York that weekend. Then my thoughts shifted to Sal, and in a moment of inexplicable deliriousness, I decided to give him a ring. I strolled towards the telephone which hung on the kitchen wall. Ma was safely tucked away in her bedroom. Nervous, I dialed his number. On the other end, the telephone rang insistently. I was going to abandon the ridiculous idea, especially since I had not figured out what to say, when a woman with a heavy Spanish accent answered.

"Hello?"

My mouth was suddenly dry. Still, I asked if Sal was available. She wanted to know who I was. I told her I was a friend, hoping it was enough to satisfy her, at the same time slapping myself mentally for the fool I was about to become. Sal had never rung me, so why was I ringing him, especially this late? There were shuffling noises, a long pause, and then muffled voices.

"Hello?" It was a familiar, deep, honey voice.

"Hi Sal, this is Ada. I was wondering if you were busy tonight," I stuttered.

"I'm free, wanna do something?!"

"If that's okay with you."

"Of course, it is!"

I felt myself breathe easier. He asked me if my mother was home, and I told him 'yes.' There was a pause, then an innocent yet heavily loaded whisper.

"What do you wanna do?"

I knew what I wanted to do, what I needed to do at that moment, and I got the impression he knew too.

"I will get you at 10 p.m. Is that good?"

"Yes, that's good," I said, relieved.

We arranged the exact location of our meeting.

Ten o'clock was perfect timing because, by nine, the light in Ma's bedroom was out as I expected. The house was now completely dark as I waited patiently by the window. At exactly 10:01 p.m., I heard my name carried by a whisper. I crammed the window open and looked down to see Sal looking up at me, grinning. I jumped and landed safely a few feet down, with Sal catching me mid-jump. The window was left open, but I did not care about the empty room being exposed to the night air. As Sal took my hand in his to make sure that I had landed safely, I wondered if I was making a mistake, going off with a boy I hardly yet knew. Then he grinned again, and my concerns evaporated like puddles on a sunny day.

"How did you get here?" I whispered, overcome by sudden guilt. I knew he lived about thirty minutes away by foot and didn't have a car. In response he said he borrowed his mother's car key and drove. I released a quiet sigh of relief.

Nudging me along, Sal told me he had a special place in mind and led me away as we threaded softly past gardens and neighbors' backyards. In the distance, a dog barked ferociously. I shivered slightly from the eeriness of the night. Sal must have felt my fear because he pulled me towards him and assured me that I was okay. Soon afterwards, we were in a small forest, an area I had never seen in all the months I had lived in the neighborhood. Deep into it, a still lake revealed itself in the moonlight. A felled tree trunk had formed a wedge between the green-hued land and the water. We were surrounded by towering trees that emerged dark green against the blackness of night. Sal sat on the back of the trunk as if he had done so a thousand times before. I gingerly sat next to him.

"You come here all the time?" I asked, trying to sound settled.

"Only to be attuned," he said, looking off into the dark distance.

I decided to be attuned too. I shut my eyes and absorbed the still air. In the not-so-far distance, I heard an owl hoot and squirrels chattering, as I felt the wet sand beneath my shoes. The ethereal and magical feeling brought me back home, to Ogu.

"In the village at dawn, I used to sit with my grandaunt by the fire roasting corn and ube. Ube is a pear with purple skin and green insides," I said with a glance at him before staring ahead. I could feel his attention on my lips.

"I used to recite stories and poems to her off the top of my head."

"Recite a poem for me," he said softly.

I glanced at him then shook my head. "Noooo, you might laugh . . . "

"You can trust that I won't," he insisted.

I paused.

"Hmmm . . . okay, this is called *The Village Bird*, something I wrote days ago in my journal . . . "

I cleared my throat, giggled, apologized, sat up straight, and giggled again.

"Come on, it's only me."

I looked into his eyes, saccharine and sincere, and reflecting traces of light from the moon. I cleared my throat. "The Village Bird," I began.

A long time ago
in a land far, far away
I arose to distant hills
in translucent shades of blue
In the backdrop
Black birds soared
flapping their wings to the rhythm of their coos
They spread gossip about other towns
Nne heard, nodded and suddenly went:
"okay!"

I only got the part about Emekuku
What happened at Emekuku?
Nne's lips were sealed
It was older people's business

I long for the days when birds could talk
and we took the time to decipher
When chickens and goats co-existed with humans
on the front porch
Swearing away the heat
each in its own tongue
Longing for harmattan . . .

Sitting under moonlit skies
Listening to tales of duality
as corn roasts with crackling sounds under the fire

Chanting:
"udara mu cha nda cha cha cha nda . . ."

At a midpoint in a story, a sad twisted story
Some of us sniffing because of the girl whose stepmother starved her
and who prays for the udara to ripe so she can eat

It's a story about a famine and in this famine.
Udara dwarfs itself to feed girl.
and grows infinitum when stepmother sings to it
That's when we cheer!

At bedtime
And with a belly filled with corn and ube
I move lethargically towards my mat
determined to rise early
to decode what the bird from Emekuku had said.

"By the way, *udara* is a fruit and *cha* means to ripen," I said, almost choking because of the tears that threatened to suddenly spill. I successfully held them back and glanced shyly at Sal, his pupils glowing in the dark.

"Wow!" he said, finally.

"It's an okay piece . . . " I started to say.

"I thought it was pretty good," he assured me. "You have talent. The way you recited that poem made me want to visit your village in Afrika."

Don't cry. Not here. Not now.

I smiled. "Let's make a bet then, you take me to Italy, and I'll take you all over Afrika ."

"That's an uneven bet, a small country for an entire continent?"

"Hey, I'm being generous."

We tittered then observed the sleepy lake, a sublime witness to our blossoming friendship.

"It's great when you don't cover your mouth when you laugh," Sal said, looking at me.

I covered my mouth to tease him, and he burst out laughing.

"You have nice teeth, don't worry."

I didn't know how to tell him that it wasn't about the teeth.

"By the way, you mentioned someone, Nne or something like that. Who is she?" he asked sweetly, looking deeply into my eyes.

"Nne is my aunt, my grandaunt," I replied, motioning the back of my foot against the felled tree.

"She must be a very special lady."

"Yes, she is," I said softly, my mind traveling to our little house in the village where Nne still lived. Nne, approximately three scores and a ten, lean and strong with locked salt and pepper hair, and determined steps. She was a trader; fresh fish and spices were her main commodities. She was also an exceptional storyteller, whose stories served as balms for Ma's tirades and mood swings and constant travels. Our many nights of storytelling under the moonlit sky, while the flickers of light, emitting through logs of firewood carved shadowy outlines of our bodies, had inspired my passion for everything poetic. Nne was my link to the simple, the ancient and wise. She was also a woman of many secrets despite her simple habits.

Sal noticing my deep reverie asked me if I was okay. I quickly returned to the present, telling him I was fine.

"You are different," I said after a few moments.

"Really? How?"

"I don't know. You just are."

He extended his hand to me, and I held it. Then we sat there, listening to nature's insomniacs until my eyelids began to feel heavy. I rested my head on his shoulder and closed my eyes. For the first time in a long time, I felt truly at ease. We stayed like that, still and resting, for several minutes. Then

Sal shook me with his available hand, telling me that it was time to head home, that I deserved to sleep on a warm soft bed and not on his hard, rocky arm.

THE FOLLOWING MONDAY, I MET UP with Stacey at the school's cafeteria during lunch, which consisted of hamburgers and fries. As I wiped the grease from my fingers, it reminded me of the re-fried palm oil Nne used for frying plantains back home in the village.

I told Stacey what had transpired between me and Sal, and she grinned. The more I told her, the longer her lips stretched. I couldn't help but wonder, once again, if our encounter with Sal behind the school was staged.

"Did you try to get us together?" I asked Stacey through questioning eyes.

"Huh?"

"Stacey!"

"Maybe, maybe not."

"Stacey!"

"Okay, shoot me! He's sweet, he's gorgeous, you are sweet, you are gorgeous . . ." She raised her hands as if she had just solved a simple riddle.

I didn't speak.

"So?"

"He's just a friend, nothing more."

"You sure?" she asked, lifting an eyebrow.

"Yes," I said, but this time my gaze fell slightly away from hers.

Even with my good grades, I was still getting the ape jokes. Some even went as far as asking me if I had ever met Tarzan or if I had ever lived on trees or if my first encounter with clothes was in America. Stacey thought I was being too much of a pacifist. She believed in peace and love and all that but did not mind slapping someone to their senses from time to time. She said this as I headed to my physical education class the following Friday afternoon.

We played dodge ball for forty minutes at the gym that afternoon. And after the game, I entered the dressing room, along with my fellow students, where I changed from my shorts and Bishop Coral memorabilia T-shirt into my uniform. The girl with the fierce green eyes, whose name I had since come to know as Ariel, bumped into me on her way to her locker. She had made sure to hit me violently with the ball earlier during the game. Now all I could think about was that the impact of her shoulder against mine had been too rough not to have been intentional. I went over to her duffel bag and methodically slammed my shoe against it, the visible dusty shoe prints produced a delightful feeling in my chest. She faced me, her dirt-ridden bag between us, her expression red with fury.

"You should have apologized," I said calmly.

Her friends, now forming a U around us, watched with excitement.

"And what if I didn't apologize, nappy-haired jungle freak? It doesn't give you the right to step on my bag."

She reached for one of the ponytails I had carefully braided the night before and yanked on it. I sensed myself about to lose control, about to give in to the totality of my rage. Just then, a pale blonde girl intervened by pulling me away and telling me not to mind her. But it was too late. All it took was a poke in the shoulder by my nemesis to result in a resounding slap. She returned the slap. I slapped her harder and she fell to the floor. A crowd was forming around us.

"Fight! Fight! Fight!" they chanted.

I observed my enemy like a wrestler hovering over a knock-out. Her legs were trembling like a leaf at the mercy of blustery weather. She rained more insults on me from the floor down below.

"Monkey! Go back to Afrika!"

But she was paper white. It appeased me greatly, made the insults inconsequential. It didn't take long for the story to get around about the Afrikan girl who had gone wild and started "punching" on a fellow student. In half an hour, I was sitting across from Principal Mason at her office.

"Ada, unless you tell me what happened we have no choice but to suspend you."

Silence.

"Fighting is not allowed at this school."

Silence.

"Ariel said you attacked her . . . now is that true?"

Silence.

I believed in solving my own problems, and besides, I doubted Principal Mason would have done much to stop the taunting anyway.

I was sent home.

Once in my bedroom, like a pup nesting under the belly of its mother, I snuggled under my blanket and fell asleep.

"So now you are starting fights in school, eh? You must be out of your mind!" Ma burst into my room.

Forced out of my dreamy state, I stared at her like she was an intrusive apparition.

"Get up from that bed, I am talking to you!" She thundered.

I sat in a lotus position, allowing myself to face the world of Ma's wrath before me. She spent the next few minutes raining curses down on my head, saying I was a good-for-nothing, stubborn child. I guess my good grades had done very little to curb those feelings in her.

As she continued to vent, my mind slipped away. I complained to the sympathetic, white, orb-like sprites by the tortured garden outside my window. With my head cocked to one side in a stance signaling defeat, I pretended to be absorbing it all to avoid Ma growing even angrier.

"You are not too big for a beating!"

Pause.

"I will tell your stepfather about this!"

No matter what you say to him to change his opinion about me it will never work . . .

"For your punishment, no dinner tonight and no breakfast tomorrow!"

What?!

She stormed off. I felt abandoned, even by my friends. A strong void floated its way to the surface, a feeling like a fetus without an umbilical cord. It was something I had experienced for as long as I could recall, something that was difficult to explain, but I felt made me *different.* It was something that I believed had its origins in Ma, and in the way she treated me like an intrusion to her perfectly planned life. It was something born out of rejection, of not being seen, and even felt as abyssal as being born in the wrong form or on the wrong plane. Whenever Ma and I had a major falling out, this emptiness rose to the surface. And in that moment, this emptiness revealed itself like a chasmic hole in my chest. The will to go on dissipated. Out in the open was a compilation of aches my heart hadn't yet figured out what to do with. Silently, I wished my existence away but the universe, as if enjoying the unfolding drama, simply watched. I went to the kitchen, retrieved a knife from a drawer, and retreated to my bedroom. I sat at the edge of the bed and made spiral motions with the tip of the sharp steel against my wrist. I cut. Black, red oozed. Raw pain.

I quickly dropped the knife, my gaze shifting to the notebook and pen by the bedside drawer. They caught my attention as if the universe was showing me another option. I flipped to an empty page and wrote: *LOVE.* It stared back at me, mockingly. I crossed it out with black ink. Truer words emerged . . .

I feel empty,
like a drum without sound
Bare—like a colorless, non-existent sky

Chapter Five

June 1966

DEPRESSION CAME AND AFTER SOME POETIC release, like the change of seasons, it fell away—or more appropriately, retreated for the time being. That summer, I learned by listening to Ma's passionate conversations on the phone that a new general, a Northerner, had taken over Nabuka. In my head I thought, *so what?* But for Ma, it was a bad omen for the burgeoning nation.

When I wasn't with Stacey, I was with Sal, usually at his house. This was of course when Ma was out working late. Before school had closed for the summer, Sal had told me after philosophy class and over the phone that he was supportive of me defending myself. Stacey too. In fact, the next time she saw me after the fight, she had said something to the effect of, "Give me five on the black hand side!" Uncertain about what she meant; I had responded with a simple handshake.

"Chick, I mean the back of my hand, the black side . . . " She insisted.

"But . . . it's . . . not . . . black . . . "

"Geez, why you got to be so literal?!" She said with a frustrated smile.

Sal lived in a house with one door and one window. It was separate from the family house and was in the backyard. It wasn't really a house, but a log cabin with a small bed and a tarnished wooden dresser. Our times there were spent playing records, lip-syncing, and dancing to Motown idols like Marvin Gaye, Smokey Robinson, and The Temptations. The few times when Stacey came over, she brought her obsession, Bob Dylan, in the form of his records. We named the room The Groove Box because of all the music we played.

One hot afternoon during early summer break, we were sitting on the rug inside the Groove Box when Stacey suggested that we play Truth or Dare. We had just taken a break after an hour of Stacey trying to teach me "the watusi" dance. I reluctantly agreed to play after she explained the rules to me. Sal agreed to play along too. We all sat cross-legged on the carpeted floor and Stacey started with truth. She asked me what I thought of her. I was honest. I told her I thought she was the hippest chick I ever knew. She smiled softly and blew me a kiss. We took turns, asking questions and daring each other to do inconsequential things like daring to stand on one foot for more than five minutes. The game seemed harmless enough until Stacey desired to change gears. With a twinkle in her eyes, she faced Sal.

"Truth or dare."

Sal considered the options before choosing the latter.

"Dare you to kiss me," she said. My heart stopped and my chest tightened as I felt myself grow dizzy.

Sal raised his eyebrows and squeezed his face like he was unsure, but Stacey was already leaning towards him with her lips pouted. Sal leaned forward and touched his lips to Stacey's as the tightness in my chest squeezed even harder and a large knot appeared in my throat. They remained that way for what seemed like a long time before Stacey pulled away.

"Wow, strong lips!" she exclaimed. She looked at me. "And if that makes you feel better, I will kiss you too . . ." she said and planted a big one on my lips before I could object.

"You see, kissing is like a high five. It's not that big a deal these days," she said to me and chuckled.

I felt my head spinning, like tangled clothes in a laundry machine.

"So, who's next?" she asked.

No response. Sal seemed unable to look at me. Stacey turned to Sal.

"Sal, do you find Ada sexy?"

This was getting worse. I felt a surge of heat that could not be attributed to the sunlight pouring in through the window. I faced the loose ends of the blue rug and held my breath. It seemed to last for eternity, that awkward stillness. I sensed him fidgeting.

"Em . . . uh . . . "

"Why don't you tell her?!" Stacey said.

My heart began to beat fast, I didn't know whether to run or to yell at Stacey for being so intrusive. Finally Stacey, as if feeling sorry for the discomfort she had created quickly said, "Gotta bug out," and left.

Moments later, I decided to "bug out" as well, glad to escape the hot room. That night, I studied my face in the bedroom mirror with an uncommon vanity. I saw a girl barely five feet tall, with virgin hair. I had never had a perm because Ma disapproved. I stared at my round eyes, button nose, and full lips on cocoa-colored skin and I wondered if, perhaps secretly hoped, it meant *sexy*.

Later that night, I tossed in bed. After Ma's bedroom lights went off, I tip-toed to the telephone in the kitchen and dialed Stacey.

"What was that about?" I whispered angrily when she answered.

"Ada, life is too short not to do what you wanna do."

"I don't know what you mean," I replied. *I certainly didn't want you to kiss me.*

She could sense the agitation in my voice.

"I apologize, I promise not to butt in again," she said in a disgruntled voice and hung up.

I didn't hear from Stacey for days. Then one night, as I sat in bed skimming through Khalil Gibran's book, *The Prophet,* I heard the telephone ringing downstairs. Ma answered. Moments later, she called me. I took the phone from Ma, hoping for some privacy and to my delight, she left the kitchen and headed to her bedroom.

"Hello?"

"Hey, Ada, what's up?" It was Stacey.

"Nothing much."

"Hey, you wanna play another round of truth or dare?"

"No, thank you," I said dryly.

I heard her chortle on the other end. "I was just kidding chick. Lighten up! Anyway, Dope Fiend, a local band, is gonna be playing at Washington Square Park in New York this Saturday. The band is great and it's free. Wanna come?"

The thought of going to New York, a city full of excitement and all manners of stimulation, made me swell up inside. It would be a great way to end a relatively quiet summer, but I knew it would require a certain level of cajoling for Ma to permit me to go. And in honest introspection, I wasn't too sure I would succeed. Finally, I found my voice.

"I would love to, but I don't think my mom will allow me . . . "

"Damn."

"I'm sorry."

"Just ask her, what is there to lose?"

Those words played in my head for hours, and when I could no longer bear the repetition, I summoned the courage to ask Ma. This would be one of the few times I would ask her for anything in my life. The last time I had asked her for a box of crayons was when I was five and we didn't have the money in Ogu. In response, she had given me a sliced look for reminding her of our impoverished state before walking off, knocking me to the ground in the process. Nne was left to pick up the crying pieces.

I knocked on Ma's bedroom door with a lumpy feeling in my throat. She invited me in. Then without hesitation, I laid out my request. In my head I was thinking, if she doesn't let me go to concerts now, in a year or so, I will be in college, free to engage in as many concerts as possible anyway. Stacey was right, there was nothing to lose.

Her back was against the bed post, her spectacles resting on the bridge of her nose, a Bible flipped open in her palm like a preacher. The space was bathed in an aura of blue light from her bedside lantern. The blue light against her red silk pajamas made her look purple.

She turned serious as I laid bare my request. She wanted to know which friend, and I told her about Stacey, and how she was a really good friend. Like a detective questioning a suspect, she queried about the nature of the concert. I told her all I knew from the information Stacey had given me. It was a good thing she had no clue what dope meant.

"You can go. I give you until 11 p.m."

I blinked to make sure that this was real life. It was as real as the wind that began to blow through the white satin window curtains. And for the first time since I was a toddler, I felt the urge to embrace Ma. That urge did not get satiated. She had already dismissed me by returning to her Bible. And so, with only myself to embrace and with glee and buoyancy to my step, I left the room and telephoned Stacey to deliver the news. She was thrilled. She kept saying, "It's gonna be a gas, chick!"

The following Sunday, I attended mass with Ma at Sacred Mount, the only Catholic church in Greensberg. During the part where the congregation kneels as the Priest blesses the bread and wine, aka the body and blood of Christ, I thanked God for softening Ma's heart towards me. After the ceremony, we drove home in our usual silence. As she turned off the engine in the driveway, I asked for permission to visit Stacey. I was permitted with a wave of the hand. I watched as she proceeded to enter the house with her flowing boubou clinging to her body from the pressure of the breeze. I got out of the car. As she struggled to unlock the door, I was momentarily overtaken by emotion. How had it come to this, mother and daughter leading separate lives? If only she and Ben had stayed together, things would have been better for everyone, I thought. There would have been more laughter, more illusion of togetherness between us for he served as a bridge, our bridge. I imagined Ma and I bonding like other mothers and daughters, having girl talk, going shopping, sharing beauty regiments . . . Maybe that was part of the problem, we both lacked interest in the activities that brought mothers and daughters together.

"Are you not going?" she snapped.

"Yes Ma, I am . . . "

She glared at me before entering the house and locking the door behind her.

I headed towards Sal's instead as I had not seen or heard from him since Truth or Dare. It was a half-hour walk, but the air was pleasantly warm. Birds chirped along the way, squirrels darted to and fro, and flower gardens of all sizes and variety displayed themselves like a contest from neighbors' lawns.

I finally arrived at Sal's cabin and leaned towards the cracked wooden door. No music. I knocked. He demanded to know who it was. I affirmed my presence and was invited inside. I opened the door and beheld a shirtless Sal in tight blue jeans. He was sitting on the bed, the sheets and blanket in a jumbled lump behind him, and he was pumping some air into his soccer ball, which I always insisted was a football and American football is something else. His hair was ruffled, and his eyes, a darker hue than usual. It made me blush, being exposed to his brawny chest.

"I can always come back . . . "

"No, sit," he said with a big smile.

I shut the door behind me. Just then, I noticed beads of sweat travel down his navel, the scent of his body heat filling the air. I sat next to him, but not too close.

"Are you playing soccer this evening?" I asked him. He played soccer at a local park with some of the students from Coral High and other neighboring schools, some evenings and on weekends. Sometimes I was there to watch, but I tried to minimize my presence as rumors began to spread that Sal and I were "going steady." Being called "checkerboard" just for being his friend infuriated me.

"Yes, I am," Sal replied, "as soon as I'm finished with this ball."

He continued with his task.

"Is everything okay?" I asked him.

"Yeah. I've just been busy competing for a local soccer championship, practice leaves me exhausted."

I nodded. Suddenly, a ladybug landed on his neck. I reached out for it, but it fluttered away. Sal jumped, his face reddening.

"Don't do that."

"Do what? Do that?" I asked. I didn't see the big deal, so I touched his neck again, hoping he would laugh. He had the most heartfelt, enriching laughter I had ever known in a person. But he wasn't laughing.

"Stop it," he said instead.

I continued with my attempts, as he pushed me away.

"Why?"

"Because . . . "

"Because what?"

He abandoned the pump, pulled me closer by the neck, and pressed his lips against mine. They felt soft and strong and sweet. My eyes slowly widened as I melted into timelessness. My heart pumped blood through pulsating veins, heating my body. I closed my eyes. Just as I was about to lose myself, he pulled away from me. I slowly opened my eyes. The fire in his eyes was gone, and he looked just like the reticent Sal of old.

"I'm sorry," he said, barely looking at me.

My head was swimming fast. I faced the ground. I knew he hadn't planned for that to happen, but still . . . I got up to leave.

"Ada . . . "

I slammed the door behind me.

THE SATURDAY AFTER I WALKED OUT on Sal, Stacey came over to the house with her black hair flapping against her tanned cheeks. She wore a hair band, a Sari-inspired mini dress, and faded bell-bottom jeans. It was Ma who answered the door after the doorbell echoed through the house. I stood a few feet away from Ma, bracing myself, unsure how she would react to meeting a friend of mine for the first time. In Ogu, when my closest friend at the time, Oluchi, would come over to visit, Nne would feed us smoked fish cooked with firewood. Then Nne, Oluchi, and I would congregate in the backyard, not too far from the ash pile, where Nne would listen to our girly stories and marvel at our free-spiritedness.

Now here stood Stacey before my mother, who had never been around during Oluchi's visits to Nne's house back in Ogu.

Stacey was beaming, unaffected by Ma's disdainful look.

"Hi, Mrs. Ekne." She meant to say Ekene. ". . . It's nice to finally meet you, I'm Stacey."

She reached out for a handshake, but Ma kept her hands firmly at her side. Stacey dropped hers slowly, showing no signs of anger or embarrassment. I did not give Ma the chance to interrogate Stacey. I simply promised to be back by 11 p.m. and joined Stacey outside. Ma suddenly seemed uncertain about the whole affair.

"Be careful and don't do anything…!" I quietly shut the door, the resounding noise drowning out the rest of Ma's words. I hoped it appeared innocent.

We were met in the school parking lot by Stacey's boyfriend, Ted. I was glad that Ted had the sense to park there and glad that Ma had not gotten to meet him. Not with his long hair, dirty fingernails, and grimy clothes.

Ted had languid blue eyes and a scraggly beard that had sprung up since the last photo Stacey had shown me. He wore a faded brown suede fringe vest over his bare chest and grubby navy-blue bell-bottom jeans with red colored peace symbols etched on it. His long hair fell loosely against his cheeks, hiding a big portion of his face. He smiled a lot, a very charming smile that could melt a glacier. He told me how Stacey had told him so much good stuff about me. It made me smile too.

We passed hills, small towns, and forests on our drive to New York. At one point, we witnessed a magnificent sunset and even a rainbow. When Stacey and Ted held hands and exchanged quick kisses, I thought about Sal's lips and mine, locked for what had seemed like an eternity. I deleted the image with a mental sponge only for it to re-appear like a chronic disease. I resolved the issue in my head. The event, I concluded, was not worth the internal turbulence and therefore needed to be discarded from memory. I stilled my mind by slowly counting down from a thousand. By four hundred, I was under.

Hours later, I was awakened by glaring guitar sounds as Ted parked among a sea of cars and drunk hippies. Back in Lagoon, I often caught our gateman smoking *igbbo* or pot when Ben and Ma were away, so I could easily recognize the sweet, pungent smell.

Blonde-, black-, red- and brown-haired people were everywhere, with their hair sitting mostly past shoulder length. As we headed towards the arena, which turned out to be a sprawling field filled with hundreds of people, the intoxicating scent grew more intense, and I experienced myself hovering in unfamiliar places in my mind. Stacey and Ted blended with the crowd. As for me, I felt conscious of my appearance. My sleeveless white dress, a few inches past my knees, seemed tame compared to the outlandish colors and styles around me, compared also to the semi-nudity. Hippies. People said they were no good. But I liked these people around me, doing whatever they wanted, telling the establishment to "fuck itself." I wished I dared to forget everything, run away from home and join them. I wish I dared to be a no-good too.

"Let's sit here," Stacey said, pointing to a space on the grass. She spread out a blanket she said was crocheted and given to her by her grandmother. The three of us sat on the soft woven yarn and watched a lanky, male figure take over the stage several feet away. He began belting a song about cosmic consciousness, swaying to music inspired by an eclectic mix of The Doors and Jimi Hendrix. I became hypnotized by the psychedelic sound, the fluid dance moves displayed by the crowd, the public display of bedroom affections. I turned to my left to see Stacey and Ted arguing over a white pill offered to them by a stranger. Ted grabbed the pill and shoved it in his jeans pocket.

"How come you never let me have one?"

"I think you should wait till you are a little older."

"Why?"

"Why?!" he replied. "I had a hell of a trip on this the last time, that's why! I was meditating with some Hare Krishna folks at a temple in lower Manhattan when I slipped a pill cos I thought, you know, it would heighten everything. Anyway, some crazy shit happened. I saw Devas in orange gowns and huge wings, and they were inviting me to join them in nirvana. Just as I was about to go with them, this belly-dancing Asian chick came out of nowhere. She wanted to make love. It felt like a test, you know? Like I had to choose. Make love to this goddess right there and then or go straight to nirvana with a group of them. Unfortunately, I blanked out before I got to choose. I just remember waking up hours later. Guess where? Lying under a freakin' tree in Central Park. Don't even know how I got there!"

"That doesn't sound like a bad trip," Stacey said, rolling her eyes.

"What is it?" I asked, stifling my laughter.

"LSD. Here take this instead," Ted said, offering Stacey a blunt he had just rolled. She grabbed it, sulking.

"Freedom and love!" the musician on stage belted after the song was over.

Was this freedom? Was this love? Whatever this was, it was certainly better than the mundane experience that was my life.

A war protest song boomed in the air. Dope Fiend, with his bare chest and black leather pants, twirled like a man possessed by a rock n' roll god. The crowd cheered; the smoke thickened. I glanced at Stacey. She was holding the pot. It burned generously at its tail. She took a drag, passed it to Ted, he took one, and in a few seconds, it came my way.

"Try it," Stacey said in the most convincing tone.

I wanted to fully be one with these people, even if for a few hours, so I did. I must have taken a long drag because Stacey went, "Easy baby," before sliding it from my fingers. Soon, blurred images induced by a euphoric feeling filled my head as it expanded as if it was going to explode. I rested my back against the grass, legs planted on the ground, knees facing the smoky sky, and giggled. Not just once, but continuously. It came out impulsively, unstoppable.

HOURS LATER, THE CONCERT HAD ENDED, and we were heading back to Pennsylvania.

In the car, I rested my head against the window, elevated, floating above everyone and everything. Stacey and Ted kept asking me if I was alright even as the lazy smile on my face produced more smiles from them, reducing their anxiety. Then it happened: the bright lights of a truck, Ted attempting to swerve sharply, Stacey screaming obscenities—then darkness.

The darkness gradually faded to reveal a dim light. I found myself standing in the deep of a forest at sunset, facing a flight of intricate maple tree branches in front of me. A silvery sprawling lake revealed itself in the distance, behind the tree. Orange butterflies murmured delicate ideas about the magnificence of flowers and the generosity of trees. I heard laughter, child-like laughter seeping through the tree trunks. Then, spontaneously, a group of them appeared, blue-black in appearance and covered in leaves. They climbed up the branches; male, female, male, female . . . but with their stubby legs and wise eyes I wondered, were these actually children or gnomes?

"*The water is running, running, running, the water is running, from the pitcher to the Sea . . . Oh Mother, Oh Mother, Oh Mother, be awakened . . .* "

The forest began to spin. The trees began to sing along too, as well as the red sand beneath my feet. More laughter emerged, intermingled with strange singing. I closed my eyes.

"Wake up!"

Startled, I opened my eyes. It had been a frantic teenage girl's voice, and it seemed to come from a different place. When I fully came to, I realized I had been visited by a throbbing headache. Stacey and Ted hovered over me from their front seats.

"Holy moly, you scared the shit out of me!" Stacey exclaimed.

"Huh? What happened?"

"Accident. You passed out," Ted replied.

I noticed red patches and bruises on Ted and Stacey's foreheads and elbows. I tried to sit up straight. It was dark, but I could still see Ted's Toyota caught in a tree, off the side of the road. There were no other cars or pedestrians in sight.

"We turned around to check on you, but you didn't respond," Stacey said. "It's almost as if you left us."

The startling realization that perhaps I did want to "leave them" and the entire world made me shudder.

"We need to get this car out of here," Ted said.

He hobbled his way to the front of the car, while Stacey moved to the driver's seat to start the engine. Though inebriated, somehow, Ted was able to push the car. Later, Stacey and I would joke about Ted's joint being laced with steroids. Meanwhile, I felt myself and the car slide backwards and adjust itself safely on the road. Stacey cheered then winced with pain. Ted resumed his position as driver, forcing Stacey back to her seat. She looked at me.

"You okay?"

I nodded, yes, and then lay across the seat.

About two hours later, I was waving goodbye to a somnolent Stacey and Ted. They drove off. I made fumbling attempts to unlock the front door and, after a few misses, I heard the 'click' sound. I pushed the door open, longing for my bed even as I felt my stomach rumbling. Without warning, the light came on, blinding me. When I opened my eyes, there stood Ma, a livid look on her face.

"Do you know what time it is?" she thundered.

I shook my head, no.

"It's four in the morning!" She pointed to the grandfather clock hanging behind her.

"Shit!"

It was silent, not intended to be heard by anyone other than my rising anxiety. But it was heard, and it catalyzed the forceful motion of her palm across my right cheek.

"I have been up waiting for you since eleven!"

Silence. Then the dreaded realization from the perceptive mind of a doctor and a mother, combined. Not another word needed to be said for me to realize she knew about the pot. She shoved me inside the house and locked the door. Then she held her breath and released it.

"Is that marijuana I smell?" she said in a seething voice.

I didn't speak. My heart was racing. My legs were weak. I wanted Ani, the earth, to drown me. I wished I had died when I had the chance earlier . . .

"Do you know what is going on right now? Your people are being wiped out like chickens back home, and you are busy smoking marijuana, eh!?" she shouted.

I stared at the floor. I didn't know then that she was referring to the genocidal attempts towards the Afa people in Northern Nabuka as a result of the coup. At that moment, in front of Ma, all I wished was for her torrid outburst to end before attempting to defend myself because I knew from experience that she did not take kindly to being interrupted when she was scolding me. I took the risk anyway.

"We got into an accident . . . "

"Shut up! We agreed at 11 p.m., look at the time!" she shouted. "I was up, worried about you, you selfish brat. *Anuofia, I na eri nsi*! Get out of my sight, you make me sick!"

I stumbled my way past her, my head bent low. Her words followed me.

"... And I better not see you with that Stacey girl again! And I swear on Nne's life, if I ever smell what I just smelled on you tonight ever again, you might as well get out of this house and live on the streets! Nonsense!"

I stormed to my bedroom and slammed the door loud enough to be felt by her, and yet not too loud as to appear intentional. That made me even angrier, that I could not even just slam the door.

I sat on my bed, freeing the tears in my eyes. I thought back to the accident, and for an instant, wished it had been more horrific. I pondered the idea of being dead from it, joining all those jolly elemental beings and how it would make Ma feel guilty for all the bad things she had said and done to me over the years. I wanted to hurt her, just as much as she hurt me. But Ma, I concluded, was incapable of feeling while my heart was soaking up every dirt and grim dumped on it, like a sponge. I grabbed my pen and notebook.

Life hurts. I hate Ma. I hate this house. I want to go away and never come back!!!

But it was Stacey who went away.

A few days after the concert, I received a phone call from her—from New York. She had decided to drop out of school and relocate to the city after a verbal confrontation with her parents over her refusal to obey house rules. She apologized for the accident. I told her not to worry about it. I thought she was lucky to be brave enough to split.

I wished I was going away too.

"What about Lady Macbeth . . . ?" I said flimsily.

"I already told Miss Pearce. A new Lady Macbeth is in order."

I suddenly felt sorry for Miss Pearce, our drama instructor. She only had a few days to get a new Lady Macbeth . . . and another backstage costume handler as I mentally made a note to turn in my resignation.

"Bye chick," Stacey said in a soft voice.

And just like that, it was over. Just like that, I was alone again.

Chapter Six

August 1966

As summer neared its end, I experienced the somber feeling that came with it just like most teenagers do. I wasn't eager to face teachers and taunting students, even though the latter had lessened significantly, thanks to my latest status as a fighting champion. And with Stacey gone, the thought of school without her felt daunting.

But eventually, school resumed. Classes opened the gate to psychological escapism, and I poured more energy than was necessary into my academics. Being so occupied helped sever my ties with Sal. Soon, he became just another face in the classroom, in the hallway. At first, he tried to reach out, but I wasn't receptive.

Then he stopped trying. After all, he had friends, soccer friends, and even girlfriends who were relieved to see that he had been freed from the "spell" of that Afrikan girl. And then, of course, there was Ariel, always lurking, always making sure she had him in her sights.

Fall came and went, creating a canvas of orange, red, and brown leaves which eventually turned crisp and fell to the ground, often scattered by dry winds.

The school production of *Macbeth* arrived as well. It received mediocre reviews due to Stacey's replacement who fumbled on her lines so much.

Then, in late April of 1967, came the night of the prom. As I lay in bed reading Khalil Gibran's, *The Prophet,* in a dramatic attempt to understand "the purpose behind suffering," Ma barged into my bedroom, demanding why I was not attending the dance. She asked me why I hadn't told her about it, why she had to hear about it from a hospital staff member. I told myself she did not understand the ritual of mothers and daughters collaborating and fussing over the perfect ballroom gown weeks in advance. To sidestep this process was to slash in half the essence of prom. We had lost that opportunity and it was too late now.

Instead, I told her I had been too focused on enrolling in a good college and I had forgotten about prom. The answer was so perfect that it caught her off guard. Void of words, she left me alone. But in my mind, I saw Sal and Ariel dancing together under ballroom lights, lost in a ballad. Sal in a white tuxedo and black tie and her in a pink lacy gown fit for a princess. I saw her *onye ocha* hair, bouncing to her swaying movements. My hair was thick and felt like thin wires and did not bounce, nor flop. I wondered if Sal liked my hair just the way it was, whether he would have a problem with not being able to roam his fingers freely through it.

What was wrong with me? Why would I leave him to be grabbed by that awful girl? Most importantly, why did I even care?

Before Sal kissed me, kissing, to me, meant nothing more than lovers swapping spit and convincing themselves that it made them euphoric. Then Sal kissed me, and I experienced a volcanic feeling too powerful to contain. And now, I was entertaining thoughts about kissing and sex even though it was too late to explain my fears to him, my concerns about being hurt, about losing control. There was something in the way he had pressed his lips against mine, the burning intensity in his eyes that made him unrecognizable and wild—a different Sal, a Sal who was unpredictable and too free, and the resulting excitement between my thighs . . .

I understood this sensation was connected to sex. Sex. What did it mean for me? For Sal?

Days later, I received an acceptance letter from Smart College, a woman's college in Wellesley, Massachusetts. I had acquired a full academic scholarship, which made everything even sweeter for Ma.

I told Ma the good news over dinner. She didn't jump around singing praises to me like Nne had when I passed the entrance exam to enter secondary school in Nabuka. That wasn't Ma's style, but she showcased her approval with a half-smile.

I am not sure if it was due to the little time I had left at home, or because I had made good decisions up to that point, but Ma was talking to me now. Before my acceptance letter, dinner conversations were stifled and dispassionate. After my acceptance to Smart College, our dinners became filled with Ma's tales about her experience at Bryn Mawr, a college she believed was the best in the world. She had done her medical residency at the University of Pennsylvania in Philadelphia, at a time when black faces were rarely seen on campuses, especially those of black women. She explained to me how she was often discouraged by white male professors from pursuing medicine. They told her she could not succeed as a woman of color. To her surprise and bitter disappointment, she received similar rhetoric from a few black folks along the way, usually black males. But racism and sexism did not discourage her, Ma concluded with pride.

"And it shouldn't discourage you either!" she said to me after dinner one night. "Now, it may look like I am hard on you, but I have had to be that way so that you can face the harsh realities of our world. That your former friend, Stacey, or whatever her name is . . . friends like that will pull you down. This hippie thing is a phase. Trust me. Twenty years from now they will wish they had gone to school and focused on their careers!"

Many did go to school, and many did focus on their careers and went on to have leadership positions in various fields, but I did not say that to Ma even though I knew she was wrong and not all hippies were or are deadbeats.

Meanwhile, Ma began to emphasize that I should take pride in being an Afa person. Not long ago it was Afrikan pride, Nabukan pride, now it was Afa pride? Where was the Nabukan unity that our founding fathers preached post-independence? The Pan-Afrikan ideology that these same founding fathers espoused while challenging the evils of colonialism? Now Afa people, my people, were being slaughtered in the North. It left me to ponder, what would be next?

Chapter Seven

May 1967

ON THE DAY OF MY HIGH school graduation in the last week of May, relatives and friends sat in the bleachers on one side of the gym-turned-graduation hall, while the graduates, with their white gowns and matching hats, faced them on the opposite side. Principal Mason stood on the podium and gave a speech congratulating us on our achievements and encouraged us to face the world with big dreams. My gaze fell on Ma as she sat across the room. She appeared to be expecting someone. Probably Mrs. McCormey, as she seemed to be the only real friend she had.

I thought about Ben and wished he had been able to make it. But we had spoken on the phone a few weeks prior, and he had said that he had urgent matters to tend to in Nabuka. What matters he did not say, but I could not extinguish the dreadful feeling that it had something to do with the tense socio-political climate happening at the time. As thoughts of Ben persisted, I was interrupted by thunderous applause in response to a student who had just finished her speech. She bowed one time too many before walking off the podium. Aimlessly, I let my gaze roam the back of the heads of my fellow graduates. That's when I caught sight of the back of his head. He was sitting only a few rows in front of me. It suddenly dawned on me, how much I would miss him—Sal.

Principal Mason returned to the podium and announced that it was time to hand out diplomas and that names would be announced according to the rows in which we were seated. So, row by row we lined up, ready to receive our diplomas amid applause, cheers, and whistles.

Later that afternoon, we all gathered inside the cafeteria, which had been set up to look like a restaurant. Everything looked and tasted many times better than it had just a few days before. We feasted on baked chicken, grilled fish, potatoes, green peas, broccoli, and white rice. I took off my graduation gown to reveal my satin blue boubou and received many curious stares, a few people walking up to me to comment on its elegant spiral designs.

I scanned the room for Sal when I saw someone who looked like my stepfather, Ben. He was standing by the main entrance, the same door I had walked through on my first day of school. I blinked my eyes and took a closer look. His broad, six-foot frame and charcoal skin made him easily detectable. It was him! I rushed towards him and threw myself into what would soon become an emotional embrace. When we let go of each other, I led him to Ma who did not seem the least surprised to see him. They exchanged a brief hug, and he joined us at the table.

"I thought you weren't coming!" I said to him.

"Me? Not coming? How can I miss my Ada's high school graduation?"

I leaned my head against his chest as Ma focused on her meal.

Awards were handed out as we ate. I received the magna cum laude award. It was presented to me by a thirty-something, overweight man with a cheesy expression. He turned out to be Jim Coral, Bishop Joseph Coral's grandnephew.

"I'm proud of you," Ben said, kissing my forehead after I returned to my seat.

"We thank God," Ma said.

I was nibbling on my fish when I saw Sal standing by the same door Ben had just walked through. He was chatting with an older woman and a young girl, maybe twelve years old. They shared the same tanned complexion and curly hair. Immediately, I hoped he would separate from them and head to the adjoining hallway where a row of lockers stood. And when he did, I quickly excused myself.

"Have to speak to a friend," I said and dashed off.

I found him at the end of the hallway, by the glass door that led to the back of the building, peering outside. He seemed contemplative. What if he was thinking about that Ariel girl? The thought infuriated, saddened, and made me squirm all at once. I turned around, deciding to leave him alone to his thoughts when I heard my name. He had seen me. With trepidation, I turned around and walked up to him. All I wanted was to say goodbye, all I needed was to say goodbye . . .

"Hey," he said.

"Hey."

I extended my hand to him.

"Congratulations."

He held it. It felt cold. He removed his hand first. I mumbled an apology for intruding on his privacy. I felt like a fool, standing there as he looked at me.

"Don't be sorry. I was just thinking of how time goes by so fast. I can still recall freshman year like it was yesterday."

I was relieved. At least he wasn't thinking about Ariel. For an instant, I wondered about my former classmates. I tried to imagine how different my graduation would have been if I had remained in Lagoon, at the secondary school I had attended for four years before I was ripped away and whisked to this Pennsylvania town. The graduation gowns and speeches would have been there, but there would have been no elaborate dinner reception afterward, I was certain.

"Nice dress," he said.

"Thanks. It's called boubou."

"Boo-boo?"

"Boubou," I said with a slight chuckle.

"Buubuu . . . I see. Looks good on you."

"Thanks."

"Wanna go outside?"

"Sure."

We used the door prohibited for student use. But we were no longer students. Soon, we were outside, facing remote slopes. Maybe it was being in proximity to the spot where our friendship began, but I felt an overwhelming urge to completely bare my heart to him.

"I'm sorry," I blurted.

"There's nothing to be sorry about."

"There are things to be sorry about. I wasn't very nice, and it wasn't because of . . . "

"... I understand."

Adamant and certain he did not understand, I grabbed his shoulders and forced him to face me.

"It wasn't because of . . . "

"... Either way, it shouldn't have happened, I'm sorry."

I felt a surge of discouragement sweep through my body at hearing his words. He must have sensed it too because he quickly added: "I am just relieved we can end things on a good note."

"Me too," I said.

Then I let go of him, thinking that perhaps I was stifling him. He suggested that we go back inside, or our parents would begin to wonder about our whereabouts. Then, as if it had been twisted out of him, he said, "Just so you know, I was also thinking about you."

Something in my chest exploded. I planted a swift kiss on his lips. Secretly, that is what I had wished for, what I had missed, the pure feel of him. He stared at me, shocked, flushed, and pleased.

"I didn't go to the prom because of you," he confessed.

A soothing, sweet, rush . . .

"But I thought you and Ariel . . . "

"Ariel? Are you kidding me?" he scoffed. "Why would I go with her after all she said to you?"

He continued, "Truth is, Ariel and I were about to go steady until I noticed you on your first day at school, and she overhead me confess to a friend that I thought you were the most interesting girl I'd ever seen."

I smiled. I finally understood Ariel's animosity towards me, where it had sprung from. Sal began stubbing his canvas shoe against the brown dirt. I noticed the way the breeze kicked his curls and how pale his skin could get after the flush ran its course.

"I'm sorry about prom . . . " I said.

"Don't be," he replied, giving me a sideways glance and grinning.

Chapter Eight

June 1967

BEN IHEANACHO WAS A MAN IN his mid-forties, regal, with broad shoulders, and a distinguished air about him. An intelligent, epicurean man with a passion for travel, romance, and red wine, his greatest asset was his charm which women of all ages often found disarming. According to what he had told me, he was born in a little village in the outskirts of Ogu but spent most of his childhood under the care of his loving, entrepreneurial parents somewhere in Northern Nabuka. From Northern Nabuka, he had moved to England to pursue a university and graduate degree in international relations at Cambridge University. After he obtained his degrees, he returned to Nabuka where, thanks to personal connections, he was recruited by Nabuka's Ministry of External Affairs. The rest, they say, is history.

He said he had met Ma in the summer of 1960, and it was love at first sight. He was in Philadelphia on vacation when he saw her in a café arguing with the waitress over the stale taste of her coffee. Her beauty and no-nonsense attitude had intrigued him. So, he approached the waitress and complimented her hairstyle before diffusing the situation by convincing the waitress to apologize. The waitress, perhaps now flattered, left and returned moments later with a fresher tasting coffee for both Ma and Ben, who by this time were sitting across from each other. Ben and Ma chatted over coffee for two hours that evening, planting the seed of their love affair.

Ben stayed with us after the graduation ceremony. His plan was to remain with us until he received further instructions from the Nabukan government. Being an Afa person meant his life was at risk, and for the moment, Afa officials overseas were encouraged not to return. He slept in the guest room in the basement. We had dinners together, with Ma making an effort to spend more time at home. Sometimes we ate in fancy restaurants in the town's outskirts. Even though they were technically separated, Ben was still fond of Ma. I often caught him staring at her womanly curves whenever she had her back to him. She rarely wore skirts or dresses except for the boubou, which was her favorite thing to wear on Sundays. Ma maintained a short fro which exposed her cinnamon complexion and striking facial features. I could tell, however, by the platonic way in which she treated him that there was no hope of reconciliation. Ben must have known this too. Being of Afa heritage was one of the few remaining threads linking them as socio-political discourse filled the house. Afa people were being killed in the north, many escaping across state lines and denying their ethnic identity to survive. From Ben, I learned that war was inevitable. He said he could sense it strongly, and he was glad Ma and I were here.

"It's a surprise the federal government did not invade the east sooner, for that would have been a faster job," Ben said to Ma at the dining table one evening as I pretended to watch reruns of American Bandstand in the living room.

"Maybe the resources were not there to perform such a task . . ." Ma said with a tint of hope in her voice.

"Maybe. But I tell you there will be more than enough resources to ensure the Afas lose. The U.S and the U.K governments will do all in their power to prevent the Afas from emerging victorious," Ben said.

"But why would they interfere?" Ma asked in an infuriated tone. "Why won't we be allowed to deal with our problems ourselves?!"

"Yes, why?" I found myself asking.

"Both governments have a lot to benefit from a unified Nabuka. Especially with oil recently discovered in the East, they cannot afford to see an oil-rich East engage in trade relations with a communist-friendly country if victory were to be achieved, for example. Already the U.S government has expressed staunch disapproval with the Eastern leader for his decision to lead his region to secession."

As they discussed, I longed for the days when Ben used to say, "Viva Nabuka," "Viva Afrika," those glorious times after our newly acquired independence from Britain. For now, it was Viva Afa! Then on the summer solstice, Ben received word from the Nabukan Government to return home, along with other government officials. They were to be absorbed into the mainstream civil service under one Nabukan government, Afa indigene or not. It was a dilemma that Ben refused to acknowledge fully in front of me, but I often overhead him discuss with Ma.

Ben understood me as a person, understood that I was a bird, a currently caged one with unspoken dreams. The evening after the solstice, while the three of us sipped on tea in the living room, my gaze travelled to the parted drapes across the room and caught two pigeons wrestling on our neighbor's roof. I was so fixated on which pigeon would cower to the other that I didn't realize Ma had said something to me. It took Ben's baritone voice calling out to me to snap me out of the action outside. Ma shook her head and complained that I was too absent-minded. Ben laughed it off and said I was imaginative. And the way he said "imaginative," like it was a romantic attribute, not a trait to be stomped out of a person. Ma repeated her question. She wanted to know if I had any ideas what I wanted to study in college. I shook my head, no.

"You see, I told you!" She said to Ben in resignation and focused on the task of stirring her tea, this time with a tighter grip. Ben snuck a wink at me.

For the rest of the evening, he urged me to write. In response, Ma said, "Artists are poor, they make no money. How did her painter of a father end up? I bet you, poor and disgruntled."

"From what you've told me, it seems the man was a revolutionary," I overhead him say after I left for the bathroom. "He used his art to protest colonial rule."

"With art?" she scoffed. "To overcome the conditions of this world, all one needs is to make a solid living, and that is rarely achieved with art." The Friday following the solstice, while Ben and I played chess on the living room floor, I asked him why I ought to stay with Ma. I let him know that I got along better with him than with her. He said it was because she needed me more. I insisted she was extremely independent, just like me, and that she seemed to fare well without my companionship, and that besides, I would soon be in college, far away from her, and then what? Would she still need me then?

He dropped the pawn in his hand and said, "Make sure you come home frequently, okay!?"

Pouting, I said that I would. He opened his mouth to say something else but was interrupted by the sound of Ma's car in the driveway.

A WEEK LATER, BEN LEFT FOR Nabuka. The night before his departure, I sobbed, face pressed against my pillow in bed. I was tired of losing him, missing him. I thought of myself growing into womanhood, soon to be in college, while Ben would be far away in Nabuka, and would probably continue to be far away for the rest of my life.

Ma and I dropped him off at the airport the following morning. We had to travel almost an hour to get there. Once we arrived at the departure terminal, Ma and Ben embraced each other in the car like comrades. As for me, I followed him outside and buried my face in his Old Spice scented suit before he nudged me to join Ma in the car.

A few days into July of 1967, a couple of weeks after Ben's departure, civil war broke out in Nabuka. We heard about it on the radio one evening after dinner. The Afa people were adamant about secession. It was officially Nabuka versus Afa—the new, mostly Afa nation. As expected, Ma was burdened by the war, even though she expressed happiness at Afa solidarity and kept saying, "It's about time we made them stop killing us like chickens." We were both worried about Ben, but he called whenever he could get through to us to let us know that he was okay and to give us updates about Nne and other relatives. I was optimistic the conflict would soon end, and life would return to normal once both sides realized the inanity of their undertaking.

Chapter Nine

August 1967

BEFORE BEN RETURNED TO NABUKA, HE told me he had deposited an unspecified amount of money into a personal account set up for me. He made me promise I would not touch the account until I was in college and in desperate need. Ma was present and warned me to manage my money wisely. She said just because I had money stashed somewhere was not a good enough reason for me not to work like everyone else my age.

Towards the end of August was when I left for college. It was also when I decided to call Sal; I suddenly found myself longing for his sweet voice and easy laugh. He had telephoned the house a few times when Ben was around. Ma had answered those calls with a look of suspicion, and I had relayed the message through her that I would contact Sal back. Truth was I didn't want to risk having either Ben or Ma listening in on our conversation. Then after Ben departed in June, I became too preoccupied with college preparations and with the happenings in Nabuka to create adequate space for Sal. Perhaps he had also become too preoccupied with his own life to create adequate space for me.

He telephoned two more times. Both times I answered, but the conversations were brief. In the first conversation, I shared with him how happy I was to be enrolled at Smart. He told me he wasn't sure what he wanted to do with his life even though he was about to turn eighteen, and his mother wanted him to attend college right away to avoid being drafted to the military. Then I heard his mom call out his name. The conversation ended there. The next time he called, which was two days later, his voice was laced with concern. He had learned about the war in Nabuka. He wanted to know if my family was safe. I felt a lump in my throat and stinging tears in my eyes. I told him my family was okay and quickly ended the call with the excuse Ma needed to use the telephone. It wasn't true. Ma wasn't home that day.

A week before my departure date, I called him once more. His mother said he was running errands and would relay the message. I didn't call again—for a while. Perhaps fear and trepidation had swallowed that space. I didn't know how to go into detail about the genocide and war that had imploded in Nabuka. About the devasting impact it was already having on family and friends, who thankfully were still alive as far as Ma and I could tell. It just wasn't something I was ready to fully discuss yet for fear of casting a shadow on whatever it is that we had which to me was something special but very fragile. Now as I dialed his number, the sweet rush came flooding back. He needed to know that I was leaving for Smart. I needed to find out what his plans were and how we would remain in touch.

"Hello?" A female, prepubescent voice answered the phone.

"Hi, can I speak to Sal please?"

"Who's this?"

"Ada."

"Sal isn't here."

"Oh. Can you please let him know that I called and that I will call him…"?

"…He's in Italy."

"Excuse me?"

"He's moved to Italy." She sounded impatient.

"Anna!" Someone in the background shouted.

"Mom, I am on the phone!" she yelled back. I imagined her head cocked sideways, away from the telephone handle.

"Hello?" She was clearer again.

"Thank you," I stuttered.

About an hour later, Ma and I drove in silence towards the train station, *The Mamas and the Papas* singing "California Dreamin'" on the car stereo, my belongings stuffed in some luggage in the trunk of the car. I looked out the window of Ma's 1966 Cadillac and caught bees buzzing around flower gardens. I noticed Bishop Coral High at a distance, atop a slope in an aura of timelessness. I recalled the moments I had spent with Stacey, and with Sal, and even my historic fight with Ariel.

Sal. My thoughts returned to Sal. In my head, I rewound what his sister had said. "He's moved to Italy." Sal was in Italy? Why hadn't he told me his plans during those phone calls? I wondered when he had decided to go to Italy or if it was more of a spur-of-the-moment kind of thing. I kicked myself for not calling sooner.

"Ada, I would prefer you select a field of study as soon as possible," Ma said, interrupting my thoughts.

We had already discussed this, and I had already told her that I was undecided.

"After I speak to an advisor, Ma, I will make a decision," I said to appease her.

I wanted to select something in the line of English Literature as a field of concentration, but with Ma's disapproval of the artistic discipline, I felt there was no use letting her in on this, at least for now.

"Decide soon," she said firmly. "And keep in touch, at all times."

"Yes, Ma," I said, but in my head I was rolling my eyes.

We arrived at the station and Ma parked in the parking lot and followed me to the platform. About ten minutes later, we could hear the puffing engine of the train, then the train became visible, and finally made a stop and opened its doors. After a brief, warm embrace, Ma watched me board. I quickly found a window seat and placed my single luggage in the overhead compartment. Once settled, I smiled wryly and waved goodbye at Ma through the window. She smiled back, one of her rare full smiles. The engine continued to puff and roar. It was just me on the seat. My time had finally come. I shut my eyes and prepared for the ride.

Part II

We Shall Overcome

Chapter Ten

August 1967 Continued . . .

I HAD DECIDED ON A WOMEN'S college because a part of me wanted to please Ma. Even though I had rebelled by not applying to one of the Ivy League schools Ma had suggested, I still on a subliminal level craved her approval. To select Byrn Mawr, her alma mater, would have been a sound declaration of solidarity that I didn't think she deserved. But Smart was the perfect middle ground, appeasing both of us. It was also a prestigious college located in the same state as Harvard.

When the train reached its final stop, several hours after I bid farewell to Ma in Greensberg, the sun had just retreated to its origins. A lazy cool breeze whispered among the trees, the sky a clear, deep blue.

A Mrs. Butler came to pick me up along with a few other students, mainly international students, who had boarded the same train. This pickup arrangement had been made a week before I departed from Greensberg. I could only make out little details of Mrs. Butler's facial features under the evening light, but I noticed her blonde bob hairstyle and her rather colorful dress that danced around her flabby cream legs. She introduced herself as the primary advisor of the international students council. We drove in a Jeep, about eight of us.

"Welcome to Smart College," she said in a British accent, breaking the silence. I glanced at the other students. They were all white. Most spoke French. They said nothing to me, so I said nothing to them.

"Thank you, Mrs. Butler, for picking me up," I said from the back of the Jeep.

"You are welcome my dear," she replied cheerfully. "You must be from Afrika."

The chatter stopped as the girls stopped to listen in on the conversation.

"Yes," I replied and held my breath, hoping that I would be swift enough to counter whatever racially driven comment might follow.

"I want to visit Afrika sometime. I hear they have the best cuisine, and I love Afrikan fabrics. So colorful, so alive!"

Relieved, I smiled. The other girls continued with their idle banter. I looked out the window. The road was wide and clear.

Smart College was a picturesque little community surrounded by colonial-style structures, tranquil trees like maple, honey locust, and white pine, and lush gardens. There were no dormitories. Students lived in brick houses, some dating back to the 19th century.

My new home was a two-story brick house with approximately ten bedrooms. Each bedroom was heavily furnished with 19th-century furniture decked in gold trimmings and housed two roommates.

The building in which I was housed was supposed to honor one of Smart College's alumna who had been a locally renowned painter. The main lounge, located on the first floor, had photographs of Frida Kahlo, Georgia O' Keefe, Sylvia

Path, and Virginia Woolf on each corner of the wall. The placarded quote under Virginia Woolf's image read: *As a woman, I have no country. As a woman, my country is the whole world.*

That day as I stood beside my luggage, a fellow freshman turned and said to me, "This building reeks of estrogen, doesn't it?" The resident director, a prickly young woman who was assisting me and other students with our housing and room placements, glared.

"What is wrong with estrogen?" she snapped.

The freshman did not respond. She chewed her gum and went her way.

"Her parents obviously forced her to come here," the director said, rolling her eyes. "Girls like that take us back a hundred years."

It did not take long for me to befriend my roommate, an effervescent red head named Anna, and a mild-mannered and introspective East Afrikan girl named Nzingha who lived next door. We met during orientation and considered it serendipitous that we were in constant proximity with each other during the campus tours and freshman meetings hosted by seniors. We laughed about it until a solid amity was formed.

It was clear Anna and I were a match. Besides the occasional, to be expected annoyances and idiosyncrasies, we proved to be a suitable pair. I was surrounded by intelligent, ambitious women who possessed higher visions than the previous generation, it seemed. Most importantly, many of the students were concerned about social issues such as the environment, civil rights, and the anti-war movement. I met interesting people from all over the world, people like me who had taken the chance to live and be educated in a foreign land. And for once in my American academic life, it was refreshing not being the only black or minority student! The foreign students on campus brought out my thirst for travel, but with the active life I was leading and my plans to work during the summer holidays, I knew international travel would have to remain in the backseat.

In mid-September 1967, I joined the campus newspaper staff and we held our first meeting in a room known as The Bennet, named after a certain Jane Bennet, a 19th century aristocrat whose funds had helped lay the foundation for the building. The room had cream leather couches, a couple of bay windows, a glass backyard door that opened to an exquisite rose garden, and several obscure Victorian paintings on the wall. There were about thirty of us in that meeting and we had different seating arrangements. The ones who made it on time planted their bottoms on couches while the late comers had no option but to sit on windowsills and the burgundy-colored carpet. I was one of those on a windowsill. Sitting there allowed me to scan the room easily. I noticed a combination of fresh-looking faces and some more mature ones. The freshmen, or freshers as they were often referred to by Mrs. Butler, gave themselves away with their unnecessary giggles and whisperings in contrast to the older students who sat mostly in a calm and collected manner, some with bored expressions. I was filled with feverish excitement, just like the other freshers.

I would have missed this meeting if it hadn't been for Nzingha. A few days ago, I had told her about my interest in writing, and she mentioned to me that she had noticed a sign in the campus cafeteria announcing the first Smart news publication staff meeting for the year. The sign, according to her, had encouraged freshmen to attend as well. When Nzingha told me that the name of the campus publication was *The Phoenix*, I grew even more intrigued. Something about that fiery winged bird, a symbol of transformation, spoke to me at that moment. I hoped *The Phoenix* would allow me to blaze a trail.

The humming in the room ceased when another student walked in. Her walk was different from the rest. It was more dignified, almost authoritative. She had a file and a few copies of what appeared to be *The Phoenix*. She sat in an empty seat reserved for her somewhere in the middle of the room. I studied her features: blonde hair, straight, skinny nose, marine blue eyes, cold as fish. You could tell right away that she wasn't the type to banter much nor was she the kind to engage the other staff in any way that was beyond what was necessary for her position as the editor. She introduced herself as Mary and went straight to the topic at hand, describing the history of *The Phoenix*, for the freshers. How it was founded sometime in the late 1800s. How her ancestor, the great Dame Bennet, had pushed for the publication of the magazine during her student days at Smart and how *The Phoenix* held itself to an exceedingly high standard, expecting only the best out of its writers.

"So, any questions?" she asked, scanning the room. A student raised her hand. She was a fresher. You could tell. She was too feverishly excited.

"I was wondering, em . . . if you know anything about the type of person Dame Bennet was?"

I heard someone in the room whisper, "What da fuck, who cares?" I forced myself to keep a straight face. Fortunately, Mary was too focused on her agenda to notice.

"What is your name?" Mary asked with a condescending smile.

"Sophie . . . Sophie Blanche."

"Sophie, one thing I know for a fact was that she was a fantastic lady. A lady of innovation, a feminist unlike any other, a pioneer . . ."

Another student, someone I had already recognized during orientation as a senior, raised her hand before Mary could complete her sentence, and opened her mouth before she was granted permission to speak.

"So are there certain things we wish to explore this year?" She asked. Her voice was strong and commanding.

"How about bringing back the poetry and short story segment?" another student interjected.

The senior nodded in agreement saying, "Yea, exactly."

Mary appeared hesitant. Her countenance had also grown a little harder. It affected the tone of her response.

"It takes time and effort to edit poetry and short stories. It is not the same as editing an article . . . " she said with clenched teeth.

"We are going to require perfectly edited submissions, of course," the senior said. "And if you need a helping hand choosing which ones to publish, I can assist you. I major in creative writing with a minor in English Literature. I am also a member of the English Honors Society."

Some of the students agreed with her, nodding their heads.

"Yea, Mary, I think it's a good idea," another student said and many in the room agreed, nodding their heads even harder.

Mary stretched her neck like a peacock. She knew she was already defeated. To disagree with what most people in the room agreed on would make her undemocratic, an outcast.

"Okay, short story and poetry segment returns, but we can only publish a few at a time, and it has to be a once in a month type of thing."

Everyone agreed. It was settled. Students interested in submitting short stories and poetry were encouraged to fill a sheet of paper on their way out. We were also encouraged to submit writing samples for review after signing up and were told that selected candidates should expect a telephone call within a week.

A week went by and no samples from me. What if my writing wasn't good enough? Thankfully, soon after, I received a telephone call from a senior who introduced herself as Kat. Recognizing that I had an accent, she asked me where I was from. I told her. Immediately she brought up that there was a war in Nabuka and encouraged me to send a writing sample and to use my poetry as an outlet if I wished. Feeling a bit more inspired, I sent her a writing sample through the school mailbox a day later and by the following day, it was approved.

EVERYONE WAS DATING, AND I FOUND myself pressured into thinking I ought to be swapping spit with a fella against some tree, or in front of a movie theater, or drive-in, or parking lot . . .

Though it was an all-women's college, there were opportunities to mingle with the opposite sex outside campus. Most times, however, I was unimpressed. It was either they were too tall, or too short, or too suave, or too dull, or too disingenuous. I had resigned myself to spending the rest of my freshman year as a single woman when Malcolm came along.

Malcolm was a black American with caramel skin, not tall but not short either. He attended a community college in Boston. My favorite feature of his was his hair. It was full and thick, and he had the slickest sideburns. He was black, he was proud, and he was highly active in his community as a civil rights activist. He had participated in the marches, attended the meetings, and had even been jailed a few times before the civil rights bill was passed. And now he was pushing for more rights and equality with his poetry.

We met at a poetry and music night at Malcolm's community college that a friend of Anna's had invited us to. Malcolm had just read a poem about police brutality that left me spellbound. What he read, and the intensity with which it was delivered, left me wanting to know who this man was. Because besides what they showed on television of civil rights demonstrators being hosed down by police, I hadn't been aware of the bitter struggles of inner-city blacks until that night.

After his performance and the applause that followed from the audience, I left Anna and Nzingha at the makeshift bar after ordering a drink. My first exposure to alcohol was at age fourteen in France. It was normal to have a glass of wine or a bottle of beer at Pauline's house or on special occasions, when Ma was absent, with Ben and his diplomatic friends. That night, bold from two bottles of Guinness in my system, I walked up to Malcolm who had returned to his table by the stage. He was alone.

"That was such a wonderful piece," I gushed.

He assessed my appearance, his face illumined by what he saw. I thanked Anna under my breath for the outfit selection—a black mod dress and white platforms, hoop earrings and shimmering lip gloss.

"I'm glad, my *sister*, that you were paying attention. The struggle needs to be fought and won," he replied

I liked being referred to as *sister*. Made me feel dignified, equal, like a comrade in some underground movement. I was certain my very feminist women's studies professor Mrs. Pearson would agree it was better than being referred to as *kid,* a term of endearment used by many old-time movie actors towards their leading ladies.

"Where are you from?" Malcolm asked me. "I see you have an accent. "

"Nabuka, I mean . . . Afa . . . " I scratched my head.

"No need to feel bad, sister. I understand. War is always a bitch."

He knew about the war. That made him even more appealing.

"Nabuka or Afa, you are definitely a Nubian queen," he continued.

I did not consider myself Nubian, but I did not mind being referred to as a queen either. If being Afrikan denoted royalty, then I would claim that royalty fully.

That night I learned that he was twenty years old and the middle child of a family of five children. That his parents were elementary school teachers who, with apprehension, supported his activism. That he studied government at school, worked at a car dealership as a repairman, and lived in a studio apartment very close to home. We exchanged telephone numbers. A few days later, after a satisfying burger and fries lunch date, we shared our first kiss about half a mile away from Smart's college campus, leaning against a tree. My lips moved tentatively at first; our lips pressed against each other's until I relaxed and surrendered to the fluid motions of his tongue. He had strong lips. I could feel his kiss throughout my body. It was a good thing I wasn't in love with him.

Ma expected me to telephone her at least once a week. I was studying in bed one evening, on one such due date, when the telephone buzzed in the hallway. I considered ignoring it, but it kept ringing, and no one cared to answer it. Finally, I rose out of the bed in my black silk pajamas and pink socks and ambled towards the telephone. Expecting to hear Ma's voice, I spoke in a somewhat dreary tone.

"Hello?"

"Can I speak to Ada Ekne please?"

It wasn't Ma. Her throaty voice did, however, sound familiar.

"Speaking . . . "

"Hi, chick! It's me, Stace!"

I stood there, saying nothing.

"Hello?"

Elated, I found my voice.

"Wow, Stacey, how have you been?"

"I'm cool, real cool."

"How did you get my number?"

"I called your house and asked your Mom. Guess what she said? That she didn't have it. Can you believe that? Then I recalled she didn't seem taken by me when I showed up at your house to pick you up for the concert. So, a few days later I called again using a different voice and name. And voila, I got the number!"

"I'm sorry you had to go through all that," I said, embarrassed by Ma's behavior.

"Don't worry about it. It's nothing," she said in her carefree way.

She was no longer with Ted and was now working as a go-go dancer. The money she earned was used to pay her part of the rent in an apartment she shared with four other people on the Lower East Side. According to her, Ted had taken the free love movement too far, engaging with multiple lovers to the point where she could no longer claim him as hers. She was still pursuing acting, even though countless auditions produced nothing. She hadn't spoken to her parents for several months. Her voice fell when she said this.

THAT CALL FROM STACEY BECAME ONE of our weekend habits. We discussed our daily lives. I vented to her about my classes, she about her failed auditions. We discussed the war in Nabuka.

"If we were all free and smoked dope, there wouldn't be any wars," was her response to almost every horrific incident.

I informed her about Ben and his most recent decision to fight on the side of Afa, albeit behind the scenes. She hoped for all to go well, whatever "well" meant, but didn't linger on the subject, knowing that it was the last thing I wanted to talk about. In one of our conversations, she asked about Sal.

"He moved to Italy," I told her.

"What a shame, he was such a nice guy," she replied.

"As you know, I am still seeing Malcolm. He's a nice guy too."

"Malcolm?"

I was pretty sure I had mentioned Malcolm in one of our many conversations.

"Yea, the boy I told you I just starting going steady with, remember?"

"Oh, right. Yea, yea," she said and quickly moved on to other topics.

Chapter Eleven

October 1967

Finally, it happened. One of Stacey's many auditions came through. She telephoned me one early fall evening to share the good news.

"I'm gonna be in a really cool musical, chick!" she announced. Something about Stacey's excitement, her minor triumphs, made me want to believe in the world again. There was an unadulterated feel about it, like it added to a grand universal optimism that held the universe together.

"Congratulations, Stace!" I replied with the same gusto. I fished for more details. She said the production was called *Hair* and was about hippies, revolution, and The Age of Aquarius—a coming period of peace, understanding, and everything well-meaning people all over had been praying for with regards to our planet. She was going to be playing a small part as a background dancer. It was last minute. A cast member had fallen ill. It wasn't Broadway—at least not yet—but it was a start. Something right up her alley! Days later, I discussed with Malcolm about going to The Public Theater in Lower Manhattan to watch Stacey's performance. We were snuggled together on a park bench, a few feet away from an ice-cream truck, feasting on our stuffed cones, our arms interlocked, my furry pink and black checkered cardigan and his musky scented brown leather jacket intertwined. My ice-cream selection, vanilla. His, butter pecan. The trees had turned different shades of yellow, brown, and red, ushering the fall season. Some of the leaves littered the ground in a pastel of warm colors. Ahead of us, a young white mother was playing hide-and-seek with her daughter, who looked to be about four years old. The toddler's giggle echoed through the air, made the atmosphere sparkle, like a slice of heaven had fluttered its way to us—like a moment in France with Ben. It even left a fixated smile on Malcolm's usually furrowed face.

"How do you feel about going to New York to see a musical?" I blurted out. It was my first time suggesting something *this* different. Our dates normally consisted of strolls, smoking cigarettes in parks, picnics, and make out sessions in his stone-washed gray Toyota Corolla. I still hadn't seen the inside of his studio apartment. He said it didn't evoke romance, that it reminded him too much of the movement—the densely stacked books penned by black intellectuals: James Baldwin, W.E.B Du Bois, Langston Hughes, and the likes. He said the walls were filled with posters of freedom fighters—Marcus Garvey, Medgar Evers, Martin Luther King, Malcolm X—and the air was saturated with the spirited echoes of passionate comrades on their way out to a match.

He hadn't seen the inside of my living quarters either. It was a building for women, celebrating white women accomplishments. Somehow, we both agreed it would be awkward to usher him into such a space. We had a lot of heady conversations, him doing most of the talking, the educating. I did not mind this. I'd rather hear him talk. It provided more comfort to me than being listened to. Honestly, at this point, I did not find myself that interesting. Perhaps if I had told him that I noticed the sun dance like a cosmic wave from time to time, or that I could hear the spirits in the air whisper when all was silent, or that I knew for a fact that trees gossiped when they leaned towards each other and their branches touched, he may have found me fascinating. But it wasn't the sort of thing that I wanted to go into with anyone except for Sal. And with Sal, it was never something I went into, it just was...

". . . is that what you want?" His silky voice jolted me out of my skin.

"What?"

"New York? The play?"

"Yes, I would love to support my friend Stacey, from high school. She's part of the cast. Perhaps we could surprise her," I responded before capturing a stream of vanilla goodness running down my fingers with my tongue.

Malcolm took a mouthful of his pecan ice-cream. I watched the gradual curling motion of his tongue as he licked his lips. It made my heart skip a bit and my knees tingle.

"Not my sorta thing to be honest with you, my queen. But if that's what you wanna do, I'm down."

"Thanks, Malcolm," I said. As if intercepting my thoughts, he leaned in for a kiss. His kiss tasted musky and sweet.

THE NIGHT BEFORE THE PRODUCTION, MALCOLM called to cancel. It was the first time, and he promised me it would be the last. He said he had forgotten that he had scheduled a meeting with a Black Panther leader visiting from Oakland, California. He had educated me about the Black Panthers a while back—how they were considered a hate group, and how the FBI was on their tail even though, in his opinion, they were community organizers interested in the protection and upliftment of black youth. I told him not to worry about it. That I understood. I also pleaded with him to be careful and safe.

After crawling up to my bed, I thought about myself marching alongside Malcolm, throwing fists in the air, putting myself in the frontlines like he did. But he always insisted this was not what he wanted for me. "There's an actual war in your country. Your plate is full as it is, queen. Keep your heads in your books," he would often say. And so, I did.

A few days later Stacey called, excited about the play and how incredibly well it went.

"If I make it to Broadway next year, I hope you can come see me!"

The rest of the year, I focused on my schoolwork, determined to end the semester with good grades. In Ma's point of view, it was one thing selecting non-science courses, it was another obtaining a less than perfect grade on the liberal art courses I supposedly loved. I found out quickly that some of my high school antics, such as the occasional class skipping, did not fare well with me here. A skipped class could mean missing out on useful information or a group project that could have secured a perfect grade or improved a weak one. At Coral High, teachers were more forgiving. At Smart, not so much. Daydreaming in class was also a luxury I could no longer afford as I quickly learned from Mr. Hall, my Shakespearian Literature Professor.

In November of 1967, during my Shakespeare class, Mr. Hall caught me etching spirals in the back of my notebook. Ever since I could recall, I was drawn to and loved to draw spirals. I would proceed with a big circle and then repeat downwards until they became such small circles that there was nothing left. Sal once told me, after peering into my notebook in philosophy class, that it was perhaps an indicator of my affinity to the infinite. Professor Hall, on the verge of being elderly, short in stature with a lopsided toupee and a habit of donning wrinkled suits, was only concerned with the finite, in particular, *Hamlet* on this day. He approached Shakespeare like a religion, and any student who approached Shakespeare with lesser devotion was treated like a heretic. And here I was being an ardent heretic, doodling in the middle of the classroom, unaware I was being watched.

"Miss Ekene," he called out mid-monologue with a voice that had grown fatigued with time.

Startled, I responded with a very meek, "Yes, Mr. Hall."

He read from his book on the desk: "To die, to sleep--to sleep, perchance to dream—ay, there's the rub, for in this sleep of death what dreams may come. . ." He paused, staring at me with opaque looking eyes.

"Your thoughts?" he continued, blinking rapidly.

My thoughts felt like mush. My heart raced, my hands trembled as I flipped through the pages of Hamlet. The silence in the room washed over me until it felt like I was about to be swallowed by it.

"Meet with me after class," he said curtly.

The next twenty minutes felt like twenty years as I waited for all the students to file out before walking up to Mr. Hall who was wiping the chalk filled board. He appeared so frail, I thought he might tumble over if he jerked his arm across the board one more time. He turned around to face me.

"You have it in you Ada. Which is why it hurts me so much to see you take this so . . ." he balled his fist, the same fist that began to tremor as he ransacked his brain for the appropriate criticism. "It pains me to see you take this class like it is a joke! Is this how you treat your other courses!?" he stammered.

I felt shame, watching my professor, timid and passionate, breaking down before me because of my uncontrollable interest in etching spirals in notebooks.

"You are on the verge of a C. You are very close. Is that what you want?!" Mr. Hall continued. He searched my face for an answer, any answer.

I needed to say something and quick. "No, Mr. Hall. It is not what I want. I promise to be better, to do better."

I meant what I said. I walked out of the classroom that afternoon with a greater resolve to excel. Shakespearian English was exacting to my fidgety brain. But I would study hard. It was challenging, juggling a quasi-romantic relationship, a social life, and loads of coursework, but I was determined to do my best.

By the end of the semester in December, I managed a B in Shakespeare (Mr. Hall said he extended some grace to me due to my efforts) and a GPA of 3.4. Ma looked over my grade report over the holidays and with a look of acceptance said, "I trust you will do better next semester."

JANUARY OF 1968 USHERED IN THE second semester of freshman year. By then I had become so comfortable with campus life to the point it felt more of a home than my actual home. My telephone interactions with Stacey had lessened significantly by the previous November due to my busy schedule (research papers, tests, exams) and frankly, our different lifestyles. Still, it was a connection we both continued to maintain even though it was clear we had, in some ways, grown apart.

Malcolm and I managed to spend every other weekend together. I chose not to pressure him. I gave him all the space he needed like the forbearing girlfriend of a freedom fighter. We ebbed and flowed this way until a shock wave hit the nation in the spring.

In early April of 1968, I strolled into the lobby of my building, after an hour of research in the library, to catch a group of students huddled over a colossal television in sober silence. I inched closer to hear a devasting news report. Martin Luther King had just been assassinated on a balcony in Memphis, Tennessee. I stood in complete horror for five minutes before rushing upstairs to telephone Malcolm. He was distraught. I could hear people in the background wailing and cursing. I don't recall what either of us said that evening. I just remember an overwhelming feeling of despondency.

About a week into the production of *Hair,* Malcolm visited me at Smart College. He was standing on the bottom step of my building. I was standing on the one above it, bringing our heights a little closer. By the redness of his eyes and the puffiness of his face, I knew Malcom was weary. And his weariness meant little room for leisure activities, such as a New York City trip to go see a Broadway show. I told him he didn't have to see *Hair* with me if he didn't want to.

"But I promised you . . ." he said, reaching for my right hand. He began to stroke it. It felt warm and grainy, like leather.

"Don't worry about it," I consoled him. "I know someone who won't mind going with me."

He pulled me closer until I was forced to stand on the same step he was on. He buried his head in my neck. "You are special. I hope to one day make it up to you in every way."

Later that month, the very thrilled Anna and I made it to the Broadway premiere of *Hair*. By then Stacey was no longer in the cast. The sick dancer had long recovered, and production felt she was a better fit. Stacey was too upset to show up. Even though I was disappointed that she didn't have the courtesy to at least meet with us before or after the show, I chose to pretend I wasn't affected. After all, she had been my first real friend in high school and, at one point, Sal's neighbor. That provided enough sentiment in my mind to put up with some of her personality traits. Anna and I sat in a back row with limited lighting due to ticket affordability, but it didn't stop me from enjoying the show.

My face exploded into a smile at the evocative dance number in which the cast belted, *This is the dawning of the Age of Aquarius!* When they sang, *Let the sunshine, let the sunshine, the sunshine in*!

I sobbed.

A FEW DAYS AFTER *HAIR*, THE evening breeze was cool and seductive, James Brown was on the radio declaring he was black and proud, and I was in front of the mirror in my bedroom admiring the mini skirt Anna had convinced me to purchase while on a rare shopping spree. It exposed my "nice legs" and made me appear less "square." I was wearing a pair of go-go boots. My hair was tied neatly in a bun, large silver hoops dangled from my ear lobes. All this was for Malcolm, who had arranged to pick me up for a movie date that evening in an attempt to "make it up to me." We hadn't seen each other for over a week, since our talk on the steps, and had chatted on the telephone only once since. Tonight, I wanted to surprise him, to prove to him that I could be more than just the "girl next door." Truthfully, it was all Anna's idea. The previous night, she had looked me squarely in the eye after I confessed that I still hadn't seen his apartment and said, "What if he has another girl?" Of course, that thought had crossed my mind. I often wondered, what if he had a girl who understood him better, his world, his life? What if I was the naïve suburban girl he ran to as a means of escape from his gritty inner-city revolutionary existence? In front of Anna, I projected a different feeling. I shook my head, no. Malcolm didn't have another girl, at least not in the physical sense, I was certain, I said to her. If anything, his "other girl" was his work. I reminded her that he juggled a lot—school, the car dealership, activism. Mentally, I admitted I wasn't completely unhappy with the way things were going with Malcolm. There was something easy about him. No intense emotions were involved. No excessive demands. We connected when we connected and that was that.

Still, Anna insisted I keep it sexy for our date. She believed in keeping it "sexy" to keep a man, and I wanted to prove to Stacey, and myself, besides the seeming inconsistences, that Malcolm was a keeper.

I was still admiring my look in the mirror when the telephone buzzed in the hallway. I heard someone answer it with an excited, "Hello?"

"Why doesn't he ever call me!" the same voice whined, after a few muffled seconds.

"Maybe he's busy," another voice replied.

Moments later, someone pounded on my door. I turned down the music before answering.

"It's for you," a blonde, noticeably bitter girl said before storming off. I watched her storm into her bedroom and slam the door shut, her empathetic friend not far behind.

Thinking it was Malcolm, I took the receiver and answered, "Helloooo . . . "

"Ada?"

"Yes?" I said, straightening my voice.

"It's you. What's with the voice?"

"What voice?" I asked, pretentiously.

"Sometimes you act weird, you know that, right?"

"Stacey, why are you calling?"

"I wanna apologize once again for not meeting up with you chicks in New York."

"It's fine. Apology accepted."

"Cool . . . um, I have to tell you something though."

Her voice was low. My heart cleaved to my mouth. Was she pregnant? Did she contract a venereal disease at her work-place? But she never said she slept with customers. She interrupted my morbid and quite frankly disparaging thoughts about her, her voice clear and crisp.

"I called to say I have decided to join the gay rights movement."

I said nothing. Suddenly the air felt deeply silent. Then like a record needle that kept skipping back, my thoughts zapped a few years back to the kiss at the Groove Box. Maybe the kiss should have been an indication. Maybe. But I was afraid to go into why, to go into further detail with her. Perhaps I was afraid to discover what that meant for her, for us.

"Hello?" I heard her say.

"As long as it makes you happy, Stace..."

"Really?!"

"Of course."

". . . After Ted and I broke up, my parents still tried to reach out and all until I told them what I was into now, ya know." She stopped, then continued. "My mom cried on the phone, then called my dad and he cursed at me, and then she took the phone from him and said it was those damn hippies and drugs and Ted's fault . . . And then my dad took the phone and said I had caused Mom much grief and that they didn't want to have anything to do with me no more," she said.

"Wow . . ."

"Yea. I thought I'd share that with you . . ."

"I'm sorry your parents acted that way . . ."

I blinked for a few moments and then shook my head. "Stacey, I'm sorry, but I have to go," I said quietly and hung up the phone.

I felt bad ending the conversation like that, but my thoughts were on my own love life, on Malcolm. Why hadn't he called?

Moments later, the telephone rang again. It was Malcolm. He was on his way to Philadelphia as he had just received a telephone call from a comrade's girlfriend who needed his assistance to bail her man out of jail for supposedly inciting a riot in Philadelphia during a protest.

"They really messing with our people. I gotta fight harder," he mumbled before dropping the call.

I became fully aware of my appearance. It no longer matched what I was feeling on the inside, dejected and out of touch. Overcome with this new sensation, I dashed to my room, jerked the skirt and boots off me and flung them in the closet, where they would remain for the rest of my college years.

Chapter Twelve

August 1968

By late summer, the war in Nabuka was waging on with morbid intensity. I was able to garner updated war information through the librarian who saved newspaper clips from *The New York Times* and *Washington Post.* She was a pleasant white woman and, for a time, an angel to me. When she discovered my avid interest in the war, she began compiling clips for me.

The death toll was climbing. Foreign journalists were traveling to the warring region to capture images and report back on stories. On campuses across the country, youths were creating organizations and raising awareness and funds for the people of Afa whom they considered victims. In London, citizens were protesting their government's involvement in the war as it became more apparent their government was arming the Nabukan side with weapons.

Stacey was raising funds for a Catholic church's Afa relief mission. She said the nuns and priests were friendly to hippies and that it made her feel less judgmental of people in religious authority. As for me, I gave up hope on normalcy and began to write feverishly as I thought of the rising death toll and the innumerable kwashiorkor cases among children.

Just as Malcolm was using his poetry to protest civil rights abuses against black Americans, I did the same for the innocent women, men, and children who were caught in the horrific thresholds of war. I vented about child soldiers being forced to shed blood because of the self-serving needs of a few sinister people in power. I was convinced most people did not want to kill or die senselessly. Most people wanted to love and partake in life. It was only through deception and manipulation that people lacking hope, passion, and love decide to destroy what they have failed to understand.

On a global scale, the world watched as prominent leaders were violently toppled off the world stage. Martin Luther King's assassination incited riots in Louisville, Baltimore, Washington D.C., and many parts of the country. It was depressing, growing into the realization that we lived in a sick world, a world out of touch with life, with love, with its essence. As if the nation had not undergone enough tragedies, in June of that year another great figure, Democratic senator and noted civil rights activist Bobby Kennedy, would also be lost to an assassin's bullet, throwing the nation into a state of grief and chaos. Including me. Except that in addition to everything going on around me in the United States, I also had more personal distresses that stretched past U.S. borders. I worried about Ben, Nne, and other relatives and friends. I worried about their safety and hoped that the United Nations would intervene and end the civil war. But my hopes were quickly dashed when I realized the war could only end with victory for one side and crushing defeat for the other.

Besides Britain's support of Nabuka, Afa had its share of international supporters, France being one of them. Afrika's first post-independent civil war was inciting global interest like wildfire!

Malcolm and I fizzled out like an open can of soda pop. Then one early August afternoon, while listening to a radio commentary on how James Brown had saved the city of Boston from being engulfed in flames after Martin Luther King's death, my gaze fell upon a Boston newspaper on Anna's hardwood desk. I picked it up and began to scan through it as was my habit with newspapers. And then like lightening, I was jolted by a photo of Malcolm with a small group of people in handcuffs. With a gaping mouth and bulging eyes, I read the article. His apartment had been raided by the cops due to suspicious activity involving the Panthers and other "hate" groups. Now I understood even more clearly why he had never invited me to his home. The risk was too high. I also knew that I would never hear from him again. He was now on their radar for more "insidious" reasons, and anyone close to him would be in jeopardy.

Malcolm's arrest fueled me even further to focus on my new cause. In my free time, I studied United Nations policies, world governments, and international development. Imperialism, I concluded, was the enemy. It was the reason behind colonialism, the reason behind the Berlin conference in the 1800s that mapped out the continent of Afrika. It was also the reason for the amalgamation of Nabuka in the early 1900s. The reason why ethnic groups were now at each other's throats. Like many of my peers, new left ideologies, especially socialism, appealed to me. My field of study became world history, to Ma's astonishment.

"Ada, what happened to medicine, law . . . something more lucrative?"

"But Ma, I want to make a difference."

"Trust me, you can do more with money."

"I am sure I will always have food to eat, Ma."

"Ada!"

"Sorry."

"Reconsider your field and stop arguing with me. History does not put food on the table!"

I might have been in college, but Ma had no problem reminding me that she was still in charge.

After the telephone call, Anna barged into our room with the local newspaper in hand.

She shoved it in my face. "Look, you are in the paper!"

I looked and there it was, a fuzzy image of me with the headline: "Afa Student Protests Her People's Plight with Brilliant, Heart Wrenching Poetry." The article printed my age, my field of concentration, and my poems.

"This is a sign you are gonna be famous one day!" she said excitedly.

"Someone must have leaked my photo and poems out," I said quietly, dismissing her comment.

I had published a couple of poems in *The Phoenix*, not expecting someone would publicize them, worst of all, without my permission. But Anna had a more sanguine outlook.

"Don't file a complaint. This is a good thing, really good," she said.

But there was more to my inner repulsion, and it had to do with seeing my name associated exclusively with Afa. Inasmuch as I was a proud Afan and abhorred the suffering of my kinsmen, I had believed in Nabuka, still believed in Nabuka. What was to become of people like me in history's assessment? Would we be considered idealistic, unpatriotic, or even worse, traitors?

Heroes

Heroes are born,
In times like these
Voices become swings,
At the enemy

The road to perdition
Was the soundtrack of their lives,
Reduced to microscopic significance,
Due to neglect by the masses

Neglect to object,
At the subtle signs of oppression
First emerging from the collective mind
Then trickling down to performances
It takes a while.

Even as one person is extinguished,
A dozen, a score, a hundred
Perhaps equivalent to a quiver of protest
Maybe just ripe enough for the next redemption song

Heroes emerge in times like these,
In times of genocide, war, disease
In times when hell is more than a state of mind

Time is on our side---God is on our side,
Who is on the side of the sacrificial lambs?

Meanwhile in another place in time, an uprising, and a hero
To be born

Loss of Innocence

Bloody Rivers
It was Nkem who caused the flow,
Barely a moon ago
He played hide n' seek in dusty playgrounds,
Under sunset skies

Groans and Moans
Ani's womb threatens to implode,
Her insides smell like death,
Flies and vultures ballooned to content,
Her thighs exposed to see.

That

Young butterflies armed with ak47s,
Rummage sacred forests
Circling the war mill
That feed real-life vampires in high places.

Stolen innocence is nothing compared,
To the rape of innocence

I wonder if these perpetuators,
Were themselves deprived.
And carried with them the memory,
Of when their wonderment was forcefully drowned
In rivers of blood

In being the initiators
Do they heal, feel justified in their suffering?

Pleased at the idea that they shall not be the only generation?
That cannot remember heaven?

She needs to be sown up, our mother,
Look at her, don't turn away,
From her gut-wrenching cries
No epidurals can silence this pain,
Manifesting in the souls of her children
Forced to perpetuate the illusion,
Of separation and disharmony
As day by day, we lose Nkems and female equivalents.
In Nabuka, America, Vietnam, and everywhere...

Moment by moment, flames extinguishing
Memories of paradise and magic disappearing

The day after Anna showed me my poetry and picture in the local newspaper, I received a telephone call from Mary, the newspaper editor, apologizing rather precariously for "lending" my poetry to the local newspaper for publication. Her excuse was that she feared I would object to the idea if she had posed it to me first because of my tendency to "hold back."

"You see, they promised to promote our publication. I couldn't bypass such an opportunity."

"But you could have asked me," I said in a quiet assertive voice.

Her tone hardened. "You were published in a major publication. You are raising awareness. Be grateful."

But you handled this whole thing like I do not exist!

"You should be happy; you are a colored girl who got published . . ." she continued over my thoughts.

"I am not colored. I am black Afrikan . . . "

"There is a war in your country. Coloreds are killing coloreds. That is the issue here."

She was right, in her way. The focus should be on the war in Nabuka.

"Okay, Mary. If it raises awareness, I am cool with it. But next time can you please ask me first . . ."

". . . One more thing," she said, interrupting me. "You need to take it easy with the tone. Don't forget I am the editor."

After that, I heard the telephone click. She had hung up.

"I can't believe she spoke to you that way!" Stacey said after I reiterated my incident with Mary. "You are too nice, Ada, too nice. In Afrika do they teach you to be that nice?"

"No, but . . . "

". . . No but what?"

I wanted to explain to Stacey that my seemingly passive attitude stemmed from my belief that there were just too many emotional battles to fight to waste needed energy on a college editor who had a goddess complex. But I feared Stacey would drag the issue on and on if I stayed on the subject. So, I switched gears, posing questions about her own life, how she was doing, what she was up to. She said she was joining hundreds of people in a Vietnam War protest in a few hours. The protest was taking place close to the United Nations building—she was joining because her younger brother, Matt, had just been drafted into the army. She wanted me to come, too. I glanced at the pile of textbooks on my desk.

"I don't know if I can make it. I have a lot of schoolwork . . ."

"Come on Ada, I don't want my brother dying over this illegal occupation of Vietnam. Besides, this will be a good opportunity for us to see each other again."

I wanted to see Stacey, but I also wanted to catch up on schoolwork. I also wondered if attending a Vietnam War protest was an indication of my misplaced priorities. There was a war in my own country that I ought to be in the streets protesting. Charity begins at home, as they say. Pick your battles.

"Stacey, I am not sure if this is a good time." I said.

"Of course, it is. It is always a good time to protest. Come on!"

"Stacey . . ."

"Look, it's either you join me on this one or you will be forced to organize a gay rights march with me next week."

I held my breath. "Stacey, my mother will kill me," I whispered.

She did not reply to this. We both knew the excuse was lame.

"Come on, come with me for this one. Just this once, please?!"

I reluctantly took an early afternoon greyhound bus to New York City. I found the city quite agreeable and disagreeable at the same time—which was a good thing as it flamed my inspirations. I had come to embrace her for her artists, skyscrapers, theaters, and Broadway. I found fascinating the stark contradictions that signified this city; that on one end of the spectrum, it was a haven for insomniacs, hustlers, prostitutes, hippies, and druggies, and on the other end, a haven for geniuses, writers, activists, movie stars, and financial tycoons. The best and the worst of people, nested here. It was the ideal city. The place where everyone wanted to be for its glamor. The place everyone dreaded for its grittiness. It was the place for anyone who longed to belong.

When I got off the bus, Stacey was right there on the platform.

"Look at you chick, you look great!" she squealed. I was wearing a lose fitting t-shirt, jeans, and canvas shoes. I thought I looked decent, but I appreciated Stacey's compliment.

Unfortunately, I really couldn't extend the same sentiments to her. In her white tank top and floral print skirt, I noticed right away that slenderness had given way to scrawniness. Even her usually full breasts appeared smaller. Her eyes bulged. Her brunette roots sneaked out through the smudged shade of black that was her hair dye. Life in New York proved more difficult than either of us had imagined, I thought. Perhaps she was now hooked on some hallucinogen, which was why she was so thin. I smiled brilliantly so as not to betray my thoughts. We embraced. She led me outside and soon we were walking several blocks to the protest site on 44th Street.

"You are just in time," she said as we drew near.

There were hundreds of people in rainbow-themed outfits, with flowers attached to their hair. Most of them carried placards.

Make Love Not War.

Peace Is The Only Way.

War Kills, Peace Heals.

There were some black activists present as well, with afros that looked like black halos, chanting that it was unjust for white people to send black people to kill yellow people.

Stacey leaned towards me and said, "Do those brothers over there look sexy or what?"

"But I thought . . . "

"You thought what?"

"I thought you were now a lesbian?"

She chuckled. "Only when I feel like it. Anyway, if I were you, I would get those digits," she said, rubbing her shoulder against mine.

"No thanks, I will pass on that," I said sarcastically. Investing in a man was a futile exercise, or that's what I had concluded after everything with Malcolm. I was going to be like Ma, single, jaded, and free. This was the 20th century, and women didn't need men anymore, right?

THE CROWD HAD GATHERED IN FRONT of the United Nations building. Their leader, a Mick Jagger look-alike in shredded spandex, spoke into his hand-held speaker.

"My fellow flower children, we are gathered here today to say no more . . . "

He turned the speaker towards the crowd.

"War!"

"No more . . .?"

"War!!"

"We are sick and tired of our friends and families being sent off to die in some jungle. All we wanna do is live . . ."

"And fuck!" someone shouted, which produced a roar of laughter.

"Well, that too . . . Is that wrong?"

"No!!"

Someone else shouted: "War Kills, Peace Heals!"

Before long everyone was chanting the same slogan. I looked around me. A soft wind rustled tree leaves. The sky was clear. The sun was shining gently. It was the perfect day for a protest. Suddenly the chants were replaced by booing—a group of policemen were now ahead of us. They were in helmets, equipped with guns and batons as they appeared behind the leader who, according to Stacey, was notorious for insulting the police and inciting riots at rallies and protests across the country.

As we watched, the leader turned around and moved closer to one of the cops. The cop, a lofty man with a sinister expression, pulled out his gun. In response, the leader did something so unexpected and amazing, it raised the tiny hairs on my arms. He pulled out the lily in his hair and slid it into the barrel of the gun. I let out a wild cheer with the crowd.

Suddenly, the man was being shoved down by the cop. Protesters rained curses, and before long, a riot broke out, scattering the group. A thick mist descended in the air, followed by gunshots. It sent people running. Stacey and I ran with the rest of the crowd. I could hear my heartbeat. I was frightened but felt alive. Then Stacey fell and let out a piercing scream. I stopped. An out-of-body stillness took over me, the commotion around us muffled by my intensified heartbeat. Determined to flee the scene, I came to and dragged Stacey off the ground, leading her across the street. We ended up on a sidewalk, where Stacey slumped to the ground. I looked for signs of a gunshot wound. Fortunately, there were none.

"Are you okay?" I asked.

"Shit, I think I sprained my ankle."

"I will call an ambulance," I said and darted to the nearest pay phone I could find.

Moments later, Stacey was lying on a stretcher in the back of an ambulance with me by her side.

AT THE HOSPITAL, I WAS EVENTUALLY permitted to see Stacey. She was in bed when I walked in, a faint smile on her face, a white binding wrapped around her left ankle. I held her hand.

"I bet you weren't expecting this, huh?" she said.

"One should expect these things during protests."

She smiled at me like a proud teacher with her student. Then her face transformed into a distant frown.

"You know what's funny? Had a staff ring my brother to tell him what happened. And you know what he said? He said I shouldn't have gone to protest on his behalf. He said he didn't mind going to die for his country. I guess I broke my leg for nothing."

I tried to console her. "It was a major sprain, but it will heal soon. And it wasn't for nothing."

She ignored my statement, stared at the ceiling for several minutes then said, "Last week we were on the beach, meditating right there on the shore . . . "

She smiled, a whimsical smile, her now luminous eyes still on the ceiling. "We were lined up. Greg appeared in a white cloak, looking like a sacred vessel. And one by one we knelt before him. One by one he fed us LSD . . ."

The first question I wanted to ask was, "Who is Greg?"

But what came out was, "You take LSD?"

"Yes, why?" she said, looking at me for the first time since she went into her reverie.

"But Ted said . . ."

"Who cares the fuck what Ted said? He isn't even in my life no more. Besides, LSD is no regular drug. It connects you to the realms . . . It's spiritual." Her gaze returned to the ceiling. "That night, under that full white moon . . . in the presence of those ocean waves, I swear, I saw God. If you had told me before then there was a God, I would have said, bullshit, I am my god, and my god is me. But that night, I knew there was a god and this god is a woman in a white dress standing by the beach with the bright sun behind her. She said to me, go, go where the sun shines . . ."

According to the health department's recent reports, symptoms of taking LSD include hallucinations, neurosis, and, in some cases, mental breakdown . . . but then again all those could have been used to describe me at one point or another and I did not use drugs. Except of course, for that one time when I smoked pot at the Dope Fiend concert.

"After that vision, I knew it was a fucking sign chick, a sign to split," she said, interrupting my thoughts. "So, my fellow flower children and I decided to relocate to San Francisco to create our own commune. Isn't that swell? All that sunshine, every single day . . ." She looked at me. I let go of her hand.

"Commune?" I was still getting over the claim she had just made about seeing God on LSD.

"Yea . . . like away from all this. We are sick of air pollution, consumerism, the military industrial complex . . . Where we are headed, we would be free from all that. It will be like our own little world, with no electricity, no harmful technology. You can join us, ya know? The lady by the ocean, she will guide us."

I stared at her, my eyes bulging out of their sockets.

"What? I can't . . ."

"Why not? All you gotta do is quit school."

I paused, waiting for her to admit that she wasn't quite serious, but it never came.

"But Stacey that's not realistic," I finally blurted out what I was thinking. "You can't just go off like that . . ."

"Why not?" She asked, shrugging her shoulders, and staring at me with wide eyes.

"Because it's not logical," I said quietly.

She frowned. "You've become one of them, huh?"

"One of who?"

"You sold out."

"What?"

"Yea, you sure did."

Her words felt like a dagger plunged at my stomach. Perhaps she hadn't noticed my reaction. Perhaps she did but ceased to care as she kept up with her rant.

"You probably think I am nothing but some lazy, sloppy, drug-addicted high school dropout, huh? You probably think I got no sense in this brain of mine 'cos I am not going to Smart or whatever college you attend, huh?" she said, raising her voice. "Let me tell ya something sister girl, I got heart, I got soul, and I got the sense to do what the fuck I wanna do!"

I opened my mouth to defend myself against this new Stacey with the street lingo, this new Stacey who was raising her voice and cocking her head at me, when four people, two young men, one of them black, and two women, barged into the room. Her expression lit up when she saw them.

"Bloody Mary, Stacey! Someone said they saw you fall, you alright?" the black man asked. They spoke at the same time, smothering her with hugs and kisses until I was completely relegated to the background.

"How did you know I was here?"

"Well, the person said they saw you enter an ambulance. We figured it was going to the nearest hospital."

As they high fived each other and continued their conversation, I began to feel a sense of alienation that I hadn't experienced in a long time. It produced a sting in my eyes that extended to my throat. I resented being labeled a sell-out. Who had I sold? Who or what had I betrayed by refusing to quit college for a life of debauchery in San Francisco? I asked myself this as I tried to maintain a steady gait. On the other hand, I began to doubt myself and started to explain away my life; it wasn't my fault that my mother was a doctor and expected more from me. It wasn't my fault that I had to attend college. Even while I was thinking these thoughts, I still could not help checking my watch. It was already evening and I had to head back to campus and finish a class assignment due the next day.

"Stacey, I have to go," I said in a low, trembling voice.

No response. I took one more look at Stacey, hoping for a sign that she cared, hoping for a lingering gaze. There was neither. It was as if in her world I had ceased to exist. I left the hospital disenchanted.

Chapter Thirteen

August 1969

A YEAR PASSED WITH NO WORD from Stacey. On the forlorn bus ride home the day of the protest, I had questioned Stacey's judgement of me, concluding that my decision to remain in college was one of common sense. It showed that I was prepared to face the world headlong, unlike her, who was choosing to escape it. I said this repeatedly to myself. Like a true college student, the experience had also brought a series of questions to mind: In the territory of idealism, shouldn't there be limits? In the search for freedom, shouldn't there be boundaries? Can we all afford to do as we will? Most importantly, could society afford it?

The questions still unanswered, I quickly focused my attention on my circle of friends and activities. I even began working as a part-time restaurant waitress, donating a significant portion of my pay to the Red Cross for Afa refugees. I didn't feel like waiting until summer break to earn money anymore.

I also visited home regularly—not because I wanted to, but out of respect for Ben's wishes. It was a pattern destined to be unbroken until I received a postcard in the first semester of junior year. The card was a depiction of a colorful, surrealist painting of the Arno River. Scribbled on the flip side, "*Hi, how have you been? Sal.*"

My chest rose, then fell, rose and fell, my lungs hammering against it. I had surrendered the possibility of ever hearing from Sal again after his abrupt move to Italy. The resulting lack of resolution had solidified in my head the belief that nothing good was meant to last forever.

Anna was in the bedroom when I walked in with the postcard.

"Is that from your stepdad?" she asked.

She was in a lotus pose on her bed, staring at me intently. I was startled. I rarely shared details about Ben with her except for the time during orientation when I revealed to her that he was in Nabuka. Perhaps her curiosity was her way of finding out if he was okay.

"No," I said and returned to the note.

"So, who is it from?"

No answer.

"So, I guess this is private too, just like everything else with you these days. It's alright . . ." she sulked and reclined against her bedpost.

I studied her large, round face and flaming red hair that added life to her green eyes and red puffy cheeks. She tended to be too meddlesome for my taste, but she had a good heart. She was also fun to be around, applying zest to every situation. I gave in.

"It's from Italy."

"Oooh," she rubbed her palms in excitement. "Who do you know in Italy?"

"A friend from high school named Sal."

"Sal . . . "

"Yes, Sal."

She wanted details, and soon I found myself providing a brief synopsis of my relationship with Sal.

"Awwww, how romantic. You could use a fella. Nothing's been happenin' down there since that Malcolm guy . . . "

Her eyes roamed to my pelvic region when she said, "down there," inducing a flush of embarrassment. I said nothing.

She gasped. "Wait a minute, don't tell me you're still a virgin?"

My silence furthermore betrayed me.

"Oh my gosh, you have to go to Italy and get laid!"

"Huh?"

"Don't huh me, you heard me!"

"First of all, I am way too busy to take a trip and number two, I am in no rush to get *laid*."

"There's Christmas break . . . even better, there's that two weeks of spring break next semester. That's your opportunity. I know you can afford it. You are always working."

"I have to do research for a paper," I said, slamming the postcard on my dresser.

"Chicken."

"What did you say?"

"Didn't say anything."

"Yes, you did."

"You must be hearing things," she said, giggling.

I snagged a pillow from my bed and flung it at her. She threw it back at me, still giggling. I flung another, targeting her. Nzingha walked into the room.

"What is going on here?" she asked.

"She needs to get laid!" Anna yelled.

Nzingha flung the last remaining pillow on my bed at her and said rather seriously, "That's nonsense!"

"Thank you Nzingha! Thank you!" I said, flapping my arms.

IN THE SECOND WEEK OF SEPTEMBER, another postcard arrived—from Italy. The image, a gothic Church building in Florence. And on the back, scribbled in black ink . . .

Knock, Knock? Hope I am writing to someone. When I called your house, your mom told me you were at Smart and she gave me this address. As you can tell I am in Italy. I'm also a part-time university student studying history and sociology. Please prove to me I am writing to someone by perhaps, writing me back?

Regards, Sal

After the second card, I knew I had to respond, and soon. I wrote back the same day, detailing my life at Smart, my fears regarding Ben and Nne, and childhood friends and relatives stuck in Nabuka. A few weeks later, in mid Fall, I received a small package. Inside, a letter with a photograph of him on a motorcycle. He was beaming at the camera, his face unshaven. His eyes darker, but more alive, like a person on the verge of a life-changing discovery. I was still drinking in this updated image of Sal when Anna burst into the room. She paused upon noticing the photograph and snatched it before I had the chance to object.

"Oh . . . la . . . la. Italian boy again, isn't it?"

"He's American . . . "

". . . Who cares? He is sexy. I'd bed him," she said matter-of-factly.

"Anna!"

"Oh hush, don't act innocent," she said with a wave of the hand. "I'm surprised you haven't yet."

She shut the door behind her, still clutching the image. I snatched it from her grip, somewhat angrily.

"Forgive me, I am suffering from testosterone deprivation," she sighed, planting herself on her bed.

My attention returned to the letter. I was desperate to explore its contents—alone.

"Why don't you just go to Italy and tell me all about it when you get back," Anna said and winked.

I rolled my eyes and sat on my bed.

"I'm serious. You could use a break. No one deserves it more than you do. And besides, you are not a woman until you have done it," she said, casually.

"Done what?" I asked, looking up.

"Done what we have been talking about," she said, raising her hands.

"That's not true," I said quietly.

"Yes, it is," she said, emitting a chortle.

I shook my head but remained silent.

That evening, after Anna finally left for the library, I read the letter.

Dear Ada,

It's great to hear from you. I am sorry about your stepdad and about the situation in your country. Your dad obviously believes in his convictions and is doing what he feels he needs to do for his people. That is one of the qualities of a man of character. I pray alongside you that he is safe and that your family is safe as well.

Life is good for me. Enjoying this beautiful region called Tuscany where at the moment I reside with my godmother, Sophia. She's the best cook ever. Have a feeling you will like it here. As you can see, also bought a motorbike. About Italy, just say the word.

Sal.

I read the letter a few more times before sliding it back into the envelope.

"So, are you going to Italy?" Nzingha asked me as she nibbled on a slice of pepperoni pizza at the campus cafeteria during dinner.

"I think so," I said. There was no food in front of me. I wasn't hungry.

She produced a hidden smile, revealing sparkling white teeth in stunning contrast to her jet-black skin.

"Are you excited?" she asked as if I had already confirmed my trip.

"I don't know," I said, lowering my gaze.

After a few moments, "Nzingha have you ever . . ."

". . . Yes," she said almost immediately.

With wide eyes, I gasped and clasped my mouth, surprised to find that the very conservative Nzingha was not a virgin.

"So, what happened?"

"He moved on. Said he didn't know how to be with a colored girl," she said with blank emotion.

"Didn't know how to be with a colored girl?" I asked, grimacing.

"Yes," Nzingha said.

"I'm sorry," I whispered.

"Nothing to be sorry about. It saved us both a lot of problems," Nzingha said waving her hand. "For six months we had to deal with the stares, the slurs, the disapproval of friends and family. It wasn't worth it."

"Any regrets?" I asked with a slight wince after a pregnant pause. She knew what I meant.

"Sometimes," she said quietly as she stared at the crumbled pizza pieces on her plate.

I said nothing more. Just wondered if there would ever come a time when I would have to explain Sal to anyone.

"Next topic?" Nzingha said with raised eyebrows.

I produced a somber chuckle.

Having such a conversation was indeed a rarity between us because Nzingha, as I had come to discover, wasn't much of a conversationalist, especially when it came to boys, sex, movie stars, and other frivolous topics. Perhaps this was because life had taught her to be serious-minded, to be focused on some goal, knowing full well she carried with her the burden of mapping the way for those to come after her. She was one of those you did not immediately notice was exquisite until you took the time to reflect on what exquisite truly is. One could also see that she was lonely, out of choice of course, and that she wore that loneliness, like a fancy shawl, with dignity.

Soon, she was complaining in her drawly East Afrikan accent that American food had no taste. That no matter how much spice you put in it, it still lacked flavor. She said she missed home, the majestic sunsets, her parents and siblings, going to the village on seasonal breaks. She complained about Uganda. Said the current prime minister was beginning to act like a mad dictator, suspending the constitution and assuming all governmental powers. Now Uganda was a republic, giving the president even more powers. The country was never going to be the same.

We didn't say much after that as we reflected on a continent filled with promises, vibrancy, wealth, and opportunities and yet so much uncertainty, poverty, and horrors. Nzingha and I had also come to embody the simplicity and the complexity, the innocence and the deeply rooted wound that was our motherland. As we ate, we moved on to mundane topics, but in the simplicity of our discussions, we experienced home in each other's expressions, words, sighs, longings, and prayers.

Chapter Fourteen

March 1970

WINTER WAS MAGICAL FOR ME. MAYBE it was because of Sal's letters. Maybe it was because, on most days, the snow descended on trees in thick flurries like a perfect Christmas morning. I didn't mind the cold that much and had even taken the time to build a five-foot snowman in front of our schoolhouse with Anna, who derived pleasure from such endeavors.

I also visited Ma during the holidays. We had an intimate Christmas and New Year's feasting quietly on *jollof* rice, chicken, and red velvet cake for a few days before I headed back to school. Classes and activities resumed as usual in January. Then spring came, and some greenery returned to Smart. The night before spring break, I had a large knapsack packed with clothes for my trip to Italy. Anna was right. I deserved a little vacation. I also looked forward to seeing Sal and realized that I had secretly nourished that thought for a while. I retrieved the money in the bank account set up for me by Ben. One thousand dollars! I had never possessed that much money at once. I would be thanking him profusely as soon as I got the chance.

As I lay in bed that night, I wondered about Sal, if he had changed, if he still laughed the same way: spontaneous, like a gush of water from a fountain. The motorcycle awakened me to the realization that he was on the verge of fulfilling his dream of biking through South America. The full curly hair, the boyish smile, the motorcycle . . . These thoughts flooded my mind as I drifted to sleep.

I left for Italy the following day, after donating some money to the Red Cross for Afa refugees. Anna drove me to the airport with a big smile on her face. On the airplane, I dozed in and out of sleep. By the time I arrived at the terminal, my eyes and face were puffy, and I could taste the tartness of my breath. After deplaning, I wandered about the crowded airport in search of a lavatory for a quick mouth rinse. There were foreign speakers everywhere, and I wasn't sure who to ask for directions. Eventually I settled for a single piece of rumpled bubble gum lodged in the bottom crevice of my knapsack front pouch.

"Ada."

The voice was unmistakable. I turned around and there he was, beaming at me, a live replica of the picture he had sent me. He wore a black moto jacket, a buttoned shirt, slightly exposed at the top, and bell-bottom jeans. I smiled. He pulled me close. In seconds, we were in an embrace. His arms felt stronger, his chest harder.

"Welcome to Italy!"

"Thanks for the invitation."

"I knew the only way I could get you to come here was to nudge you a bit."

"That's not true," I retorted, guilty.

"Yet it is." He let out a laugh. "I was hoping I'd fly you over . . ."

We had discussed it briefly over the phone, and I had declined his offer to pay for my flight.

"I'm here, that's all that matters," I said.

He carried my knapsack. We chatted about the flight and other generalities as we exited the airport. Then he led me outside to where his motorcycle was parked about half a mile away. The sun was making its descent on the horizon, as I observed the natives stroll the streets, speaking their palatable language and using a lot of hand gestures. They reminded me of Nabukans: full of passion, full of life.

He tied my knapsack to the tail of the bike and insisted that I hop on. I did, cautiously. He gave me a helmet. It had a few scratches. It was used. I imagined by a girl. I wondered if he was seeing anyone.

Observing my unusual silence, he asked, "What's the problem, you scared?" he asked, concerned.

"Never ridden on one of these before."

"I've been riding this baby for almost three years now. Don't worry, you are safe with me."

After a few pumps on the pedal, the bike produced a roaring sound, and off we went, my heart almost jumping out my mouth. I roped my hands tightly around his stomach, hoping I wasn't sucking the air out of his lungs. At the same time, I tried to take in the hilly landscape. Through winding roads and scenic routes, we zipped by houses, churches, museums, and restaurants. After a while, the view transformed to apartment complexes and acres of vegetation and farmland. We rode past a vast vineyard, the intoxicating scent of fresh grapes producing excess saliva in my mouth. I was starting to get used to this!

Several minutes later, we arrived at an expansive cream-colored rustic bungalow in a hilltop town in the outskirts of Florence. It was isolated; we were ushered in only by cypress and olive trees along a dirt road. To the left side of the house was a rose bush. The bush and home belonged to Sal's godmother, Sophia.

"Wasn't so bad, huh?" he said as we got off the bike.

"Sorry if you couldn't breathe," I said sheepishly.

He chuckled. "No worries, I'm used to being held like that."

I again pictured a girl, fair-skinned with lustrous hair, a typical Italian woman. Immediately, I reprimanded myself for being so self-deprecating.

Soon we were in a parlor with a green sofa and burgundy rug. On the peeled ocean blue wall was a painting of Mary, ebony in complexion, cradling the infant Jesus. The serene fixture in Mary's dark-hued face pierced my heart with what felt like tongues of healing fire. Later, Sal would point out to me that she was the Black Madonna, a version of the Virgin Mother and child Jesus highly revered in Italy, Spain, France, and a few other places in Europe. It was a maternal energy that radiated throughout the room and from the old petite woman who faced the painting while we walked in.

Sophia had a generous amount of white hair that fell loosely on both sides of her face, and a pleasant smile that was activated by our appearance. No wrinkles. I convinced myself that she couldn't be more than seventy years old, so I was surprised to discover later that she was actually way into her eighties!

Sophia had five children. All males. All grown and married with children and grandchildren scattered across Italy and beyond. Sal's father and his mother, who was an international student in Pittsburgh, Pennsylvania at the time, met and got married in the late 1940's. Shortly after, they relocated to Greensberg, Pennsylvania because Mrs. Giacalone believed in the security and close-knit community that a small town often provided. It was in the late 40s, while honeymooning in Tuscany, that Sal's parents had met Sophia and her husband, Antonio, while taking a stroll in the neighborhood. They struck up a friendship, and after Sal's birth in Greensberg, his parents asked Sophia and Antonio to be Sal's godparents. They agreed. Over the years, the couple had kept in touch with Sal. To Sal, they were grandparent figures since his grandparents on both sides were already dead by the time that he was old enough to form a meaningful relationship with them. Unfortunately, Sophia's husband would also pass away when Sal was in 10th grade.

Even though Sophia's children had insisted that she move in with any of them, she had adamantly refused, insisting that she was going to die in the same house she and her true love shared. Upon hearing about Antonio's death, Sal decided he would visit her as soon as he got the chance. Visitation extended into a permanent stay after they discovered they enjoyed each other.

He introduced me to his godmother in weak Italian. The more he spoke, the more her scant teeth came into view. She said something I did not understand. He translated.

"She asked me why I didn't tell her you were such a beauty," Sal said bashfully.

I blushed, sneaking a vanity-filled glance at my floral turtleneck blouse over a bohemian skirt.

After Sophia embraced and pecked me on both cheeks, I followed Sal into a different part of the house. Another parlor surfaced, partitioned by a red curtain. The floor was covered with a dark green rug. A black leather sofa stretched across the room facing a colossal television. To the right of the television stood a record player with piles of records on top. Hanging on the wall, a South American tribal mask.

His bedroom was behind the curtain, he said. The mention of the bedroom quickened my pulse and transformed me once again into an untainted schoolgirl.

"Err . . . didn't know you spoke Italian."

"Just a little. But by the time I start working, I will be fluent. Come with me," he said, not picking up on my nervousness.

He led me through the curtain, still carrying my knapsack. He dumped my bag on his bed. It was a double mattress covered in red satin sheets. The window blinds on the right side of the room filtered sunrays that illuminated a small section of the bed and the back wall. Displayed on the back wall was a map of the world. To the left of the room was a closet.

"It's my humble abode, hope you like it," he said.

"Of course, I do," I replied and meant it.

I noticed the fresh pink roses in a black oblong vase on a miniature dresser beside the bed. I had told him years ago that my favorite colors were pink and black, and he had said something about how it meant I was sweet but imbued with a certain enigma, which had made me blush at the time.

He studied me with his sweet yet slightly intense look and said softly, "I can't believe you are here."

My heart began to beat fast, and I felt my knees almost buckle. I couldn't believe I was there too, standing in the middle of a bedroom in Tuscany—with Sal.

"One day I will take you to Tuscany."

Those words, said years ago, behind a high school several miles away. I wanted to ask him why he had left for Italy so suddenly, without even a goodbye, but I did not want him to know that this abrupt act of his had affected me so deeply. Pride, I guess.

"So, how is your stepdad?" he asked. The question was drawn out somewhat apologetically. I recalled the bloodshed, the destruction, everything I longed to wish away, and an ominous feeling took over me, draining my energy. He noticed the change that swept over me.

"Please relax, you must be tired."

He led me to the bed. I sat on it, no longer shy. He sat beside me.

"You okay?" he asked.

"I will be."

"You know you can talk to me about anything." He was looking into my eyes now.

"I know."

Soon after, I was stretched across the bed. I closed my eyes and sensed him shut the blinds, blocking off the sunlight. Then I heard his footsteps gradually disappear through the curtain.

When my eyelids fluttered open, the room was dark except for a yellow light streaming below the curtain. I could hear voices, Italian voices, emanating from the television. It took me a moment to recall where I was. I sat up in bed, experiencing the drowsy effect of a sleep hangover. I gingerly moved towards the curtain when Sal, sliding the curtain open at the same time, bumped into me. We found ourselves laughing with wild abandon after apologizing to one another. He turned on the light switch and asked me if I was hungry. It was the right question at the right time, for I was indeed famished.

THAT NIGHT, AFTER FRESHENING UP, WE ate a heavy meal of lasagna that Sophia had prepared. Extremely delectable, the sweet, tangy taste of lasagna sauce lingered in my stomach for a few more hours. After dinner, Sal and I reclined on his sofa. There, we discussed high school memories, the teachers, the students, Stacey. I told him how Stacey and I had recently reconnected and about the protest and her decision to relocate to San Francisco and create a commune.

"Now, that's interesting!" Sal exclaimed.

"I think she was mad at me for refusing to go with her," I said.

"I doubt it. Disappointed, yes, mad, no."

I was grateful to Sal for making me feel better. It didn't matter anyway. With no means of contact, it was unlikely that Stacey and I would ever see each other again. For some reason, the idea created a hollow feeling in my stomach. I ignored it.

"Remember truth or dare?" Sal said.

I swallowed and nodded. Of course, I did. For a few minutes, silence settled in the room. I was pondering something, a suspicion, an inkling I needed to resolve for good.

"Sal, did you two ever *get together?*"

He produced a boyish grin. "She's beautiful, and she's cool, but nah, we didn't get together. Truthfully, she is not my type."

I wanted to ask what his type was but said nothing. At least I knew what his type wasn't.

OVER THE NEXT COUPLE OF DAYS, Sal showed me around Florence with his bike. Like a tourist, I made him stop often so I could snap a photograph of that building, cathedral, or museum. One of my favorite sites was the Basilica di Santa Maria del Fiore, a Gothic-style cathedral, capped with a dome. The building, Sal told me, dated back to the 12th century, with renovations that spanned hundreds of years.

Beneath the dome was a painting known as the *Last Judgment.* It was a painting of Jesus clad in a robe, surrounded by angelic and saintly beings in a sort of heavenly whirlwind. I often wondered what heaven was like. If the saints sang daily praises to God with their harps as the Bible suggested. I considered the idea of praising God for eternity boring—perhaps that made me a sinner.

Sal had once introduced me to Khalil Gibran, beginning my love of esoteric literature. Along the way, I had read somewhere that heaven was a state of mind, that we judged and punished ourselves when we strayed from the path of light, the source of our being. I wondered what the artist would say regarding this concept of heaven as I scrutinized the painting.

I was drawn to paintings. They were my only link to a father I had never known. As a child, I had been denied exposure to his work, his art, his life's joy. How can you know someone without knowing their life's joy?

We left the building. Moments later, I stood with Sal before the statue of Michelangelo's *David,* in awe. This sculpture stood close to twenty feet tall—David depicted as a Goliath. Sal grinned, leaned in my ear, and said, "I told you so."

We spent most evenings strolling in rural areas, feasting on fresh fruits and conversing with the locals. Whenever we returned home, I experienced bouts of melancholy, wondering if I ought to telephone Ma to request the latest news on Ben and Nne. A bad idea, since she had been unaware of my trip to Italy. It would have disappointed her to learn that I had chosen Italy over spending time with her. When my countenance betrayed my feelings, Sal would respectfully create some distance between us. However, he always hovered nearby as if to say, "In case you need to talk." The truth was, being in this countryside kept me in a state of denial about the war, Ben, Nne, and all the people I knew back in Nabuka. In the States, the images of skeletal children with distended bellies played like a horror flick in my dreams, the death tolls splashed across newspapers hung like banners in my head. The Italian countryside and Sal made those images less frequent.

One evening, Sal and I leisurely entertained ourselves to some James Brown music. It was good to see that Sal hadn't lost his passion for good ol' American soul music. When James Brown's "I Got You" came on, he slid to the center of the room, comically imitating the soul singer's dance moves. I sat on the sofa, tears rolling down my cheeks, laughing. Moments later, I begged him to stop. The sweet tickle in my stomach was too much to bear. He stopped the record.

"Do you wanna see my photo album?" he asked, raising his arms like a Las Vegas showman.

"Sure!"

He disappeared into his bedroom, returning moments later with a family-size album. He plopped himself next to me, placing the album on his lap, before flipping through the pages. First, there were the baby pictures: Sal crawling on a carpeted floor, Sal on his mother's lap revealing his scant teeth, Sal posing between his parents at age two in a family portrait. It was uncanny, how much he resembled his father.

"Sometimes I miss the old man," he sighed. "And other times . . . "

. . . *I hate him for the indelible emptiness he created in my heart,* I said inwardly, completing his sentence for him, for us.

"You look like him," I said out loud. I wanted to add that it went beyond looks. That just like his father, he too had a nomadic spirit attached to him, but I said nothing. Sometimes too much honesty opens more wounds than heals.

"Do you find yourself wondering about your dad?" he asked.

He was facing me now, daring me to be transparent. I knew he meant my birth father.

"I do think about him," I admitted with a sigh. "Sometimes I try to imagine what he looks like, his passions, his dreams, the reason why he left Ma, or rather us," I said the last part with a quick glance at his direction. He looked away somberly.

"Whenever I look at a painting, I imagine him making colorful strokes with his paintbrush," I continued. "I overhead my step-dad and mom say something about him being a revolutionary painter."

"Revolutionary painter?" Sal asked with raised eyebrows.

"Anti-colonial stuff."

Sal remained quiet. I didn't want to dampen the mood, so I flipped to the next page: Sal on his motorbike. Sal posing with friends at a restaurant somewhere in Sicily. There were girls in this photograph—gorgeous girls with copper skin. I quickly flipped to the next page: two photos of him and a girl sipping beverage in a cafe. Her long, brown hair cascaded over her face. Her sensuous gaze flirted with the camera and anyone who happened to stumble upon her image. Her lips were voluptuous and red. She looked familiar and then it hit me—this was a Sophia Loren look-a-like leaning against Sal's arm. And the worst of it . . .

". . . She's this girl I'm seeing . . ."

"Cool," I replied, but a knot was forming in my throat.

He cleared his uneasily. "Never asked you if you had a boyfriend."

I was tempted to formulate a lie, to say, "Yes, Malcolm," but changed my mind.

"Well, if I had one, I wouldn't be here, that's for sure," I replied instead, with false gaiety.

He chuckled nervously and nodded. Suddenly, I was aware of myself melting like steamed butter. This night belonged to me. Sophia Loren wannabe could kick rocks.

"Sal . . ." I said softly.

"Yes."

We gazed at each other, my heart pounding, his eye lids lowered, my face leaning forward until surrendering to the sentimental current passing through us. Our lips met, and we kissed, slowly at first, then passionately, sending currents through my body. We paused for air after several minutes as he held my face with his hands. His soft touch activated my pulse, made me shiver. At the same time, I felt alive and warm, like a soft flame in an encased candle.

I could feel his breath on my cheek when he whispered in my ear, "Let's go outside . . . "

I followed him out, relieved that I still had him, that we still had each other.

We strolled past the front yard to the back. The pink roses in full bloom danced softly to the tantalizing breeze, the night caressing her petals. With the gentility of roses, a stranger to this world would never suspect they had thorns.

We sat on the back porch steps and gazed at the waxing moon, which reminded me of an orange partly buried in the shadows. The night was perfectly still except for the faint sound of rambunctious party music coming from several miles away. I wanted us to continue from where we had left off on the couch . . .

"I like nights like these."

I wasn't sure if he meant nights like the one we were sharing or just regular nights with moon lights and sweet breezes, but I concurred. We gazed at the moon more closely. In it, I saw the outline of what looked like a woman's face at first, then a baby's silhouette . . . but then a few moments later, it transformed into a solitary landscape. I heard the sweeping flow of a tide from an invisible ocean, patiently gathering and picking up momentum and then slashing itself against the shore.

Mmiri na eje, mmiri na eje, mmiri na eje . . .

The water is running, running, and running, the water is running, from the pitcher to the Sea . . . Oh Mother, Oh Mother, Oh Mother, be awakened . . .

Chants from the night air . . .

"I meant, I like nights like these, with you," I heard him say and then I felt his warm, ticklish breath on my right cheek once more. When I returned his gaze, we were only inches apart. In a swift move, he laid me across the scanty grass before us. We kissed some more, his fingers roaming under my dress to reach for my boxer shorts. I didn't care about my yellow polka dress gathering dust. I didn't care that a neighbor looking out of one of the high-rise concrete buildings might see us. All I cared about was getting more of him, his mouth, his taste, his flesh. I felt his fingers between my thighs, igniting euphoric pleasure. I felt those same fingers move slowly, meticulously until they began toying with my pelvic region.

"I'm a virgin," I blurted out.

He stopped, then pulled away.

"It's okay," I said.

I was giving him the green light, something no other man had been given the privilege to receive from me.

"I think we should wait."

"But I don't want to."

To my dismay, he came off me and stood up. I slid my boxer shorts to its proper position, embarrassed, wondering if I had done something wrong. If I had broken some sort of sexual code. An awkward silence fell between us.

Finally, he said, "It's kinda late, let's get some rest."

THE FOLLOWING DAY, HE RESUMED HIS platonic banter. And by dinnertime, sitting across from each other and next to the placid Sophia, my feelings had transitioned to rage. Was this some silly game he was playing? Payback for what had transpired at the Groove Box years ago? How dare he treat me this way? How dare he? It was illogical, my rage, but I was blinded by my pride. For the first time since my trip, I craved a cigarette. The deep inhalations, flick it and toss it out the window type craving.

Sal said something in broken Italian to Sophia. She said something back then gazed at me sweetly.

"Just told her you are leaving tomorrow," he said.

I smiled at her but did not as much as glance at Sal. Even for her lack of English, I was certain she could sense the tension between us by the quick, uneasy glances she gave us from time to time.

After dinner, I took care of the dishes even though she insisted with adamant gestures that I leave them up to her. Like the days before, I refused to give in and washed and cleaned amid her protests. Her simplicity reminded me of Nne. Each time I helped Sophia with a chore, I imagined myself helping Nne, a woman caught in the nightmare that had become Nabuka. It was the least I could do under the present circumstances.

After we were finished, she retired to her favorite spot in the main parlor to gaze adoringly at Mary. I headed towards the bedroom to pack my things. Sal was planted on the sofa, watching a travel show.

"Ada, is there anything else you want to see in Firenze besides the museums and . . ."

"I need to pack that's all," I interrupted sharply.

I stormed into the bedroom and flipped the light switch. I stopped. Before me, pink petals lay sprinkled over a bed draped in black sheets. My torrid emotions quickly fell off, replaced with a glowing sensation. Sal emerged beside me, our arms slightly touching. I was consumed by the intoxicating smell of fresh wildflowers and the heat he was exuding.

"I changed my mind. I don't want to think about tomorrow, I just want to be with you now," he said softly.

I noticed a squeezed condom pack in his right hand and felt foolish and sorry for having wasted so much time fuming. I reached out for his hands and held them. We faced each other, lost in our internal fire, the scent of flowers, and *l'amour* under Tuscany skies.

We kissed our way to bed. We undressed each other carefully down to our underwear before landing on the petal-covered sheets. The flower skins stuck to our trembling bodies. I focused on his lean, brawny chest. Even though he wore boxers, I wasn't quite ready to look down, at least not yet. With his eyes, he drank in the outline of my neck, shoulders, and chest, parts not hidden by my lacy shelf bra camisole.

"You have very beautiful skin, the color of malt," he whispered in a hoarse voice.

The way he said it made my heart stop. I started to breathe heavily. He kissed my temple.

"I will be gentle, I promise," he said.

His eyes shone in the dark, blanketing my thoughts. I smiled a nervous smile. We squeezed each other tenderly, making intimate discoveries. He kissed me from the top of my head to my toes until I felt myself trembling. I closed my eyes to soak it all in. Then I felt it, the feel of his hand trying to go deep, and I froze. He hesitated. I told him not to stop. He came off me gently and lay beside me, staying in deep thought for several moments.

"You worried it's gonna hurt?"

"I dunno," I said, feeling like a failure.

He said nothing.

"Sal?"

"You know I care about you, right?"

"Yes," I said, wondering where his mind was going.

"We don't have to do this if you don't . . . if you are not ready. It doesn't change anything, frankly."

I sighed. "But I want to . . ."

"But are you ready?" he said softly. "This is beyond physical, Ada. It's about mind, it's about spirit, it's about the soul. And you are a very soulful person, intricate, gentle like a flower. You deserve a love that waters you and makes you bloom. Frankly, you deserve a love that takes you higher to God."

For the first time, I saw Sal for who he was, what he was becoming, and I was touched like a heart set ablaze. I was touched because I knew he saw me, had made contact with me, the real me. I felt tears trickle down my cheeks. My body grew warm. The rose petals on the bed oozed a richer scent, as if his words had activated their very souls. He reached for my hand. We breathed in unison. Our hearts pounded away in unison. The air was meditative. This was what we needed. This was stronger than anything. I found my fears vanishing, I found myself wanting to surrender to him, like a sacred offering. My body burned feverishly with passion for him. But by the sublime look in his expression, I knew this was exactly how he felt it should be, at least for now.

THE NEXT MORNING, I WOKE UP to the crow of a rooster, took a slow shower, and packed my things, ready for my return flight to the States. Fully dressed and packed, I shook Sal's leg to wake him up, even though I knew he had woken up when I did. He asked me how I slept. I told him I slept well, omitting the fact that my spirit felt full, and was on the verge of running over. He told me to sit by him. I did, timidly. He kissed me on the neck.

"What happened last night," he said with a dark, penetrating stare, placing his hand on my thigh, "means we are forever linked."

I held my breath, my mouth tied, my throat stuck. I watched him timidly, the whole of him, as he gingerly rose from the bed and stumbled into the shower room. I was still this flower, this very untouched flower, and here I was forever linked to this man not because of a night of lovemaking, but because of a union that took us beyond this world.

About an hour later, we said goodbye to Sophia who we found in the kitchen flipping omelets in a blackened skillet. But Sal and I had decided to skip breakfast. She pouted. As compensation, I embraced her a little longer, kissing both cheeks with increased fervor.

On the dawdling motorcycle ride, we chatted about the countryside, Sophia's endearing spirit, everything but the experience of the night before and the unavoidable separation that was to take place. Even though the night before had brought us closer, it still left a feeling of "now what?" For me, the answer was obvious, the end of spring break escapism and last-minute passion and back to the real world. But I could sense that Sal was still fidgeting with the issue by his unusual pauses. At the airport, he sat with me in the terminal as we waited for boarding time. I retrieved a JET magazine from my knapsack and began to read. I felt his gaze, questioning, devoted, loving. After a while, I couldn't bear it anymore.

"You keep staring at me," I accused him.

"Staring at you?"

"Yes, staring at me."

"And what makes you so sure?"

"It's obvious."

"You are so full of yourself, aren't you?"

I could tell he didn't mean it to come off that way by the pained look on his face. Things had just become more complicated. I tickled his underarms. Initially, he maintained a stoic expression, but after a few more tickles, began to chuckle, pushing me away from him. I persisted until boarding was announced. Then I stood up from my seat. He stood up too. Here it was, the farewell moment, and it didn't look like he was going to say anything, so I decided to begin.

"Sal, I had a great time, thank you for . . ." my voice trailed off.

This was more difficult than I had imagined. His watery pupils landed on my lips and in an instant his lips were pressed against mine, leaving me gasping for air. He finally let go, his pupils saturated with longing. Teary-eyed, I shook my head, waved him goodbye, and rushed towards the boarding line.

"So?"

"So?" I replied even though I knew what she meant.

"How was it?" It was Anna, prying as usual.

Just moments ago, I had been dropped off by a taxi from the airport on what proved to be an emotionally turbulent flight. After meandering into the bedroom, Anna had overpowered me with a welcoming embrace and a mischievous grin. I couldn't lie, couldn't pretend I didn't understand what she meant.

"It was divine," I found myself saying.

"I knew it would be!" she squealed, "Now details!"

I laughed at her. What did she know about love?

"You really like this guy, huh?"

"Good night, Anna."

I slumped on my bed, not even bothering to shower or change my clothes. I shut my eyes. I heard her pace the room.

"By the way, your mom called while you were away."

I opened my eyes.

"Did she say anything?"

"She said you should call as soon as possible."

"Did it sound like an emergency?"

She shrugged to suggest she didn't know. It was late in the evening. Ma would probably be fast asleep, yet I had the pressing feeling to telephone her, so I did.

She questioned me about my whereabouts. I fibbed, saying I had been extremely busy with schoolwork, hoping Anna hadn't already divulged to her my escapade to Italy. There was silence, the kind that assesses an opportune moment to reveal something grim.

"Ma, is everything okay?"

Bumps began appearing on my flesh, my heart started to pound and air gradually sucked its way out of my stomach.

That is when she told me about the explosion in an abandoned warehouse near Ogu where Ben and his comrades made grenades. That was a week ago. They found his body days later, laying protectively over two of his comrades.

Chapter Fifteen

April 1970

I WAS IN A FETAL POSITION staring at the wall, though my thoughts were in places beyond it. Two knocks on the door. The door swung open. Ma's face emerged from the crack.

"I made *jollof* rice with fish stew," she said.

"I'm not hungry."

My voice was hoarse, and as she had for the past few days, she quietly exited the room. My attention returned to the wall, then onto images of shattered buildings with black smoke imprints—residue of explosions. Homes dilapidated and blackened with smoke, cars, trees, even the grass mourned in the East. The war had ended in late March, a few days after Ben's death, with Afa surrendering. In early April, Ma and I returned to Nabuka to bury him. When we arrived at Lagoon, we were met with otherwise contented people—people who considered themselves fortunate to live in the capital, to be predominately non-Afa, to be on the side that won. The crowded streets hustled with activity as usual; music blasted in the air from someone's car radio, and street vendors brought attention to their wares by chanting product names.

We spent the night at the home of a distant relative from Ma's side. I later discovered she was a woman in her sixties whose wittiness had now given way to something more acrid and vindictive—though she still had her maternal inclinations if you were under her good graces. I had not met her before, but from the conversations Ma had with her, it became clear to me that she was one of the people Ma conversed with on the telephone before the war. They discussed the war, Ma threading carefully around the topic of death, disease, hunger. Defeat.

Mrs. Ude, the woman, had managed to escape to safety after losing her husband and three children, twin boys and a girl, to a Nabuka army raid while in Ogu. After the soldiers had raided her house and shot everyone, thinking she was dead, they looted food and money then departed. Several minutes later, a Nabukan soldier who she, at first, feared had returned to finish the job of destroying her life, carried her to safety in his jeep to a refugee camp. It was after the war that she made her way to Lagoon to escape the memories of her past. Her story came out sporadically, her voice sounding haunted as Ma listened.

As she provided details of the attack, which included being raped by one of the soldiers, I gradually drifted to the farthest area of the house, away from the conversation.

"Is she alright?" I heard her ask Ma.

"She's okay," Ma replied. "*Biko,* continue."

I ended up in a vacant bedroom with a heavy chloroform smell. There was a worn mattress on the floor. The yellow foam stuffing leaked out in different areas from the mattress's pink flowery pattern. I lay on the mattress, holding my stomach, and fell asleep. In my sleep, Mrs. Ude's story followed me in the form of military men with menacing expressions, brandishing their firearms on a group of unsuspecting men, women, and children.

The following morning after Ma and I embraced and thanked Mrs. Ude for hosting us, Mrs. Ude's nephew Paul drove us to the East. He was a young man in his late twenties with a meek disposition. It was at his house that Mrs. Ude had settled after the war ended. Fortunately, his parents and sister had been in London during the war and therefore had not been directly impacted by it. He drove us to Ogu.

The melancholy in the East was palpable. It had its own life, was well fed, and ballooned with intoxicating misery. While one part of the country cheered in victory over a united country, another wallowed in the loss. Ma and I visited some of the surviving members of Ben's family, including his parents, with whom I had spent a couple of memorable Christmases in the past. Their defeated stance and broken spirits induced bouts of tears, moving me to retreat to the bathroom repeatedly to release them. It was obvious that nothing would ever be the same, at least for a long time.

Shortly after, we drove to Nne's house and my early childhood home. A house that once seemed large to me now appeared like a tree house perched on land. Nne had lost a significant amount of weight, her bones protruding through her skin, just like almost every man, woman, and child Ma and I encountered. We held each other for several minutes, all three of us, thanking God that she had made it alive.

Afterward, I demanded to be taken back to Ben's family compound so I could face the reality of his death. Upon arrival, we were shown a rectangular concrete grave in the backyard, his final resting place. My legs gave way at the scene, leaving me collapsed to the ground. Right there I let out a primordial scream, asking God and whoever would listen why he would let this happen. Ma simply watched with slumped shoulders.

We stayed in Nabuka for a few days before returning to the States. Ma had to resume work. I had school.

However, once in Greensberg, the desire to further my education quickly dissolved. I felt deprived of purpose, of meaning. What was the point of aspiring for anything if one could lose it all in a flash? My mind stayed hooked on Ben, and on the horrific stories of rapes and killings and children, some of whom I had grown up with, forced to kill and be killed as child soldiers. For a time, I found myself blind with hatred for the government that had caused this. Later, I discovered Ma shared the same sentiment. It was something she would never recover from, Afa's defeat.

I heard another knock on the door. Thinking it was Ma, I responded with a voice worn out by nightly cries, "Yes?"

"Ada?" It was a man's voice.

I lifted my head and stared at the door, blinking rapidly. It creaked. A face emerged.

"Sal?"

I blinked a few more times to make sure I wasn't hallucinating. He beamed and sat next to me.

"Hey . . . "

I tried to sit up. He gently shoved me back unto the bed. He sat next to me, grabbed my hand, and stroked it.

"Decided to visit my family. I called the house after your roommate told me you were home." He stalled. "She told me what happened . . . I'm sorry."

"Thanks."

He was indeed real, and he smelled like grass, sweetgrass, and like a man who was about to cross many rivers.

"She's concerned about you. She says you are not eating," he said.

Ignoring him, I toyed with the edge of the blanket.

He placed his arms around my shoulders. The sound of our breathing permeated the air.

"You know, I never imagined the last time I saw him would be the last . . ." my voice trailed off.

He said nothing, only listened.

"I have cried so much I don't know if I have any more tears left in me . . ."

He kissed my forehead and stroked my left cheek.

Sal visited daily. He usually arrived before dinnertime and left before midnight. We ate dinner together, all three of us. On night one, we had discussed mundane things, countries we had been to and the ones we looked forward to visiting, the rise in unemployment. On the third evening of his visit, over spaghetti dinner, we discussed the draft and the updated lottery system that had been implemented in December of the previous year to select men for military service.

"The new military draft lottery system is really at work. Mrs. McCormey's nephew just got drafted because of it," Ma began the conversation before taking a sip of her water.

I had heard about the lottery system but hadn't taken the time yet to truly understand it. I asked Ma for clarification.

"From what I understand, they are now going by the letters of the alphabet with each letter assigned to a number. Men with the same birthdays would be picked according to the ranks of the first letters of their first, middle and last names. It's a pity . . . Nixon had promised last November to pull out of Vietnam. Yet, here we are," Ma said, shaking her head.

"How have you been able to avoid the draft this far?" I asked Sal in a low voice.

"I got a medical exemption from my Doctor for acute ACL . . . "

"Anterior cruciate ligament injury," Ma interjected.

"Yes Ma'am."

"When was this and how come you never told me?" I asked in an accusatory tone.

"It was last summer. I was playing soccer with some friends one weekend and suddenly, I felt my knee pop. Excruciating pain to say the least. Was rushed to the hospital and had to undergo surgery to replace the torn ligament. And of course, do some physical therapy."

"You okay right now?"

"Oh yeah," Sal said before biting into his meatball with a fork. "I just can't do anything too strenuous, which means no soccer. Before my return visit to the U.S, my doctor wrote me up an exemption letter stating I wasn't fit for military service."

"Thank your lucky stars," Ma said as the shrilling sound of the telephone ringing travelled through the house. She left the table to answer it.

"I wish you had told me all this in Italy though," I said to him.

Sal leaned his face close to mine, his wood brown eyes piercing through my skin. "I was having too much fun knowing you in other ways Ada, I forgot my manners," he said with a boyish grin.

I blushed and looked away.

"How is the spaghetti Ma asked as she made her way back to the table from behind us.

"Mrs. Ekene your spaghetti sauce might just be as good as my godmother Sophia's!" Sal confessed.

And thus Ma was completely won over.

Ma had taken to Sal so swiftly that it astonished me. When he spoke and his brown eyes exposed the saccharine nature of his soul, I could sense Ma's sighs from across the table, from deep within her being. I wasn't sure if it had something to do with her missing Ben or from missing having a man around in general. Sometimes I chided myself that I was being paranoid, but then she would gaze at Sal a little longer, smile a little wider, allow her shoulders to descend with each word that poured out of his lips.

It lasted several days, the rhythm of Sal coming and leaving. Then one gusty evening after dinner, Sal rushed home to his mother to help with errands. As I carried his emptied plate to the sink, a smile dangling from my lips, I felt Ma's eyes on me.

"Yes, Ma."

"Did I call you?"

"With your eyes, you were." I dropped the contents on the kitchen sink.

"You are becoming so rude!"

"You were judging me with your eyes. I'm not sleeping with him if that's what you think."

"Ada, are you mad?!"

"Ma, I'm old enough, relax."

She rose from the dining room chair, stunned and angry. I relished the reaction. It was about time she knew how I felt.

"I will choose to attribute this nonsense as an effect of mourning!"

"You have a problem because he's not Afa, or wait, I guess it's back to Nabuka?"

"Eh?"

"Never mind," I said and sighed.

"I don't know what you are trying to say, but I was indeed looking at you because I feel sorry for you."

"Why? *Maka gini*?"

"Because you two can never be happy."

I dropped the sponge I had picked up to drench in soap.

"Why?"

I was staring at the sink, not particularly concerned about the sponge and greasy plate and cutlery.

"Too much feeling. Such things never last."

I stood still like a person struck suddenly by an unrecognizable weapon. I watched her head towards her bedroom, her anger from a few moments ago snuffed out with each stride.

"I AM GETTING TIRED OF THIS cold already. It's supposed to be spring!"

It was Ma's attempt at conversation. Maybe it was the guilt, who knows, but throughout that morning, she had been unusually cordial. She had just parked the Cadillac in the driveway upon arrival from church. I said nothing to her.

"Who's that?" she asked.

I peered through her side window. It was Sal on the front porch, grinning. He looked like a rugged movie star in blue bell-bottom jeans, a checkered shirt partly hidden by a black leather jacket, and matching shoes. I couldn't get out of the car any faster. Ma trailed behind. I leaped my way towards him. My arms eclipsed his neck, then I ushered him in. He shook his head and moved towards Ma. And that's when he asked her, as if I were a sixteen-year-old on a first date, if he could take me out. Ma responded with a crisp, "Sure." I slid my arm under his as we strolled off.

"Where are we going?"

"Wherever you want."

"How about we just walk around?"

"As I said, wherever you want," he smiled.

The snowplows had cleared the streets early that morning for cars and pedestrians, leaving the rest of the snow on the sidewalk. There was no wind. And no humming sounds. No cars. No pedestrians. Just leafless tree branches observing our steps, and Bishop Coral High revealing its scholarly head in the distance.

"I kinda miss high school," Sal said.

I recaptured images of Stacey and I skipping class and smoking cigarettes in the school backyard. The thought of cigarettes made me twitch, made me want to purchase a pack. I quickly shook the thought away. Somehow, I had the feeling that Sal would not approve of my smoking habits. I was convinced that most non-smokers were unsympathetic to the plight of smokers, making them very judgmental. I did not want Sal to judge me. I wanted him to consider me his ideal girl.

"Yeah, I think we made the most of it," I said, responding to Sal's statement. "Back then all I did was dream of freedom."

"Freedom, ahhhhh," he said and smiled.

"Freedom, freedom, freedom," I said stretching my arms and skipping. "I want freedom."

"Haven't you heard we are living in the age of freedom?" Sal said in a lighthearted satirical tone.

"I thought that was the 60s," I said mockingly.

"Who says we can't bring the spirit of the 60s into the 70s . . ." Sal replied in the same tone.

Suddenly, he scooped me up and placed me on his right shoulder and began trudging along.

"Sal, what are you doing?" I squealed. "What about your knee!"

"But you are light as a feather!"

An elderly couple emerging from a corner caught sight of us. The woman snarled at us before whispering something to her husband.

"Fuck racism, genocide, war, and whatever else!" I shouted.

"Yea, what she said, 'cos we are living in the age of freedom, and we are lovers!" Sal shouted and spun me around.

With a horrified expression, the couple hastened their steps. We arrived at the woods laughing wildly. He let me land on the grass. The bright ray of the sun pierced through stoic tree branches. The light made the snow on the ground look silver. We moved closer to the lake. She was frozen. The felled tree trunk remained as before. I wondered if anyone ever came here, hid here to "bug out" as we used to say.

As if sensing my thoughts Sal said, "Sometimes I wonder if I'm the only one who's discovered this place."

With a wink, I urged him to follow me. He did in anticipation. Side by side we threaded softly until our feet touched the edge of the crystallized water. I leaned forward as if to kiss him before shoving him into the water. He proved niftier than I previously thought, for as he descended he managed to grab both my hands and take me along with him. We went through the icy surface.

The last time I was underwater was in Ogu, by the edge of the river, where some villagers took baths, washed clothes, and made offerings. Some mornings, when I wasn't in the mood for a regular bath, which consisted of a bucket of water and shea butter soap on the cemented portion of the backyard, Nne would accompany me to the river for a swim, my naked flesh soaking in the fluid motions of the river's embrace.

There was a particular woman who always fascinated me because she spent many days by the river praying, "*Ezenwanyi*, dear Mother, beautiful one, show yourself to me!" She often crooned this way, sometimes going into swoons—perhaps entranced like Stacey, with her woman of the ocean. Once, while swimming with Nne, I asked about her, what her problem was.

Nne smiled a knowing smile and said, "It's devotion and with it comes many blessings."

"From a river goddess?" I asked with a hint of skepticism.

"From the river of life," she replied as if correcting me.

Meanwhile, the water was painfully cold. Sal and I staggered onto the frozen muddy surface that was the shore. He zipped his jacket to his neck. I folded my arms across my woolen peacoat.

"What was I thinking?!"

"You weren't thinking, that's what," he grinned, his teeth chattering.

"I'm so cold," I groaned.

He pulled me closer. Our lips touched. For seconds we forgot where we were, and then a gust of wind wheezed by as if to remind us. We had had enough adventuring for the day.

The next day, Sal came to visit. As usual, we had dinner. As usual, Ma observed us closely, reserving the least critical attention for Sal. After dinner, we retreated to the bedroom. In bed we wrestled, we giggled, we played, we exchanged heated squeezes, and kissed hungrily in hushed tones. I didn't want the moment to end. It ended when Sal opened his mouth.

"I am returning to Italy in two days."

Something knotty and heavy tanked in my stomach. As the news settled in my mind, I felt impending tears sting my eyes. I shriveled away from him. It was happening all over again, people having to pick up and go.

"I am sure we can make this work," he said and leaned in for a kiss.

I got off the bed. He sat up, planting his feet on the ground, his eyes widening.

"What's wrong?"

"You think you can just say all the right things and all of a sudden everything will be okay?!"

He looked at me like a prince who had just discovered that his princess was a venomous toad.

"And what's with this?" I continued, making the quotation sign with my fingers on "this."

"This?"

"Yes, you said, this could work. There's no this."

"What?!"

"You know what? I need to go wash my face for bed."

I stormed to the bathroom. But I was more concerned with cloaking my tears than having a clean face. I began lathering my face with soap, letting the sink tap water run. He came after me. I scrubbed even more fervently.

"Ada . . ."

"I appreciate you coming over to make me feel better, and yes, we had some moments, but let's just leave it at that. Let's not complicate things."

He stared at me, perplexed.

"There's no complication here. I want to be with you."

"One, it's not going to work. Two, grow up, life is not a movie, in case you haven't noticed."

"I am not a child, don't tell me to grow up!" he yelled.

Startled, I halted my rinse mid-way. It was Sal's turn to shock me. He inhaled deeply.

"What is it with you? Why are you this way? On one moment, off the next?"

He paused, roamed his fingers through his curls.

"I thought you had a girlfriend anyway. Why are you here?" I shouted.

"What? I never said I had a girlfriend."

"You are seeing someone in Italy, Sal, go to her!"

Exasperated he said, "I thought you knew what we had was different." He lowered his voice. "Sometimes I don't get you."

"Maybe that's the problem. Now, I think you should leave!"

It was happening so fast, the torrid emotions, the spewing of reckless words. He stared at me, emotionally gashed. I completed my facial rinse, turned off the tap, and grabbed a pink towel by the rail. I pressed the towel against the minuscule bubbles on my skin. He stormed off. I held the pink towel against my chest, entered my bedroom, and shut the door. I found myself lying in bed, still clinging to the pinkness. Tears descended rapidly on my cheeks. A few moments later as Sal attempted to open the front door, I heard Ma's footsteps behind him.

"Are you alright?" she asked him.

"Yes, Mrs. Ekene, we just got into a little squabble, that's all."

"Your problem is you dote on her too much."

I heard the door close behind him. Ma's thumping feet arrived at my door. She knocked belligerently. I dried my face, rolled off the bed, and opened the door.

"What happened?"

"Huh?"

All I could think of was what Ma had just said to Sal. Did Ma believe I wasn't worthy of anyone's attention?

"I'm asking you what happened!"

Furious, I said, "Ma, what happens between me and Sal is between me and Sal."

"If you decide to fight in my house, I deserve to know what happened!"

"You have never cared about what happens with me, so this is clearly about Sal. Guess what, he's single and available!"

Ma's mouth flung open. "Are you mad?!" When she was angry, her Ogu accent became more pronounced. "Is that how you talk to me? After all I have done to cheer you up . . ."

"Cheer me up? Ma, Ben died . . . he died . . . like an animal. Like he was nothing! I didn't fail some exam that I need to be cheered up about! The only father I ever had died!" I screamed.

Ma continued to stare at me, unused to my hysterical side, unused to being in a situation with me where she wasn't in control.

After a few minutes she said, "You have to move on with your life Ada. What about school?"

"Do you even care that he died?"

"Of course I care, how dare you . . ."

"If it weren't for you only thinking of yourself and leaving him, maybe he wouldn't have died, we would have been a family. I would have at least been able to convince him not to get involved!"

"Don't put this all on me. Your so-called father was seeing other women in all his travels, and you know it!"

Her tone was vinegary. The man who had agreed to marry her, a single woman with a child, a man who had been supportive of her all these years had just died and all she could focus on was some flimsy sexual affairs?

I responded with what came into my head.

"I hate you."

A solid smack went across my face. I could still feel the handprint moments later.

"What has gotten into you? You need to get over yourself and don't forget I'm your mother!" She stormed off.

It was cold outside, but my sheets were soaked with sweat. Ma had turned up the heater before retiring for the night, transforming the house into a live-in sauna, intensifying the hellish feeling I already felt. My bedroom was bathed in an ominous white light from the pregnant moon. I knew she was pregnant because she kept me up with her laborious sighs. *This is going to be a night of labor,* a voice within me said. I sighed. Then I broke down in tears, snuggled against my pillow. I saw Sal's broken face, the pained look in his eyes, the disappointment written across them when I yelled at him like a woman deranged. I felt Ma's slap and the fire in her eyes that followed it after I said I hated her. The truth was I was starting to hate everything: the house, Ma, school and the pressure to surpass my previous grade every semester, separations. Nothing made sense. It made no sense that Ben had lost his life for a cause that would have divided a nation. It made no sense that an intelligent, handsome man with the world at his fingertips, a man who was able to change the world and realize his dream of a united Afrika would lose his life over a separatist state.

Nothing seemed to stand still. Everything was constantly moving. The world felt like it was moving towards an unknown destination. And like a lost ship being carried by the tides we were unwilling passengers heading towards some obscure end.

And then there was my birth father. Who was he? Where was he? Why hadn't he shown up for me all these years? Was he dead? Was he alive? Did I care? Should I care?

Yes, I should care. He is my father. He must think of me from time to time. Yes, he must. I must seek him out for me—for him—for the both of us.

What if he was also dead from the war? I quickly shook that thought away and arrived at another thought. Ogu.

When we left Ogu years ago, it was a tranquil fishing village full of joyful expressions of life. Now Ogu was desolate. Broken spirits hung in the air. The plants and animals, dried up, withered, confused. Most of the people I knew were in transition. Many had already transitioned to the other side.

Transition. Change.

You have become like the rest of them . . .

"Not true, dammit" I sobbed, "Not true . . . "

Part III

Homecoming

Chapter Sixteen

May 1970

SHE WAS IN THE LIVING ROOM, her face buried in a newspaper, when like an intrusive apparition I appeared before her.

"I am going back home," I announced.

"When?" She did not look up from her paper.

"In a few days."

She dropped the newspaper on her lap. "I think it is too soon, we just returned."

"I know. But that's what I want to do."

"Okay. You are officially an adult now. You are free to do what you want," she said in resignation, returning to her newspaper.

The following evening, I booked my flight. Several days later, in the middle of May, I was catching a taxi to Pittsburgh International Airport for the next flight to Nabuka. My decision had been cemented the night I fought with Sal, and then Ma. I had awoken the next morning with puffy eyes and dried patches of snot on my pillow and hadn't known what to do with the denseness in my chest except to start anew—by escaping to a faraway place. And the only place I could think of was the land I had been forced to leave, my ancestral home.

The airplane arrived at Lagoon International Airport just when the Afrikan sun, like liquid light, had emptied itself into the horizon. The only contact information I had was the one Ma had grudgingly scribbled on a piece of paper after muttering something about me being impulsive and unreasonable. The paper had the name, telephone number, and address of Mrs. Ude.

Once outside, I was swarmed by multiple baggage carriers wanting to assist me with my luggage.

"Madam, I carry 'em."

"This way, over here . . . "

All in the hopes of being given some *dash,* otherwise known as reward money.

My second greeting was by the sweltering temperature. I had on a loose t-shirt and jeans, but even that didn't seem to provide any relief. Beads of sweat congregated on my forehead, neck, and underarms like raindrops on a windowpane. After giving away some *dash* and freeing myself from the men, I led myself further to the main road, still carrying my luggage. I flagged a taxi, which screeched before stopping just a few inches from my feet. I opened the back door, shoved my luggage inside, and planted myself on the torn leather seat. The driver was a man with crinkly eyes and a disarming smile. I assumed him to be of Uoba origins by the vertical tribal marks across his cheeks. From the stereo, which was really just pieces of colorful wire arranged intricately, arose the most delectable high-life sound.

"Who is that?" I asked him.

"I no know him name," he replied, grinning at me through the rearview mirror.

"Wetin he dey sing about?" I asked, hoping my pidgin didn't sound amateurish.

"Unity," he replied. "We thank God for one Nabuka!" he shouted over the lyrics, raising his fist.

We drove in silence for several minutes, sucked in by the lyrics of the song.

"Madam, where you dey go?" the driver asked suddenly.

I rummaged through my back jeans pocket to find the address.

MRS. UDE WITH HER ELECTRIC PERSONALITY extended her arms to embrace me once I arrived at the corrugated red gate in Ikeda. She had been waiting for me outside.

"*Nwa mu*, my child, *kedu*?"

"Fine, I mean, *o di mma*," I said, returning the embrace.

"*Onye* America, American girl!" She teased, grabbing my shoulders. I could smell *anyara*, garden egg on her breath. "You eat yam, *okwa ya*?"

"Yes, Aunty."

Once inside, she had me wash my hands and we sat by the dining table where yam, tomato stew, and a glass of water were laid before me by a teenage houseboy. He was a new addition to the house, hired by Paul to run errands for his aunt. There were six garden eggs in a white bowl on the table as well.

"As you know, garden egg is an Afa staple. I *choro*? You want some?"

I shook my head, no.

After I dipped a piece of yam in stew and began to eat, she asked, "So, how is your mother?"

"She's fine," I said as the spicy tomato sauce fired my mouth. It didn't help that the yam, usually white, was brownish in some areas, indicating a bit of spoilage. I took a sip of water. Though the food wasn't exactly to my taste, I was grateful for the home-cooked meal.

Mrs. Ude adjusted her wrapper. "She told me you were on your way. It surprised me. You two had just returned to *Obodoyibo,* the white man's land."

"It was a last-minute decision. Don't worry, I won't be staying at your house too long."

"Is it me you are doing *nyanga* for?" she said, clapping her hands for dramatic effect. "Don't forget I wiped your mother's behind when she was still running around with snot in her nose."

"I'm sorry, Aunty. I didn't mean it like that."

She hissed. Then after a few moments . . .

"Where are you headed?"

I took another bite. "Ogu."

I took another sip of the water. The houseboy knew nothing about portion control when it came to red pepper.

"Oh, okay . . . your Nne, *okwa ya*?"

"I am also looking for any other family members I can find, including my biological father and his people."

She scrutinized me at the mention of my father. "*Chukwu gozie gi,* may God be with you."

I hesitated briefly before asking, "Aunty, do you know anything about my father's family?"

"*Osu.*"

"Huh?" I said, dropping my fork.

"What is huh?" She shouted. "Didn't you know your great grandfather dedicated himself to a god as a slave? It is for this reason that an *osu* cannot marry a non *osu.* To do so is an abomination. The fact that your mother went ahead and got with someone in that bloodline is the reason why it did not work out."

I knew about the *osu* but hadn't been aware it ran in my father's bloodline, making me one as well. However, personally, I didn't understand the big deal. It was a choice an ancestor made, a thing of the past, and had nothing to do with my life today, or. Or so I wanted to believe and felt should be.

"Aunty, is there anything else you can tell me about them?"

She eyed me. "No, not really. They kept to themselves. Not an open sort of people . . . Is that food too peppery for you?"

"Aunty, no," I lied.

"I *dikwa* sure?"

"Yes Aunty, thank you, *dalu,*" I said and took another sip of water.

PHYSICALLY DRAINED YET STILL MENTALLY ALERT, I spent the next few days listening to Mrs. Ude speak further about the war, how people consumed lizards and insects and drank rainwater to wade off starvation during the Nabukan military starvation campaign against Afa. She talked about how she had lost a lot of family members, friends, and acquaintances. Some had died. Some had simply vanished, not to be heard from again. Finally, she spoke about a massacre in a major city in Southern Nabuka. The Araba Massacre, she called it. She said the day would go down in history, when Nabukan soldiers gathered a group of unsuspecting Araba men and women under the guise of reconciliation only to open fire.

Her eyes were cold and distant as if relating events she could no longer feel; the ones she felt, mostly indicated by the wetness in her eyes, she rapidly blinked away. She was determined to move on, start a business and make some money by any means necessary.

Finally, she said, before announcing her need to retire for bed one evening, "Your stepfather was a good man. He died for the Afa cause."

On the morning of my departure to Ogu, Mrs. Ude shoved bills down my pockets. I refused to accept them, but she insisted, saying I was a young woman starting over like the rest of them. I told her that unlike her, I had lived a comfortable life in America. In the end, I won. She kept her money.

I caught a commercial bus from Ikeda, Lagoon to the East Central State. The heat was a combination of the warm climate and compressed body temperatures of a crowded bus. I had no option but to plant my bottom next to a middle-aged man with rubbery textured skin whose bouts of sleep meant my right shoulder would become his pillow. A few seats up, a lady about my age was passing out a flyer proclaiming, "Celebrate One Nation." She professed it was destined to be the concert of the year.

A teenage boy two seats over, with Johnny Cash-type sunglasses, was attempting to convince peeved passengers to buy his portable radio that his uncle supposedly got from London. He carried it around mid-air, like a snooty lady displaying her handbag. Through the rubber-skinned man's side window, I observed women and children with basins, trays, and baskets on their heads chanting their products: *Moi-moi! Agidi! Plantain!* Area boys roamed the streets with shredded clothes and yet with a certain stoicism that marked them as true Lagoon boys.

The bus galloped frequently through potholes and stalled several times due to traffic; to Lagoonians it was *go slow.* Eventually, the landscape transformed to reveal lush rainforests on each side of an endless road. The rubber-skinned man having been dropped off at an earlier stop, I could slide to his former seat and lean against the window. It was only then that I fell asleep.

At Ogu, I found my way to Nne's house using a taxi with three and a half doors, a disgruntled engine, and weak tires. The ground was wet, the result of a tumultuous rainstorm the previous night. It created a muddy surface that tainted my white moccasins.

Nne and I embraced for several minutes before planting ourselves on wooden stools on the veranda. One wonderful attribute of rain is its ability to create a pristine feeling in the air afterward; after all that had taken place, more than an overnight rainfall was needed to cleanse us all. I thought I imagined it, but I heard a still, small voice say, "*we suffered too.*" It seemed to come from a location beyond the window, by a cluster of blooming *udara* trees.

Nne apologized for not having food, interrupting the thoughts in my head. I insisted it was no problem even though I was quite famished. I focused on the second point of my trip, which was to know if any other family members could be found, including my birth father and his people. Nne remained in deep thought for a while before giving me directions to a place I was vaguely familiar with—I had only been there once when I was a child—then reminded me again how much food she didn't have. I promised to cater to her needs. She studied me keenly for a while, her head cocked to the side.

"You are your mother's child."

My initial impulse was to protest by listing several things Ma was that I wasn't but said nothing. I didn't want to give Nne any more things to worry about.

She wanted to know about Ma, how she was faring all by herself in the white man's land. I told her she was doing fine.

She sensed the tension in my voice, readjusted her drooping wrapper before saying, "She's all you have, eh."

"Besides you, I'm sure I have others."

"Someone should be alive somewhere on your father's side. But if I were you, I wouldn't even bother looking for him or them. After all, none of them bothered to check on you your entire life."

"That's because they probably didn't know I existed," I said stubbornly.

She sighed and shook her head, and I knew she wanted to drop the topic. She commented once again about the lack of something to eat. Getting the hint that she wanted a solution right away and feeling awfully ashamed of myself for my lack of perception, I reached for my pocket and handed her two hundred pounds.

She clasped the money in her hand and said with intense gratitude, "*Immela, nwa mu*! You have done well my daughter!"

I smiled vaguely. Then I hesitated. I opened my mouth anyway.

"Nne . . . "

"Yes, *nwa mu*."

"*O eziokwu abum osu*? Is it true I am *osu*?"

I heard the sigh from Nne's lips and watched her shoulders descend. "*Onye gwa gi*? Who told you?"

"Mrs. Ude."

Nne shook her head several times. "That woman talks too much. That has always been her problem."

I couldn't argue against that, so I simply waited for an answer to my question. Nne did not disappoint. "*Eh, o eziokwu*, it's true. But does it matter, eh?"

I said nothing, just lowered my gaze. I knew in Nne's mind it mattered because, in our part of the world where people were becoming more westernized and Christian, it mattered. *Osu* tied you to the past in ways you could not escape. It tied you to pagan gods, to indigenous ways, and had psycho-spiritual generational ties. Who wanted to remain enslaved to a god who was by many now seen as primitive, outdated, pagan? The latter evoking all manner of pious snobbery by the growing evangelical elite.

"Ada being *osu o buru njo,* is no sin," Nne said over my thoughts, outstretching her arms as if in supplication. "Back then if you wanted to escape persecution or enslavement you could choose to become a slave to a god. That was what we knew back then. As for me, even though I am Christian I still practice *omenani,* the sacred laws of the earth mother, Ani, and I am sure it will take me to the realm of the *ndiiche,* the ancestors, and to the heaven of the Christians."

I smiled, wider this time. "*Dalu Nne,* I must go now."

I stood up intending to head towards my father's supposed family compound by foot, as directed by Nne. Since Ma and my birth father had grown up in proximity to each other, I also hoped to discover for myself who Ma's parents were and other mysteries surrounding her. These were topics I had been discouraged from bringing up as a child. But now I was no longer a child. I was a young adult in need of some answers.

Nne trailed behind as I walked. "*I dikwa* sure? The place is far by foot . . . can't you wait until we find someone to drop you off?"

I insisted I would be fine. I had just taken another step when he emerged—a man somewhere in his mid-twenties and wore an afro. He had on a blue silk shirt and pants to match. His face was plain, but his eyes were bright and magnetic, his body lanky and almost tall enough to be considered lofty. Physically, he wasn't my type, and I would have easily dismissed him if he hadn't engaged me. His eyes roamed freely from my face to my feet, then traveled back up and lingered on my breasts.

"Hello foxy," he said, "the lord must have made you on a Sunday."

He had a trace of a Bostonian accent within a pronounced Afa one. I rolled my eyes.

"Classic, but not effective."

"Feisty too, what's your name honey?"

Nne stood beside me like a protective tree.

"Obinna, *biko,* leave the girl alone. She's not like one of these useless girls you carry around. She's a good girl."

"Aunty, *ekwuru ihe nka,* don't say things like that about me. I also have a heart."

Nne rolled her eyes. "Until the day you marry, I will not take you seriously."

He laughed. His laughter was so unrestrained, so careless, it seemed out of place with the current atmosphere. He said he had just returned from one of the very few operating markets several miles away and stopped by to ask if she needed anything else besides the tubers of yams that were in the backyard. We turned a corner to find six fat yams leaning against the wall. Nne flung her arms around his neck and praised him plus the mother who bore him and every other ancestor of his she could name. Then she shifted away from him as a person held captive by a brilliant idea.

"Did you come with your car?"

"Yes, Ma."

By the look she gave me, I knew it was settled. He would help me find Ma's people and my father's people and whoever else my wandering behind was itching to find whether I liked it or not. He was extremely willing to oblige.

OBINNA OKORO DROVE A 1969 PEUGEOT. The outside was a sparkling white color. The inside was brown and snug and oozed a vanilla scent from an air freshener sticker planted on the dashboard. On the car radio, the seductive Afrobeat sound of Fela Kuti's *"My Lady Frustration,"* tantalized the air. During the drive, I learned that Nne and his grandmother had been fish trading partners turned best friends for seven years before his grandmother succumbed to tuberculosis last year. That was how he knew Nne. I also learned that he had recently returned to Nabuka from the United States.

He had initially fled to the United States after receiving a wound on his chest from a stray bullet from a hunter's gun while he was at Ogu. He was sitting on the front steps of his grandmother's house when it happened. This was back in '66. It was a bad omen he said, so he decided to flee the country soon after. In 1967, His brains led him to Harvard Graduate School where he was inspired by the black student groups who fought for campus representation, equal treatment, and social justice. After the war broke out, he helped to organize numerous fundraisers for refugees with fellow students and locals. After acquiring a master's degree in psychology (because he believed understanding the mind is the root of solving most of the world's problems), he had decided to return home and help his people rebuild now that the war was over.

"What about your family?" I asked.

His father had been the minister of commerce and industry, and upon sniffing the potential outbreak of war quickly resigned from his post in 1965 and fled with his wife and Obinna's sister from Lagoon to Boston. At first, Obinna had not sensed an imminent threat and decided he would remain in Nabuka. He changed his mind the day the stray bullet grazed his chest, which he took as a sign to join his family. He indeed felt extremely fortunate.

We drove in silence for a while.

"So, what about you?" He finally asked.

I told him about Ma and I moving to Pennsylvania before the war, about my attendance at Smart College, about Ben and his violent end.

"So, we both have Greater Boston in common as well!" he exclaimed.

I smiled and nodded.

"Besides the death of your stepfather, which I am deeply sorry to hear about, you are in many ways also fortunate."

I shrugged, not entirely convinced.

"Even though we lost, we are winners at heart," he continued.

I knew what he meant by "we." He glanced my way, but I had nothing to say.

"I'm glad to have met you, Ada, I think we can do a lot of good here."

I had nothing to say about that either.

We arrived at the location Nne suggested to be Ma's parents' compound, also about a mile away from my father's family's compound. We got out of the car and faced small concrete houses, about six of them, demolished and sad looking with weeds sprouting around their foundations. I wondered which house Ma had grown up in. I had never traversed either compound before that day, but I couldn't help but react to the wasted condition before me. Obinna lingered behind me as I went inside each house. They were empty, except for some broken furniture.

At age six, I learned my father's last name was Okpara when Ma in one of her tirades referred to me as the "absent-minded child of Mr. Okpara!" So we left and asked people if they knew of any surviving Ekene or Okpara family members. People said no and moved on.

The evening ended up being unfruitful. No mention of anyone from either of my parents' side. Seeing my downcast expression, Obinna encouraged me to give it time—people remained dispersed but soon the ones that survived would return to their homes in search of loved ones. I feared that no one was going to search for me.

We surrendered for the day, deciding to indulge instead in a leisure drive. It filled a curious part of me to have a taste of my mother's childhood in the broken trees and miles of red dirt we encountered. During our drive, we came across naked children playing war games behind trees as nearby adults murmured to each other.

"As long as these children see it as a game, maybe there is hope for them," Obinna said.

I knew it would not be the case for many of these children later, that many of them would be psychologically damaged for years, even after they got married and bore children of their own. That there would be different reactions to their experiences. That some would be vocal, warning the next generation to never forget while others would remain mute for fear that speaking out would somehow introduce the horrific past to the safety that was to become their present.

Obinna turned a corner and told me about the counseling center he had just launched in the neighboring town of Owe for child war victims and soldiers, using all his savings in addition to some borrowed money from his father. A glowing light burst through the murkiness that had previously threatened to invade my chest.

"It's such a wonderful idea!" I said.

"You think?"

"Of course . . ."

"I didn't always agree with the general approach to psychology I had acquired at graduate school. I believe indigenous peoples require different processes to mental health because the worldviews are different and often contain ancestral and supernatural elements, etcetera, but I support psychoanalysis across the board. According to Sigmund Freud, childhood trauma has the potential to shape who we are as adults in more ways than previously thought. It is for this reason, I wrote my thesis on the importance of unveiling the unconscious in the mind of child war victims as part of the healing process, and also the reason I founded New Life Counseling Center." His expression grew distant as he spoke.

"That's really wonderful Obinna."

"So, you are open to helping me?"

"Absolutely."

He produced a half-smile. After a few moments, he held my hand. "Don't worry, you will find the answers you are looking for," he said.

I smiled back, a wry smile. Then through the corner of my eye, I studied his profile. Maybe he wasn't so bad after all.

The village was engulfed in darkness when we returned to Nne's house and found her asleep on a mat in the living room. I tiptoed to the room that was once my bedroom, Obinna trailing behind me like a man unwilling to lose sight of a woman whose bride price he had just paid. Moonlight pierced through the singular window, revealing that the room was bare except for the mattress Nne and I used to share. I could hear Obinna breathing in the darkness. I was going to have to send him back to where he came from, I thought to myself.

"You need mosquito nets," Obinna said.

I had forgotten about mosquitoes. As if to remind me, a swarm of them rushed towards me. I slapped the air to wade them off. Obinna tee-heed behind me.

"This is not funny!" I fumed.

"You can hang out with me at my place."

"No way!"

"Why not?" He pouted, now serious.

"Because . . . I don't know you that well," I found myself stuttering.

"I would like to think that by now you know to trust me."

I analyzed the situation for a while.

"And guess what, I also have a generator," Obinna said.

A generator. Yes, this was crucial. I had grown unused to sleeping on a mattress for an extended period, had grown unaccustomed to dealing with mosquitoes. I thought about the future, not having access to a shower or constant electricity for months, having to squat in a communal pit latrine and not sit comfortably on a toilet.

"It's up to you. Unless you are willing to brave them out . . . but you know what is going to happen, you are going to wake up with black spots all over your body," he chuckled again.

I bit my lower lip. To the front of me, the insects mapped their territory in zig-zag motions.

"I'm about to leave. . ."

His gold watch sparkled in the dark.

"Okay, I'm willing to see your place. Not tonight. But soon enough. But please, no funny business!" I wagged my finger close to his face.

"Agreed. No problem. I have too much respect for Nne to dishonor you. "There is just one thing you should know."

"Which is . . .?" My chest rose, anticipating the worst.

He leaned closer to my ear until I caught a whiff of his wild mint scented aftershave.

"I guarantee you will end up falling in love with me."

I REMAINED IN THE HOUSE WITH Nne for a few days, catching up with Oluchi, who thankfully remained physically unscathed along with most of her people. She and Nne shared some war stories in Nne's compound one mid-week afternoon—about moments when everything would feel normal; villagers taking strolls, having makeshift weddings, villagers swimming by the river, washing clothes by the same river. . . only for those moments to be interrupted by bouts of wailing and pillaging and other sounds of terror. I found it surprising that Nne's house remained the same, as if by some supernatural force. The house held no evidence of an attack, no damage from a bullet or grenade or bomb. It just sat there, anchored and secure like before. Nne's skeletal structure and the occasional sadness in her eyes were the only evidence I saw of her trauma. Otherwise, she sang the same, smiled the same, cooked her meals the same way, with lots of crayfish.

One evening, when the light came on after hours of power outage, she encouraged me to mend things with Ma. The flame from the kerosene lamp flickered from the corner of the living room. I was tempted to blow it out but went against the idea. Electricity was a luxury here. It came and went like a god bestowing its radiance only to withdraw it at a whim.

"But Nne, why would you think I need to mend things with Ma?" I asked, wondering how she could have known about our last fight.

"*Abum Nne gi*, I am your mother in every sense. I know everything," she said.

A few minutes later, I called Ma using the only telephone, located in Ma's former bedroom. I apologized for the fight and let her know that Nne and I were well and safe in Ogu. She accepted the apology somewhat grumpily, but I could also sense an underlying relief in her voice. Moments later, Nne took over the telephone, chatting with Ma for the duration of the call.

A WEEK AFTER MY RETURN TO Ogu, I went to the river for a swim at sunrise draped in one of Nne's wrappers. Underneath, a polka dot 1950's bikini suit which smelled like mothballs that I found in Ma's former bedroom drawer the night before. It was a ten-minute walk. Upon arrival, I noticed in the far-right corner, a couple of fishermen dipping their nets in the water, and on my distant left, a woman beating a cloth against a rock. I dropped the wrapper on the shore, slid into the water and exhaled as the warm water took me in like her child, held me close and caressed me with the emerging sun looking on until I felt parts of myself mend back together. Thirty minutes later, I came out of the water, tied the cloth around my body, and made my way back to the house. Nne was sitting on her favorite stool in the veranda chewing on ube pear.

"Good morning Nne," I greeted.

"Good morning *nwamu*. How was the river?"

"Comforting, just like I remembered it."

Nne smiled. I went inside, dried myself up with a towel, applied some of Nne's shea butter (which I preferred over the lotion I had brought with me from the States because of its glossy effect on my skin and the protection it provided from the elements) and adorned a sleeveless gown. When I came outside, Nne had food in a plate for me: fried yams with stewed fish. Thanking her, I sat on a stool next to her and began to indulge in the warm crunchy yams and tomatoey sauce.

"Obinna is coming over today. He comes every Saturday."

I nodded my head. "That's nice."

"I think you two should spend more time together. *O di mkpa*, it is important to spend time with people your age group who can help you find your way here, besides just Oluchi."

"But I thought you said he is a womanizer?" I chuckled.

"I said spend time together, not marry, ah ah!"

"Okay Nne," I said and chuckled some more.

That afternoon, after Obinna visited and had some ube with Nne and me in the veranda, he drove me to where he lived. I convinced myself that if he proved to be dodgy I would hike to Ogu, which was no small feat! The bungalow had two bedrooms, a parlor, a kitchen, two bathrooms, and a dining room. It was adequate for a small-size family to co-exist comfortably.

Obinna proved to be a gentleman on day one and by day seven, I had become such a regular visitor that the guest room slowly began to fill up with my things—clothes, toothbrush, hair pomade and comb, shea butter. It wasn't just the comforts the house provided that kept me coming back, it was his jovial attitude, the curious way he treated me like a sister and suitor at the same time, which I began to find endearing. He cemented his gentleman status, especially after he set me up in the guest room, a good distance away from his bedroom, and did not once trespass my door except when necessary. He had also been right about the insects. Thanks to window nets, there were no mosquitoes in the house. Except for a few bugs that popped up occasionally and geckos that crawled on the walls, I had no complaints.

Then one night in mid-August of 1970, while it rained and stormed and it felt like the world would be wiped away in part two of the Biblical flood, I appeared by the edge of his bed. His bedroom door had been left ajar. He was wide awake. He grinned when he saw me.

"You are afraid, eh?"

"No," I replied.

Lightning flashed across his window, and I hit the floor. He poked fun at me.

"Amadioha, the god of the storms, is coming to get you. What sins have you committed?"

"Stop teasing, Obinna! I swear it doesn't rain like this anywhere else in the world!"

He directed me to the bottom part of the bed, pulling his legs up to create space for me to sit. I planted my bottom on the soft white sheets.

"So how does it rain like?" he asked.

The texture of his voice had changed. It was softer, not comical. I had never witnessed this side of him before and it gripped something in my chest.

"It just doesn't," I whispered.

Suddenly the rain condensed to a drizzle, the ferocious thunder and lightning muted as if by some higher command. I felt a pull, a strong pull towards his lips. I surrendered to it. An amorous feeling reflected in his eyes. He smiled at me as a person high on something sweet. That gave me the impulse to kiss him more fervently. His eager response sent shivers through my body. He flipped me over like a doll until I was lying on my back. We continued to kiss, my fingers toying with his scant chest hair and lean muscles. The bullet wound on his right breast stared at me, inches away from his right nipple. I pecked it. He groaned. He kissed my lips again, my brows, my cheeks, my nose, my at the time wild, stringy afro.

"Ada, I loved you the moment I saw you. For me, it has always been more than physical."

"There's something you should know Obi," I said in a very low voice.

He nodded for me to speak.

"I am *osu*. I recently found out."

For what seemed like timelessness he said nothing. Finally, he exhaled and said, "Is that all?"

"Yes."

"As long as we never marry, we will be fine."

Something flipped inside of me. "What do you mean?"

"I mean that our first child might come out deranged. Or die young. Or you might die in childbirth. Or something like that. The gods are not to be messed with."

I was quiet for several minutes before asking him if he really believed what he had just said.

"Yes, Ada *oma*, beautiful one, yes," he said, blinking solemnly towards the ceiling.

Chapter Seventeen

October 1970

OBINNA AND I GOT ALONG QUITE well. At least we seemed to have the same ideas with regards to development in the East. He often teased me that he was my knight in shining armor, that if I had not met him, I would have been a lost soul in a strange, new nation. And I kept insisting I would have been fine even though I knew I was fibbing.

We formed a rhythm that worked in the house, his house, that we lived in. But it wouldn't take long before I caught a sneak peak of Obinna's philandering ways. That Sunday evening, I caught him flirting with the house girl of one of the neighbors. The neighbors in question were Mr. and Mrs. Onyeagali, a British educated lawyer and his generous wife. Mrs. Onyeagali, in her Sunday outfit; a red and white sequined gown and matching Church hat, had caught sight of me leaving out the gate that Sunday morning and proceeded to welcome me to the neighborhood. As a welcome package to me, she had made a gift basket of oranges, assorted bread, *suya,* and groundnuts and sent it through Gloria, their house girl that evening. Obinna was quick to rush to the gate when the girl arrived. And as I peered out the parlor window I noticed the overfamiliarity, the lengthy interaction between them, the way he leaned towards her when he talked, the way she threw her head back when she laughed at his jokes. It brought to mind what Nne had said about Obinna and the "useless girls" he associated with. I immediately shoved the Gloria incident in the corner of my mind. Obinna and I had something special going, something that was bigger than just us, that affected the lives of many, and I wasn't going to let a dallying house girl get in the way of that for the moment. With that thought, I walked away from the glass shutters, settled on the nearest couch, and pretended to read a newspaper.

A WEEK LATER, I WAS ABLE to apply for and get accepted to teach at an elementary school in a very rural part of Owe, despite the absence of a college degree. The need for teachers in addition to my "stellar American education" was enough to qualify me for the position.

The school was a small compound filled with several sheds topped with zinc roofs and separated by walls constructed with blocks of cement. I taught primary four a.k.a. fourth grade English to children whose education had been halted at that level due to the war. I soon fell in love with those young brave souls eager to learn in a world that had proven unpredictable only months prior. But it was challenging having to observe the effects of post-traumatic stress disorder on these children. A day barely went by when I did not pick up a drawing from the floor with images of guns, grenade explosions, dead bodies, and blood etched in red crayon. Of course, you can imagine, I would have rather known they spent more time working on their pronunciations and spellings than scribbling on paper, but as a poet I understood the process of needing to release one's feelings to avoid being suffocated and potentially destroyed by them.

There were other instances where a child would be dozing off during my lecture and a little shout from me to wake them up would produce the most startling response followed by a sudden flood of tears and panic. Feeling guilty at having induced such a response, I would appease the child in front of the entire classroom with promises of sweets and candies at the end of the school day. I had never been trained as a teacher or a counselor and no one could blame me for my inadequacy in those areas. The children in my classroom got away with things children in other classrooms did not. I was known as the "soft" teacher, the teacher who did not even use a cane—ever! It was a policy that I strictly adhered to. I knew the effect Ma's caning had on me, the fear it instilled, and I wanted more for my pupils. I wanted my pupils to be inspired by passion, not fear. To love learning and not be forced into it. However, the other teachers were not appreciative of this fact. They complained that my students were extremely interactive and that I encouraged them to be too bold towards teachers.

"Too bold?" I once asked a fellow teacher while taking a stroll in the playground during lunch hours. He was a very frigid light-skinned man about my age with more experience and confidence in his position. His name was Charley.

"Yes, too bold. They ask too many mind-boggling questions."

"But Charley, isn't that part of the learning process?

"Yes, it is, but after a while they must be trained to have the discipline to keep quiet, especially when an adult is talking."

I paused, confused.

"And I was walking by your classroom the other day. Your children don't even stand up to ask questions."

"They raise their hands . . ."

"They are supposed to stand up. It is disrespectful. This is not America, you know," he said.

I was tempted to reply, "And this is not England," but bit my tongue. I was already rubbing other teachers the wrong way. There was no need to add one more to the list.

Gossip went around, according to Charley. The gossip made me out to be a snob, made me out to be too condescending, too liberal. Perhaps it was because I saw and noticed things others did not seem to notice or pay attention to. For example, the fact that the curriculum was in serious need of adjustment. There was no denying that the British standard of education was quite superb, but the cultural element—our cultural element—seemed to suffocate over time. My feelings about this created complexity in my being that I could not explain to anyone. What no one could accuse me of was being uncommitted. The miniature school board saw that I was committed to my job, and the children, and that I was willing to tolerate other idiosyncrasies—at least for a while.

I sparked up a cigarette as we got farther away from the playground. The beach-colored sand was so deep it filled up our shoes rather quickly, getting into our bare feet as we strolled. The long stretch of sand led to a forested area. It was an amazing thing no child ever got lost in the dense foliage even though we were all aware the children performed bodily excretions in there during recess because the school latrine often proved too sullied for use, an unfortunate consequence of a growing lack of infrastructural support.

"You know this is not permissible here," I heard Charley say, referring to my smoking.

I took a drag and hid the stick behind my back.

"I can't help it. That's why I do it here, where no one can see me," I said, wincing.

"Do you plan to quit?"

"One day, so I don't die of cancer," I replied with a sigh.

IN EARLY NOVEMBER OF THAT YEAR, I began to contribute to the New Life Counseling Center with my fundraising efforts. The one-story center, a fifteen-minute drive from Obinna's house, was vertically short and horizontally wide. It had a waiting area, seven offices, and a lavatory. The outside was an amaranth pink color and it rested in the center of a sparsely grassy area like a pinnacle of hope in a famished land. Obinna had recruited three licensed therapists, two men and a woman who rotated an average of ten patients a day, but there were talks by Obinna and other board members of expansion. More children were being enrolled and this required more staff.

With a telephone book and hours to spare, I made numerous telephone calls to philanthropists and prospective givers. Because many Easterners in the region had lost their sources of income, a lot of help came from people visiting from overseas: London, America, France, and so on. On the national level, the federal government had provided funds to cover operating services for the East Central State for an interim period. Over time, Afa military personnel received leniency. Infrastructure expanded. My hope for Nabuka was rising, but to Obinna the government's efforts weren't enough. And it would never be enough until, according to him, Afa people were guaranteed socio-economic equality and protection in Nabuka.

Obinna and I contributed in other ways by providing food, medicine, and money to clinics and relief centers across the

Eastern region. We also continued to drive to Ogu whenever time permitted us to check on the people we knew. It was rewarding to see Nne's ample hips returning. It was equally rewarding to see members of Ben's family thriving. Though I was finally able to contact a few distant relatives on both sides, I still searched for more.

On the third Saturday of the month, I telephoned Ma to deliver news about Nne's wellbeing and other general updates. It was a weekly habit I maintained after my apology over the telephone in Ogu.

"Ma, I am calling to say Nne is doing well, and that I am in Owe at the moment."

"Good. Please make sure you visit her often."

"Yes, Ma."

"And what are you doing in Owe? Who are you staying with?"

I inhaled deeply and released it.

"A friend. His name is Obinna."

She hesitated. "Obinna? From what family?"

"I met him through Nne."

Before she could toss anymore questions, I blurted out, "Ma, I hope you don't feel too *alone* with me being here."

"Why should I?" She said defensively.

"I don't know. I just thought maybe. . ."

"I have been on my own a long time. Independence runs in the blood," she said.

I wanted to say more, to tell her about my search for her immediate family and in-laws, but the words could not form. She had been defensive, sometimes even angry, when I had probed her about her family as a child. And during our last visit home, she hadn't mentioned nor expressed concern over her parents and siblings. I found it extraordinarily odd. Surely being intimately affiliated with *osu* couldn't be *that bad*?

As time progressed, I provided more details about Obinna and the work we were doing during my conversations with Ma. I also let her in about how my life was finally starting to make sense.

"Oh," she said at the latter comment as if I had betrayed her in some way. Then she revealed to me that Sal had telephoned the house a few times from Italy to ask about me. I chortled, though it was more contrived than pure mirth.

"What is funny?"

"Ma, I have moved on, and he needs to move on too."

"Okay, well . . . If you say so."

She didn't seem convinced. But it didn't matter now. We went on to other topics. She complained about the people at her workplace and how they were starting to irritate her with their overt racism.

"Can you imagine some of these patients have the nerve to demand a white doctor when they see it's me attending to them?!" She decried.

Sometimes I wanted to remind Ma that she was a foreign black woman in a white man's country. In Nabuka, she was used to being respected to and referred to as madam. But in her current environment, she was just another fortunate negro who made it. But I said nothing, just listened as she went on to vent about the unpredictable Greensberg weather, how she needed a vacation, and many other things.

The conversation was going relatively well until she said, "By the way, I spoke to Nne about Obinna. She had nothing bad to say about him, and she says his father is quite well off."

I rolled my eyes.

"But you should know by now that it is immoral to live with a man in an unmarried situation. Ada, I thought I raised you better than this. I thought I should give you a break so you won't think your mother is out to ruin your life, but I must speak on this because this is unacceptable!"

The small opening in my heart shrunk. This was the same woman who had gotten pregnant with me out of wedlock, what did she know about relationships anyway? I wanted to call her a hypocrite. I did the second-best thing.

"Ma, I have to go," I politely said and hung up the telephone.

In December of 1970, during the early stages of harmattan, when the temperature was just starting to drop, and the dust began to collect and blow in people's faces, and leaves turned brown and crisp, threatening to rip off their branches, Obinna and I in our cardigans lounged on the veranda as was customary for us most evenings after a long day's work.

"So, what were you thinking, seriously, moving back to Nabuka on your own as a woman?" he began the evening's conversation.

"Why are you acting like I'm the first woman to do this, like it's a big deal," I replied.

"It's a big deal because number one, it seems to me that the decision was sudden, and number two, you left your mother by herself."

"I've told you many times that she can take care of herself. We talk a lot these days, trust me she's fine," I snapped.

"*Na wa o*," he replied, shaking his head and looking at the distant sky.

"Women don't always need men you know," I said.

"That's what you feminists say to hide the bitterness of being lonely and horny broads. Trust me, I know. I met a number of them during my grad student days . . . "

"Excuse me!" I said, pulling away from the chair. "I am not a feminist."

What followed was a burst of long, exaggerated laughter that left me wondering if I had indeed said something incredulous.

"Ada is not a feminist," he said mockingly. "*Nnem . . . biko* make pounded yam for me."

"I thought it was your turn to cook today. Besides, you know I don't like pounding yam," I replied innocently.

"You see what I am saying!" He said, almost leaping out of his chair.

I stared at him, surprised. He had never complained about my lack of cooking skills, even after I explained to him that Ma and I often thrived on quick spaghetti, rice, and sauce concoctions. And that even when we ate something close to resembling Nabukan food, Ma was the one who prepared it because she had more experience with that than I did. At the time, he had simply said okay, not to worry, that he would do most of the cooking. He had learned how to cook from his mother.

"You don't like cooking, cleaning, washing . . . you are lucky you have me or how else would you have found a husband?"

I found myself bubbling with rage. "And that makes me a feminist because I don't like doing these things?" "You have a problem with feminism?" he replied with an impish glint in his eyes.

"No, I don't. I support it. It's a man's world and a woman must do what she has to do, but I Ada am not defined by labels. This idea that I am looking for a husband or should be looking for one and that my lack of domestic skills somehow places me at a disadvantage is not only chauvinistic but also backwards!"

"Calm down. . .we are just having a conversation," he said and chuckled.

I found myself breathing slowly to calm myself. Somehow, I was becoming convinced Obinna took pleasure in getting a rise out of me from time to time. He always knew the right buttons to push and when, and each time I fell for it, which infuriated me even more.

"I am going inside to get some beer from the fridge," he said, a slight smile dangling from his lips.

"Get one for me too," I said.

He arose from his recliner. "See this woman, oh. I didn't know you drank."

"And just to put it out there, I am an occasional smoker as well. I have just been doing it behind your back all this time."

He eyed me for an instant before disappearing into the house and emerging moments later with two bottles of Guinness. He returned to his recliner, handing me a bottle.

"You are a woman, you shouldn't smoke or drink," he said rather seriously.

"Why?"

"Because here in Owe people will think you are loose."

"Let them think what they want."

I watched him shake his head in resignation.

"American girl," he teased.

"Nabukan man," I chided.

"No-ooo. Nabuka is a failed state."

"Why would you say that?"

He turned serious. "Aren't you watching the news? Don't you live here? Don't you see the dog-eat-dog mentality, the corruption, the police brutality on the city streets, the lack of electricity, the poverty?"

"We are still young as a nation, Obinna. It took America a hundred and something years to get to where it is now. And some of the things you listed, they have experienced and in some cases still do. And they too had their internal divisions that led to a civil war."

He shook his head like a stubborn little boy, took a sip of his drink then dropped the bottle on the ground.

"You are not getting the point. We were not designed by our colonial masters to be unified or successful. We were designed to be exploited for generations to come."

"You need to stop being negative," I insisted. "Every country has its problems. In my days in the States, all I witnessed was a constant cry for change and revolution. And this is the world's superpower. What Nabuka is going through will pass and it will take all of us coming together for that to happen. A united Nabuka, a united Afrika is the way forward. That is what my stepfather, Ben, taught me and that is what I believe."

"I suppose your stepfather was thinking of a United Nabuka when he voluntarily gave his life for the Afa cause."

I sprang to my feet and headed inside.

"Ada, wait a minute."

I responded with the resounding slam of the door behind me.

Later that night, he cuddled next to me in bed and apologized.

"It wasn't a nice thing to say. Seriously, Obinna, was that necessary?"

"I know, I know, it was very immature of me to say what I said. *Ndo,* sorry," he said and held me close to his chest. "Please forgive me."

But even as he apologized, I knew in my heart that he was right. Even with all his talk on pan Afrika, Ben, a staunch Pan Afrikanist and Nabukan diplomat, did choose his ethnic identity over his national identity, and this was something I had to grapple with for the rest of my life.

THE HARMATTAN BREEZE BLAZED ITS TRAIL as the weeks went by. It was one of the worst we'd had in a long time, people muttered. On the streets, I often observed people rubbing their eyes to remove restless sands that had made their way in, leaving behind red eyes like conjunctivitis. Everything was dry, parched, and felt quiet on the day I decided to leave work early and stop by the center to surprise Obinna with a visit.

It was a Friday afternoon when I strolled into the building. Inside, there was a room with chairs lined up in what was the lobby. Straight ahead, behind the chairs, were about seven doors. One of them was Obinna's office. The rest were offices for the counselors and their patients. Displayed on the right wall, weak-handed wiggly drawings. Child drawings. There were about twenty of them, mostly of people falling from gunshot wounds, dead bodies, and destroyed buildings. Art therapy. I looked away. I heard humming noises from behind one of the doors. A young man was describing something to a counselor.

"*Anyi nile nwere egbe.* We all had to take the guns. And we were commanded to kill without blinking."

"*Igburu mmadu?* Did you kill?" the more mature voice asked. Even though he spoke Afa, he did not sound like an

Easterner. In response to his question, the boy said something I did not catch. At the same time, a young woman, not more than eighteen surfaced. She had very round eyes, a thin linear face, and made slow deliberate movements. I noticed the dull blue dress she wore and how it looked like a smudged charcoal painting, against her chapped dark skin.

"Can I help you?" Her bland voice matched her appearance.

"Mr. Okoro, is he available?"

She eyed me. "Who are you?"

"His girlfriend," I said, glaring at her.

"What do you need him for?"

"Excuse me?" I said, standing at akimbo.

"*Nne nne*!"

It was Obinna's voice. From the lavatory tucked in a corner, he emerged with a big grin. He strolled towards us, slid his lanky arm across my shoulder, and planted a kiss on my right cheek. "*Nne, nne,* my mother's mother" was a term of endearment he used for me occasionally. Culturally, it meant I was respected and special to him. In reality, I wasn't always so sure.

"This is Grace, my new secretary. Grace, did you greet her?" Obinna said, pointing to Grace.

Grace's audacious expression crumbled.

"Good afternoon." She nodded before scurrying off.

He extended his arm and greeted me. "*Kedu*?"

I pulled away from him. "What is going on with that girl?"

"Which girl?"

"Obinna!"

He laughed.

"I was just playing. But what is the problem? Was she rude?"

A woman strolled in from behind, wide hips the size of a buffalo, light-skinned like banana skin, with a straight nose and shoulder-length hair extensions that reminded me of a horse's mane.

"Mr. Okoro, oh . . ." Her voice sounded like a parrot's.

"Miss. Akudo, *kedu*?"

He darted towards her. They chatted animatedly. Her wrapper, while attempting to pull out something from the fold that held it in place, began to unravel. I watched Obinna swiftly reach out to assist her. I expected her to protest. She didn't. She smiled, as they both adjusted her wrapper. Enraged, I stormed off.

An hour later, Obinna met me at the house.

"Why did you leave?"

"What do you mean why did I leave?"

We were standing in the living room, the white walls adorned with multiple paintings of nude Afrikan women. The portraits of the shamelessly voluptuous women, an aesthetic element in the past, now became evidence of his philandering ways.

"You just walked off."

"It seemed you two needed some privacy!" I replied.

"You mean Miss Akudo? Ada, don't be silly."

"Silly? You are the one who cannot control your fingers. What is the matter with you? You embarrassed me today!"

"Embarrassed you? I have known that woman for years!"

"You must think I am a child!"

I planted myself on the nearest cushion.

"A lot of these women endured so much during the war. All I try to do is exhibit some tenderness, some gentleness. Would you prefer I behave otherwise just to make you happy?"

"But you do it everywhere, with every woman!" I said recalling the incident with Gloria.

"Baby, you need to relax, it's just my personality. I mean no harm," he said.

I felt something. Like deja vu. Then it dawned on me. The scene was a replica of Ben and Ma years ago. Back then, I had chosen to side with Ben over her. After all, he was the one who understood me, the one who could do no wrong, while she . . .

"You know what? Do what makes you happy. If you like, tie and untie wrappers all day. I am finished with this conversation!"

I stood up and dashed towards the bedroom. He trailed behind.

"I know you are not finished with this conversation for you will begin to sulk for days at a time. You women are all the same."

I turned to face him.

"Look, stop categorizing me with other women, you hear?! Goodness gracious, you are driving me mad!"

"Okay, I didn't mean to . . . ah, ah stop walking away, eh?"

I slammed the bedroom door behind me.

AN HOUR LATER, HE JOINED ME on the bed. I was lying in a fetal position. His hips grazed my backside.

"Ah, ah, you can be feisty, oh."

I rolled my eyes.

"Look *nne, nne*," he continued, "I'm sorry. I didn't mean to embarrass you. You are the only one for me. You should know that I will never be unfaithful."

I refused to turn around even though my insides felt like jello on what had previously felt like sand. My stomach growled. It was way past my lunch time. As if responding to my stomach, he said, "I bought you your fa-vo-rit-eeeee."

Then the steamy, piquant, *moi-moi* aroma reached my nostrils from the kitchen. Nne had made me fall in love with the delicacy while growing up in Ogu. She seasoned hers with a mix of stimulating ingredients that included crayfish, chopped boiled eggs, and onions before wrapping them in banana leaves and then steaming them.

"You want some?"

My stomach growled again. There is no pride in hunger, so I nodded, yes.

Chapter Eighteen

February 1971

IN THE BACKYARD, UNDER THE SHADE of the metal roof, I squeezed my last wash of the day, a soapy burgundy and cream-colored wrapper, until most of the foam flowed back in the basin. Next to the basin was a bucket of clear water. I dumped the wrapper into the water. I would have to change the water a few more times for a thorough rinse. The air was dry, and the occasional dust hissed through it. The harmattan wind was no longer ferocious, just mild and cooperative, like the glare of the afternoon sun which seemed to keep a fair distance thanks to the shade.

"You think we need a house girl?" Obinna said over my shoulder, startling me. He was shirtless, wearing only a pair of jeans.

"A house girl?" I replied, suspiciously.

"Okay, house boy. Whatever."

I shoved the sheet into the fresh water with both hands until the bubbles floated to the top. I rose from the concrete step, grabbed the bucket handle, and made my way to the tap a few feet away.

"I don't want to act privileged, Obinna. I may not care too much for housework, but as you have seen so far I don't need help. Nne taught me well. The same way your mother taught you well."

He smiled as if unconvinced.

"Okay. . . if you say so. But as you know house help is not just for the privileged. In Nabuka, you can be relatively poor and still have house servants, just so you can feel better than the next man," Obinna said dryly.

I poured the murky water into a nearby bush, making sure to hold the wrapper in place with my available hand. Then I tucked the bucket under the faucet and released the water, watching it flow generously for the next rinse.

"I am a lady, not an elitist," I said playfully.

"Excuse me, lady!" Obinna said in an exaggerated female voice, planting an arm on his hip, leaving us both chuckling.

After the chuckle subsided, he went on, "Speaking of the elite, my parents are moving back to Lagoon in a week. I want you to meet them."

I felt a surge of anxiety, right from the pit of my stomach. I looked sharply at him, neglecting the running water which was starting to overflow from the bucket. On the one hand I felt honored that he wanted me to meet his parents. Perhaps validated. It would be my first time meeting the parents of a romantic interest. But then again, Obinna was my first real relationship. But there was also this hiccup . . .

"Obi, are you sure?"

"What do you mean?" he said, walking over to me. He turned off the faucet.

"I'm *osu*," I said in a quiet voice. "Remember?"

He bowed his head to confirm that he did remember the night I told him I was *osu*, the very rainy night after our first kiss.

"Don't worry, it will be okay," he said with a smile, but I could see the light in his eyes grow dim.

We drove to Lagoon to visit Obinna's parents for the Easter holiday. In the months prior to the visit, I spent hours prepping myself on what to say, how to act, how to counteract any potentially insensitive comments about my absentee father, about my *osu* status. Obinna was happy to see his parents even though I observed the occasional brooding expression whenever I brought up the topic on what to say and how to say it. He would have loved to see his sister, but she had decided to remain on a college campus in Virginia where she studied engineering.

Obinna's parents lived on Vicky Island. It was exclusive, surrounded by palm trees and towering mansions with massive gates. It took us seven hours to get there by car. When we arrived at the shiny black gate, Obinna honked his horn and within seconds the gateman, an elderly gentleman with an exaggerated smile and steps, swung open the gate. On the paved front yard were two parked cars—a shiny yellow Mercedes and a black Lincoln. Obinna parked his car behind the Mercedes. We got out the car with the gateman stretching his arms to "relieve us" of our duffel bags.

"*Oga*, and madam welcome. It is nice to see you. They are expecting you, sir," he said, bowing one time too many.

Obinna patted him on the back, muttered some thanks, and headed straight for the sliding patio door. We walked into a parlor; white porcelain tiles, mirrored surfaces, large television, velvet couches, yet the most auspicious thing to attract my attention was the warm, brothy smell of pepper soup from what appeared to be the kitchen. The smell was followed by a youthful middle-aged woman in leggings and a colorful beaded shirt. Obinna's mother was beautiful in ways I could not have expected since Obinna wasn't particularly handsome. Her eye liner intensified her almond shaped eyes. Her pink lipstick accentuated her full lips. Her perfectly red manicured nails, long and natural, clicked against each other like the claws of a regal bird. Her only resemblance to Obinna was her toffee brown complexion which she adorned perfectly with a hint of glossy face powder.

She and Obinna fell into each other's arms, swinging from side to side. "My son, *nwa mu*, it is so nice to see you, oh! It's been too long!"

Moments later, Obinna's father strolled in from an adjoining room. He was tall and robust with thick hair and a twinkle in his eyes. He was the direct replica of Obinna, except for the robustness. Obinna disengaged from his mother and gave his father, who patted him on the back several times, a tight embrace. I was soon introduced to them by Obinna who said something in the likes of, "This is Ada, my special lady" In response to my feeble courtesy, Mr. Okoro senior gave me a big smile and a nod. Looking at his mother, Obinna added for emphasis, "Her Grandaunt and Mama, I found out, were good friends before she passed."

Mrs. Okoro smiled, but I noticed a slight twitch around the edges of her pink lips.

The next couple of hours was filled with a delicious *fufu* and pepper soup dinner, some champagne, and how happy they were to have not experienced the war first-hand. At dinner I had learned that Mr. Okoro had resumed his ministerial position and that Obinna was expected to follow in his father's footsteps. Obinna responded that he was proud of his counseling center and would continue to focus on that work.

"But what about your future?" Mr. Okoro asked, swinging his glass of champagne from side to side. "We sent you to Harvard with the hopes that you would use your knowledge and skills to acquire a lucrative government position. Maybe working for the Department of Health, or something related."

"Dad, why should I work for a government that our people can't trust? Wasn't it the other day that they tried to exterminate us?" Obinna, seated to his father's right, retorted.

Mr. Okoro waved his hand, "It doesn't matter now. We are now under one Nabuka. Let's move on and progress as one, *abi*?" he said, looking over to Mrs. Okoro for approval. Mrs. Okoro nodded vehemently, staring deeply at her son.

"If the government hadn't been willing to allow me to resume my position, we wouldn't be here now. Let bygones be bygones."

My gaze shifted to Obinna. His eyes exhibited a maroon-colored glare, his body appeared stiffer. I had never experienced this side of him before and wished for the ability to end the conversation immediately.

Nothing was said for a while as we sipped on our wines, my sips now creating a queasy bubbling sensation in my stomach.

"Don't you want to have your own money one day? Be rich? And as for you Ada, what are your plans? A teacher's salary can only take you so far." Mr. Okoro, unwilling to surrender the topic, turned toward me.

I felt his verbal punch right in my gut. I had to swallow hard not to spit pepper soup and wine out my mouth.

"I'm still figuring things out, em, Mr. Okoro, I mean, sir. I do enjoy making a difference in the lives of my pupils at this time," I responded quickly, albeit nervously. I was still waiting for the barrage of questions, for the big *osu* reveal. It surprised me his parents seemed not to care much about the "special lady" Obinna had driven seven hours to meet them. I cut another quick glance at Obinna, who was poking a toothpick at his teeth. I could see his temple muscles throbbing.

"Money should be used to elevate the poor among us, to uplift our people," Obinna said in a grumpy tone.

"Sure, sure, my boy," Mr. Okoro said dismissively, rising from his chair. By the slight stagger in his steps, it was apparent that he was tipsy, perhaps fully drunk. He squeezed Obinna's shoulder. "Let's continue this discussion next time. You two have had a long trip and need some rest. Just like my tired knees," he said and staggered off. Mrs. Okoro walked up to Obinna and kissed his forehead. "Goodnight *nwa mu*, my child. Please go to bed so you can wake up early for Easter service tomorrow," she said. She looked me over, producing a plastic smile and pointing at a hallway across the dining room. "The guest bedroom is at the end of the hallway. Nice meeting you," she said and left the room, her gold-plated slippers slapping against the polished floor.

Obinna and I remained in our seats, caught up in our own mental gymnastics. It was then a sudden realization hit me.

"They know, don't they?"

"What?"

"Obinna, you already told them that I am *osu*!"

It made sense, the dismissive approach, the plastic smiles, the heavy drinking. They didn't care about me being there.

They were just too sophisticated in their approach in expressing it.

"Yes, I did," Obinna admitted waving his hands in defeat. "I wanted to give them a heads-up just in case.

I got up from the chair, making my way to the guest room, where I could privately release the wrangled emotions I could sense bubbling in my throat. Obinna followed after me. I turned around, looking him in the eye.

"Look, Obinna, I don't want to be the woman that you have to prove to your parents. I am twenty years old, and marriage is not on my radar, and may never be on my radar. I never knew my father and my stepfather and mother were as good as divorced. Please remember that."

"Okay," Obinna said, raising his hand in a surrendered stance. I went inside the guest room, quietly shutting the door behind me.

The next day they went to church, Obinna and his parents. I remained in the guest room, pretending to have menstrual cramps. Three days later, we drove in silence to Owe, back to my life and my pupils, the way I preferred it.

Chapter Nineteen

March 1972

ALMOST A YEAR LATER AND THERE were still no signs of the whereabouts of my father except for an abstract painting that a neighbor had found partially buried in an abandoned maize field in September of the previous year. The person had given it to Nne in the hopes that it might provide me some comfort. Just like the good samaritan, Nne was convinced that the painting belonged to my father. She said he was known to paint outdoors in proximity to the field. But as I scrutinized the aged canvas in Nne's veranda, I saw no trace of revolution or anti-colonial sentiments. All I saw was a burst of tertiary colors now smudged with dirt and rain. The brush strokes resembled an inferno passing through a tunnel. Obinna felt it was the passionate expression of a man struggling to contain his burning emotions. I felt it was the depiction of a man whose passions destroyed all in its wake. I stashed the painting in a drawer next to my journal after we returned to Owe.

Obinna remained in close contact with his parents. I was rarely discussed. Besides my being *osu*, they were perhaps used to Obinna having girlfriends, switching them, perhaps even professing each one to be the "one" until something occurred to replace "her." It was different for me. I didn't love easily, and I imagined if I did love it would last forever. It was while musing over the idea of eternal love that I decided one late March evening to scribble my thoughts on the topic in my journal.

> *What is love? Who can define it? Who or what can lay claim to it? Is love an it, a she, or a he? Is it a plump babe shooting arrows at random? Or is it a nymph or a god or simply a whirlwind that picks up whoever is near?*

Later that evening while Obinna and I ate fried rice and plantain for dinner, I asked him if he had ever been in love prior to me.

"Yes, I have been in love a few times," he said quietly, stuffing a spoonful of rice in his mouth.

"And you? Were you ever in love with the black American?"

I had briefly shared with him my relationship with Malcolm during the early stages of our relationship.

"I wasn't in love with Malcolm," I said and hesitated.

"Was there someone else? I know you women are full of secrets," he said with a slight jeer.

"Sal . . ."

It would be the first time I would bring up Sal's name since I left the United States. Sal belonged to a treasured part of myself that was vulnerable. It was a part of myself I was afraid to explore for fear that it would re-route me from the safe reality I had carefully crafted for myself. But here it was, his name coming out of my mouth, like a loose cannon.

"Sal? That doesn't sound like one of us."

"No, he wasn't black, if that's what you mean . . ."

The clang of Obinna's metallic spoon dropping on his plate made me jump. "Ada, wetin concern you with *onye ocha*? What is your business with a white man?"

I was taken aback by this. Even though Sal didn't identify as white I wanted to object to what I deemed to be a comment laced with prejudice, but I said nothing. I wish I had said something though. I wish I had asked Obinna if love was a spirit or a person.

In May, we visited Nne in Ogu for Mother's Day. She fed us smoked catfish in the backyard. Even though the smoke from the firewood stung our eyes and attacked our lungs and the wooden stools made our buttocks sore after several minutes, it was as close to enchantment that I had felt in a long time. Nne was spirited, laughing at Obinna's jokes, insisting I eat more fish to widen my hips. The sky went from azure blue to blue black; the merriment continuing even after the winged sounds and iridescent glow of dragonflies filled the compound. This was my family. I loved them. They loved me. Yet as I smiled, and cackled and ate, there was this gnawing feeling in my chest, this feeling that a part of me was fading away.

Perhaps Obinna felt it, the fading away. Maybe he felt it in the way I seemed to drink one too many of the beers stacked in the fridge, or my increase of cigarette inhalations, or the way I occasionally zoned off in spaces where my full attention was required. Or maybe he noticed it when I didn't flinch when in late December 1972, our second Christmas holiday in a row, Obinna visited his parents without me while I stayed with Nne in Ogu for a few days.

Perhaps it was because this that one mid-July day in 1973, after downing a few cups of fresh palm wine gifted by one of Obinna's colleagues, Obinna surprised me under the pretense of going for a quick drive. He took me instead to the house of an eccentric shamanic figure who wore a red hat covered in feathers and a loin cloth—who, like a fleeting dream, married us with a simple invocation to the ancestors, the earth, and the heavens. It was an act of rebellion. It was late at night. I could see the stars so clearly, could feel them so close that it felt like I could touch them just by extending my hands. Even though we were both quite intoxicated with alcohol and the marijuana smoke oozing from the fat joint in the shaman's hand, I took those vows in that spherical mud hut surrounded by bushes dripping with elemental forces.

During the short drive back, as the effects of the intoxication began to wane, I turned to Obinna and posed the question; "What have we just done?"

"We got married!" he said and raised his fist. "There's no reason an *osu* and a non-*osu* cannot marry!"

The rebel in me agreed. We looked like teenagers breaking the law, telling the restrictive aspects of our cultural traditions to kick rocks. The high it created was more powerful than any alcohol or nicotine or marijuana. It masked the anger I was feeling, the anger of returning home only to be made to feel "less than," for something in my lineage I felt powerless to change.

"And besides, I feel better as a man making an honest woman out of you," he said with a wink. The way he drove and smirked and pounded at the steering wheel for the rest of the drive . . .it was a wonder we got home safely without incident.

ELOPING DID LITTLE TO CHANGE OUR reality as Obinna and I continued to function in our usual peaks and valleys over the next several months. In 1974, the dry season came and went as in previous years. After the dryness, came the wetness.

It was the first stage of the rainy season when Nne's transition to the other side began. It was Sunday afternoon, the second Sunday in April, and I was on the telephone located atop a small mahogany table Obinna had bought from a local carpenter. To Obinna, buying furniture from the man was his way of supporting the local economy. The hardworking, middle-aged carpenter, Mr. Okonkwo, had constructed two for Obinna. One of them became a telephone stand. The other was used to serve food and drinks.

"I think you should make your way there," the grave voice on the other end said before saying goodbye and hanging up.

Oluchi, who was kind enough to promise to give me updates about any direct surviving Ekene and Okpara family members, had called to inform me that Nne was very ill. I was mortified and blamed myself. If I hadn't been too busy focusing on Obinna, work, and the center, I would have taken the time to ensure Nne's wellbeing, I thought. I was thankful for two things. One, that I had a car, and two, that I could drive. Obinna had made this possible. He purchased a used but efficient black and white Audi for me weeks after my return to Nabuka and patiently taught me how to navigate the automobile.

About a half-hour later, I arrived at the village to find Nne shivering on her mat in the living room, a wrapper over her body. A handful of flies roamed the space, an anomalous occurrence since Nne was neat. My heart sank.

"*Nne, kedu?*" I greeted her and sat on the dusty concrete floor, next to her.

She produced a faint smile.

"Nne, I didn't know you were ill. If I had known I would have . . ."

"Shhhhhh," she said, silencing me. "How is your mother?"

"She's fine."

But was she? We hadn't spoken in weeks. The last time we had spoken, we had argued about my life's choices. She was convinced that I had become a loose, degenerate woman. I was convinced she did not know what she was talking about.

"I'm so proud of you, Ada. I have watched you grow from this peculiar child into a confident woman."

Nne, writhing on the floor, began to fill me in on more details about my childhood—all I ever really knew was that I was born nine years before Nabuka's independence and sixteen years before the war, thanks to Ma's refusal to talk about anything in her past. Nne explained that when I was born on a smeared hospital room bed after three days of intense labor, I did not cry. I looked upset, almost angry at the idea of being born into this world. She said the nurses pinched and slapped me several times and the only response I could satisfy them with was a yelp. She also told me that around age three everyone knew I was different when I would suddenly walk up to people and tell them things about themselves with such seriousness they didn't know whether to laugh or be concerned.

"As a child, you were quiet, you didn't talk much. But when you spoke, you had so much to say. Everyone who saw you called you an old soul," she concluded.

I chuckled somberly out loud but inside, I wondered what had become of all that promise I supposedly exuded during childhood. Currently, I spoke using words like a regular person but did not speak enough, especially on the important things, the detrimental things.

Nne coughed, bringing me back to the present moment. She was opening her mouth again. I wanted to urge her not to speak, to get some rest. But she was adamant. "Do you know what gave me courage with all the grenades and warplanes flying about?"

I shook my head.

"Ani."

She released a subtle groan. I pressed her fingers tightly. They felt icy and thinner than usual. She smiled faintly, "No matter what happens, don't forget you are never alone, and that everything works well for the person who flows with life."

Maybe it was because her life force was gradually making its exit that the history of Nne's life flashed through my mind. What I knew was mostly what had been told to me by Ma in one of her rare talkative moods.

Nne had what some said was bad luck with men. Her first two husbands had died of some mysterious ailment. The last had disappeared with another woman. No one could understand it, how the belle of the village in those days could be so ill-fated. It was after her third husband and the death of her mother that she decided to devote her life to Ani, the Earth Mother. Nne had revealed to me when I was a child that she used to see her mother in the dreamscape, beckoning her to her destiny as an Ani devotee. Ani would henceforth be her strength, her support, together with the women in her bloodline—as well as Mother Mary. Nne had been one of those to accept the new religion the missionaries brought with them without completely doing away with *omenani*, the ways of the land. As she had once said to me, "*Biri kam biri*, live and let live. Who is to say that a God who is infinite did not dictate there be various paths to Him?"

Looking back, I now realize Nne had more mystical inclinations than anything else. She was not bound by any system of belief or organization but simply chose to express her spirituality in ways that made sense to her.

"A woman's life is wrought with many changes, that way she can keep renewing herself," Nne said in Afa.

She gave me a few moments to ponder her words.

"I know you've been wondering about your father and his people . . ."

"Any news?" I asked with hope in my voice.

"No. No news," she said.

Crestfallen, my gaze fell on the floor.

She sighed. "In our culture, family is everything. But not everyone is lucky to have it. Even then, you have to ask, what is family anyway? You have friends that are family and families that behave worse than enemies."

I remained quiet.

Slowly, she pointed to a box a few feet away. Taking that as a cue, I reached for it. It was brown, dusty, and faded.

"I thought you might need it. All I know is that your mother used to write on that thing when she was younger. I am sure she can forgive an old woman for giving it to you."

Suddenly Nne began to breathe quite violently. "I trust that you know what to do from here on."

Before I could utter a word, she closed her eyes. I shook her arm vigorously but was met with silence.

Nne's arm felt cold as I held it, that once crinkly, warm flesh that had made me feel protected, loved. She seemed asleep, her eyes closed, years removed from her face as if making a tranquil journey on a soft sea. I was swimming in a sea of thoughts and emotions, each clamoring for attention, for its right to be expressed and acknowledged. I wasn't aware of time, of space. I was just there, holding her arm, feeling the cold floor against my thighs, my skirt bunched between them. I might have remained that way perhaps for hours if a shuffle on the cemented floor hadn't forced me to slowly shift my gaze to the door. Oluchi.

"Ada, what happened? Please say it isn't so," Oluchi said, quickly kneeling next to me with her robust, warm flesh. That is when the tears began to fall freely down my cheeks. I opened my mouth to say something, but the words couldn't form.

Oluchi stared lovingly at Nne's face. "At least the war did not kill her. She died on her own terms. What a brave woman."

Finally the words came, hoarse and wet. "We must bury her right away."

As soon as I said this, a handful of people walked into the open door as if sensing the presence of death nearby. They clamored around *Nne*'s body, asking what happened, then folding their arms across their chest and shaking their heads. I knew these people, and they knew me—somewhat. Truth was I had encountered them in my growing up, but *Nne* had been the one to befriend them as Ma and I seemed too busy or perhaps too distracted by our importance to take the time to know our village neighbors. You don't realize how much you need people until you need them.

I heard someone mention something about the mortuary. Another mentioned something about an elaborate burial ceremony. It was then that I found my voice again and insisted that she must be buried right away. Oluchi, that simple, loyal, timeless friend who expects nothing from you but gives you everything when the time is right, as people born and raised in communal settings, untainted by modern artificialities tend to be, quietly stroked my back. I got up and began to slowly walk away. Eyes followed. A couple of women, motherly and supple, asked me if I needed anything. I could tell they wanted to embrace me, to hold me as was their custom. But I was giving off a subtle message that said don't, please don't. It wasn't that I didn't need it, I did. I craved it, hungered for it like air. I just wasn't used to it, being held, being rocked and stroked by women, except for Nne, in bits and pieces when she could, but she was gone now.

HOURS LATER, I HAD RETURNED TO OWE.

"What are you doing?" Obinna asked upon strolling into the living room from a visit to a friend's house. I was sitting behind the dining table. The table had a yellow finish, peeled off in several places, and a dented leg that made it lopsided. It too had survived the war, which was why Obinna refused to fix it or replace it with a better one after he found it in abandoned farmland close to the house.

"Writing," I replied. The pen in my hand stood suspended in the air as I glanced at the paper.

"Writing what?" he said teasingly, snatching the paper from me.

Death, mysterious, unavoidable
Same as eternity

He stopped.

"What is this?'

"Nne passed away hours ago. She was sick."

He went from shock to being distraught in minutes.

"Why didn't you tell me she was sick?"

"I didn't know!" I said in exasperation.

"I'm sorry." He sighed. It was a grave sigh, from the belly of his soul. "When did this happen? I should have been there, we should have . . ."

I stood up. We held each other for a while, a very long while.

"I don't think she would like us to blame ourselves," I said, tears rolling down my cheeks. Those were indeed true words but did little to ease my conscience.

We finally disengaged. I sat down.

"Where is she now . . . I mean, her b . . . body?"

"She is being prepared to be put to the ground."

Obinna looked at me, blinking, confused.

"Nne was deeply tied to the land. She would have wanted to return to it right away, not later, and not in an extravagant way."

I heard him sigh as if releasing some tension. After a few moments of silence, he asked me if I had relayed the news to Ma yet. I told him no, but that I would soon. He rubbed my shoulders and walked away, his shoulders slumped, his skinny fingers having done little to alleviate my dampened spirit. I knew he was heading to the village, to finish what I hadn't been able to, and to pay his respects. Later I would learn Obinna had gone to the village to make sure Nne was kept in a mortuary for at least two days before she was put to the ground—just in case she changed her mind and made a U-turn to the land of the living.

Alone at home, I let the tears fall. Then I noticed the box. It lay inches away from my notebook. With little hesitation, I opened it. Inside, a small black book, about a hundred pages. Sniffing, I flipped through the pages like an unscrupulous detective. Delicate scribbles in black ink. A diary. I returned to the beginning.

March 8, 1949

Dear Diary, I am in love with a man named Simon. It is for this reason I have bought you. We met last week at Ifeoma's birthday party. Papa and Mama say he does not come from a good family, but he treats me well and that is all that matters. Mama says his father was the village thief before he was punished by the gods with blindness, and that he is from a line of osu, but what does this have to do with Simon? He is kind and sweet towards me. And I love his cocoa-colored skin and that he is a good painter.

There were more entries, detailing their courtship, first kiss, and first sexual experience. They had had their first kiss in the middle of a maize field, the same field where Obinna found my father's painting. Days later, Ma would lose her virginity in the same location. In Ma's fluid penmanship, the intensity of love and rebelliousness revealed themselves through the pages. Then a particularly verbose entry caught my eye, and I stopped to read carefully.

February 18th, 1951

Dear Diary, I am pregnant, for the third time. I cannot believe that I have miscarried twice. They say it is the same child, returning again and again to punish me. Mama and Papa say they cannot handle this, that I have made it difficult for them to reveal their faces to the community by getting pregnant again and again by an osu, who I have been forbidden to marry. Together with Uche and Nnamdi they threw me out of the house last Eke day. Simon says he doesn't want to marry me anymore. After the death of each child, he disappeared for a while. Now that I am pregnant again, I never see him. People say it is because he doesn't want to deal with a child who cannot make up its mind whether it wants to live or die. Everyone says that he has abandoned me, the only daughter of the Ekene, because of this. Mates make fun of me. The neighbors jeer at me. I cried and wailed and begged Mama and Papa to forgive me, and that I would never disappoint them again. But they refused. All this happened outside, with passersby and neighbors watching. For now, I am staying with Nne who lives several miles away. I wonder how she does it with no husband and children. Around here they say she is a witch who is bad luck to men for as soon as she marries them they die. Her third husband just left. She took me in, so I do not care what those rumors say. I will never forgive Mama and Papa and my brothers for what they've done to me for as long as I live. As for Nne, I will do what I can to make her proud and to prove to everyone else that I am somebody . . .

I stopped scanning the page. I had just delved into Ma's secrets, the dark recesses of her youthful mind, yet I felt no sense of having achieved something. I felt worse, like I was drowning. My eyes stinging with dry tears, I rummaged through my purse and pulled out a cigarette and a lighter I had recently purchased, lit up, and smoked for several minutes. With a new sense of calm, I ambled over to the living room after snubbing out the little that was left of the cigarette on the blackened ashtray next to the telephone. I dialed Ma. She picked up. I informed her of Nne's death. She went silent. I waited several minutes on the telephone. Finally, she said, "I always wanted to bring her to Lagoon when we were there, then to the U.S. after we moved. But she wouldn't leave. She was so attached to that place."

*No tears, no screams. Did this woman ever cry? Ever feel a thing these day*s?Rubbing my temple, I told her the other news, that the whereabouts of her parents were still unknown. That these people, if they were still alive, needed to be contacted about their sister. Ma remained silent on the telephone for a long time. At some point, I was convinced she was no longer on the line and called out to her a few times. When she finally spoke, she said in a steely voice, "The only parent I ever had was Nne, and that is the parent I am returning to Nabuka to bury."

Chapter Twenty

May 1974

Two weeks later, Ma was in Nabuka for Nne's burial ceremony with me, Obinna, Oluchi, Ben's parents, the group that had assembled at the house on the day of Nne'sNne death, and a few other people Ma knew. These were relatives, distant ones. Still, I was happy to see them. At least some family members cared even if the ones I longed to connect with seemed to have vanished forever, dead or intent on not being found.

A local priest officiated the burial ceremony over the mound of dirt that was Nne's resting place.

The ceremony was not met with much music and festivities, as is often the case in Ogu burial rituals of the elderly. That day, the atmosphere was dry. People wept, but internally. No one showed wild emotion, but you felt it— a result of too many burials in a land still recovering from the loss of many lives. The hours seemed to drag on. Even the officiating priest seemed to get tired quickly, and it was as if Nne was telling us to move on with our lives already and leave her the heck alone to journey in peace.

After a few hours, which included a sermon, dry hymns from the Roman Catholic hymn book, followed by dry eating, everyone went their separate ways except for Ma, Obinna, and me. We sat on the veranda steps. We were outside, gazing at the raised sand as if expecting Nne to pop out at any moment to reveal she had been alive all this while and was just playing a trick on us. Ma broke the silence when nothing happened.

"So now what?"

"Huh?"

"I mean, now what? What do we do with the house, with the things?"

I noticed for the first time that Ma's eyes were wet. Hard, but wet. It made for a strange appearance. It was difficult to imagine it was the same Ma who snuck out from the home to have passionate bodily encounters with my father in the bush.

"What do you mean, what do we do with . . .?" I asked.

"I am thinking at this point to sell . . ."

"Oh, no, no, no, no. Nne would not like that."

Ma stared at me, taken aback by my abruptness. When she recovered, she asked me how I knew what Nne would have liked or not liked.

"I just know she would not, Ma. And besides, she is buried right here. It makes no sense!"

"The problem is that you are becoming too stubborn, too rebellious. Ever since your stepfather died, it's like you decided you were going to be a whole different person."

"Ma, please . . ."

". . . Em, if I may say something . . ." It was Obinna, awkwardly trying to diffuse an escalating situation and make a point at the same time. I glared at him.

"Excuse me?" Ma said, staring him down.

He cleared his throat, shifting in his seat.

"Ma, I know we have not had the time to get to really know each other because we just met, and we had this burial today, but I think Ada has a point."

"Oh, really?"

"Yes Ma, if you don't mind my saying."

"Really!" Ma exclaimed, folding her arms across her chest. "You think you have the right to address me so directly when you haven't even had the decency to speak to me on the phone to say you are seeing my daughter. What are your intentions? Do you even plan on marrying this girl? What is wrong with you young people these days?"

Obinna, startled, said nothing. It hadn't been his fault. I had discouraged him from making that call. Frankly, I hadn't thought it Ma's business to know who I was dating, living with, married to, or not married to. And the fact that she had just called me "this girl" certainly didn't help.

"Ma I . . ." Obinna said.

". . .Shut up, I am still talking!"

"Ma, enough!" I shouted.

I could feel Obinna nudging me to relax, but I would not budge. Enough was enough. I was finished with Ma's bullying.

"What can he give you?" Ma shouted back. "Tell me! First, I heard through Nne he had acquired some money from his father after I asked her if he was capable of taking care of you. Then I thought wonderful, good news. Now I am hearing he is running some rundown psychological center with that money."

"Ma!"

"Giving back to society is great, but the bohemian lifestyle is not sustainable."

I stood up and yelled, "Ma, I said, enough!"

She stood up too, toe to toe with me. "Just like your father. A waste!"

"And you being three times pregnant out of wedlock makes you what, perfect?" I blurted and immediately regretted it.

Ma blinked a few times before responding rather calmly. "I am a Christian woman, Ada. I am no longer bound by my past."

"Of course not, I should never have. . ." I said squinting and rattling my head.

"And besides, is this how you talk to me and treat me after all the sacrifices, after everything?" she interrupted. "Stupid, wasteful, ungrateful child, you have always been a thorn in the flesh since you were born!"

A cut in my heart, my emotions gushed forth like rain. It showed up quickly as tears.

"You picked up and left too, just like your *osu* of a father!" She said and stormed off.

I found myself breathing very deeply, trying so hard to contain turbulent emotions bubbling all around me. It was strange, but at the same time I was also thinking about her. *She felt abandoned.*

"Ma, where are you going?" I asked, sniffing.

"Hotel," she said and kept walking.

"But Ma you can stay with us."

She stopped, turned around, and eyed me till I felt myself coil inside.

"Don't be ridiculous! I may not have been the best example, but it does not mean you can't make better choices," she said in a hissy voice and stormed off, this time for good.

Obinna and I watched her make a bend, and a few moments later we heard the car she had rented roar, bitterly spitting engine smoke, before zooming off.

"Wow, your mother is something else," Obinna whispered behind me.

"Obinna, not now," I said, and headed for his Peugeot.

IT HAPPENED THAT NNE HAD DIED of malaria after refusing to take quinine tablets. According to what Oluchi and other neighbors told me, Nne had refused the tablets because they had an acrid taste and made her skin itch. Usually, she depended on herbs from local herbalists to cure her bouts of malaria, but after the war, certain medicinal plants were difficult to obtain, worsened by the fact that many herbalists were either dead or missing.

Occasionally, I convinced myself that if I had been more attentive I would have known about her ailment sooner, I would have been able to convince her to take those quinine tablets. Whether this was true or not, only the earth knows.

Add to that the fact that I was still dealing with all I had garnered from Ma's diary. I hadn't been aware that I had two siblings born before me who had died. I hadn't been aware that the *ogbanje* accusations hurled at me since childhood were actually true, that according to tradition I was that obstinate child who had incarnated multiple times to the same mother due to an unwavering attachment to the spirit world.

As for my most recent fight with Ma, whenever I thought about it I felt tired, emotionally limp. I would never be good enough for Ma, I lamented out loud whenever I was alone. Even if I ended up being the perfect daughter she would still find something about me to complain about. On her last day in Nabuka, I had made attempts at some form of reconciliation. But Ma wasn't having it. She departed for the United States carrying with her two bags, one loaded with clothes and the other, the invisible one, with umbrage. I had expected my return to Nabuka to usher in some personal triumphs, to deepen my appreciation for my heritage and ancestors, but instead it brought many pains and increased isolation.

"Maybe your mother clashes with you because she still harbors strong feelings for Simon. You know that first love is hard to forget," Obinna said to me two weeks later as I complained to him about Ma.

"But if I remind her of the man she loved, shouldn't she love me just as much?" I asked. As if realizing the *faux pas* of his analysis, he simply rolled over to the other side and dozed off.

Later that, night while scrutinizing my father's ruined artwork in the moon lit bedroom, I asked myself if my being a spirit child truly made me unworthy of love. And which was worse, being a spirit child, being the daughter of a roaming or dead artist whose father was the village thief, or being a descendent of a distant ancestor who dedicated his life to the service of a god, thereby tainting his bloodline forever?

A small voice called out from within, *It is what it is, deal with it!*

Complying, I started to deal with it by slowly placing the painting aside, getting out of bed and heading to the kitchen. It was a small kitchen with a gas stove, a fridge, and a small set of drawers. I slid open a drawer. I took out a bread knife. I heard the voice say, "Don't pretend life isn't cyclical."

I dropped the knife. I reached for the fridge, took out two bottles of Guinness, and downed them. The rush of bitter foamy beer felt invigorating. Next was the bedroom to find the necessary means to complete this emergent ritual. In the tenebrous space, I observed, for a moment, the flow and ebb of Obinna's breathing as he slept. I refocused my energy to the mission at hand. I was certain I had seen one. Not a full one, but almost enough to be complete. I roamed my fingers through the dresser searching for a familiar texture. The texture found me, fumbling into my grip. Obinna's lighter was the easy part, it rested on the same spot by the lamp. Under the orange glow of the living room light, I could see the cigarette was exactly three quarter of its usual length, the other quarter consumed, apparently in haste, for whatever reason. It was flimsy, somewhat bent at the shredded tip, borderline wasted, like me. I checked the lighter. Its fluid was low though not completely worthless. I could make it work. I meandered my way outside to the veranda and noticed the new moon, a thin slice of time. I fed the end of the stick with a touch of flame after lodging it between my lips, after several motions of my thumb against the spark wheel of the lighter. The wooziness of beer and the rush of smoke opened me up to a sea of expansion. The smoke touched the moon and the moon touched me, and I felt the earth hold me down until I was forced to lie in a fetal position on the concrete and close my eyes—smoke, earth, moon, and I as one. I was going to make it through another moment, another hour, and many more days perhaps. How? Only time would tell. For now, it was the oneness that mattered, and the oneness, though induced, felt reassuring.

Chapter Twenty-One

August 1974

Grief is the worst kind of pain. It clutches at your heart and tries to pull it out of you. It beats you to pieces, kneads you like dough, and dares you to challenge its force. But even death with all its cruelty is a great teacher. Death reminds you how important life is. Why life must be lived. Why truly, there is nothing to fear since we must all suffer the same fate in the end. Death can force you out of yourself, out of your excuses, into the reality of what is. And the reality for me was that I needed to speak, I needed to shout, I needed to bare my soul to feel a sense of purpose, to survive. And I felt I had no other place to begin this process than with Afrika, who I had come to equate with a profound, mysterious part of myself.

Afrika to me was like the Black Madonna, revered but largely ignored, acclaimed but denied, wooed only to be dismissed, credited, and yet discredited, a lady of sorrows unrecognized by her lost children. And being one of her daughters, I felt it was my duty to save and recapture her dignity. It was in this spirit that I began infusing my teachings on nouns, pronouns, and verbs with historical anecdotes the first Monday into the new month. Channeling some mysterious force behind me, I began to lecture my seven to eight-year-old pupils about Afrika's glorious past.

Usually, my teachings went something like this: "A is for Ashanti! Ashanti is a what?"

A student would raise their hand. "Pronoun!"

"Noooo! Anyone else wants to try?"

Another student: "Noun!"

"Good job. Ashanti is a noun. Remember a noun is a name of a person, place, animal, or thing. And Ashanti is the name of an ethnic group. Does anyone know anything about the Ashanti?"

Blank stares.

"The Ashanti is an ethnic group in Ghana. In the past, they had a great kingdom, a kingdom that for a while resisted colonial domination under its Queen, Yaa Asantewa. And she's not the only symbol of female power in Afrika. In Afa land in the 1920s, thousands of women rioted in the streets to protest a law that required women to pay taxes to the British."

I taught my pupils about Afa Ukwu, considered the hub of ancient Afa culture. I mentioned the Benin Empire and how its architecture and system of governance fascinated the early Dutch explorers, the great pyramids of Egypt built by Afrikan hands. I mentioned Timbuktu as a major center of learning in the ancient world that drew curious minds from diverse continents. This knowledge was delivered in fragments, in ways suited for elementary school minds.

Then one day, I made the mistake of letting myself get carried away. Out of excitement that can only be compared to religious fervor, I got inspired to mail a letter to the educational council.

To the Educational Council:

I find it despicable that our history textbooks begin with the amalgamation of Nabuka by a British man and his mistress in the early 1900s. The timeline is too recent for a region that has been pumping with culture and civilization for thousands of years. For example, a terracotta civilization dating back to at least 500 B.C, which was discovered in the Northern plateau in the 1920s and acknowledged for its distinctive terracotta sculpture. I want my pupils to know their history, to ask questions, to conquer the spirit of mental slavery. In addition, even though we are now in the oil boom, I do not foresee any significant economic change in the absence of an acceleration of consciousness. Colonization has led us to believe on a collective level that we are somehow mentally inferior to the rest of the world. It is time for all of us to challenge these notions at least for our children and the future of our nation.

Sincerely,
Ada Ekene

A few days later, I was summoned to the headmaster's office. He was sitting behind his desk when I met him. He was of very average height and had a bald head with a glaring sheen and beady eyes that seemed to hang loosely on his tumefied face. He was also very stocky, a consequence of his extremely beneficial relationship with the commissioner of education.

"What is this?" he asked, waving the letter in my face.

"A letter suggesting that we change our curriculum," I said and gulped. My mouth was suddenly dry, my palms moist.

"Really? And what is wrong with our curriculum?" he asked, his eyes reddening.

"It is in the letter," I said quietly.

"I see it is in the letter. Miss. Ekene, do you have a problem with the way we do things here?"

"What do you mean, s . . .sir?"

He glared at me. His lips tightened. "I mean the way we educate our children, the way we discipline and train them."

"You mean the colonized method?" I found myself saying then wishing I could take it back. But it was too late.

"So, you have a problem with the British?"

"I don't have a problem with anyone. I just think we should teach our children our history," I said slowly.

He relaxed his shoulders, resting his back against the leather seat. I always found it incongruous that while government-funded school renovations took so long to complete, the headmaster's office included a new décor each time. The subtle hum of the air conditioner as the room swelled with cool air was the latest evidence of this.

He sized me up. "How old are you?"

"Twenty-three . . . s . . . sir."

Why was I struggling with that word, sir? The word felt strange, odd, like a bitter ripe mango. *Mister, uncle,* I could handle those, but *sir* just like *oga* sounded too docile.

"I know your type," he blurted out, interrupting my thoughts. "Young and full of revolutionary ideas. You go abroad, stay for a few years, come back, and all of a sudden you think you can change the entire system. It is not that simple. The system was constructed for a purpose, and it has its role, believe me. Nothing left out or added into the school curriculum is by accident."

I said nothing even though I suspected he expected me to say something. After a few minutes of silence, he went on to pose questions to me.

"Miss Ekene, what were you hired to teach?"

"English."

"Miss Ekene is that not what you are being paid to do?"

"Yes, sir."

"Are you a history teacher?"

"No . . . but . . ."

"That is what I thought. You are neither a history teacher nor were you hired to impose your snobbish ideas on us. We have a standard of education that we shall continue to maintain. The education board is doing its job and it is not in your place to condemn or suggest anything to them."

"But sir. . ."

He pointed his stubby finger at me. "I get complaints that your classroom is rowdy, that your children are rude to other teachers . . ."

"Sir, they perform well."

"Shall we encourage animal behavior from children because they perform well in class?"

"No, sir," I said, gulping. My heart seemed ready to jump out of my chest. I found myself wishing the earth would swallow me.

"It is a combination of things, Miss Ekene. The liberal lifestyle and manner of teaching, the disregard for authority . . . in fact, you are dismissed."

"Yes, sir," I said and promptly aimed for my exit.

"For good," I heard him say.

I turned around, alarmed. "Sir?"

He gave me a vindictive stare. "Since you think you are better than all of us here, you might as well pack your things and go. You are dismissed."

Even though my heart was now on the floor and I felt like

I was going to keel over, even though I felt myself being shattered into several pieces like broken glass, I still managed to ask him on what grounds I was being fired.

He leaned against his chair, a sinister grin on his face. Counting with his fingers he began to list them.

"On the grounds that since you buried your relative you have displayed a fragile emotional state and condition which has spilled over to the classroom. On the grounds that you have been caught smoking on school property, setting a bad example for our children. On the grounds that you have family issues deep-rooted in your lineage making you prone to anti-social and uncooperative behavior . . ."

My lips swung open. He said other things, but I did not recall them. I only recall walking out the door like a zombie who had lost track of its grave site.

BY THE TIME I ARRIVED HOME, I looked like a full-blown living corpse. This was how Obinna found me on the couch. Deeply concerned, he sat next to me and asked me what happened. I told him everything, the best I knew how. He shook his head deeply.

"I am not surprised."

I looked at him sharply. "What do you mean?"

"Did you expect him to jump *alleluia,* immediately change the school curriculum, and make you head teacher?"

"No . . . but . . ."

"You did, didn't you? You expected that praise! That is the problem with you . . . your idealism pops up at the wrong moments. When it is time for you to be practical you get idealistic, when it is time for you to become idealistic, you get practical. But you have to understand everything has a season and you must know how and when to act because, my dear, in this life you have to be strategic to win."

I rubbed my temples. The tears followed.

As if remorseful of his criticism, Obinna grabbed me by the shoulders and squeezed tight. He whispered into my ears not to worry, that we would be fine. But something in his voice made me sob even more.

"How did he know all those things . . .? How could he . . ." I whispered after sobbing for a few minutes.

"It's a small-town, Ada. Everyone knows everything about everyone," he replied, with a sigh.

Perhaps I had expected praise, some acknowledgment for being a true daughter of Afrika, a true advocate of a cause which we could all believe in. Being fired fell in the least of my expectations and so when it occurred, I entered a state of shock. Once I recovered, I sent a farewell letter to my students through Charley, who promised to read it to the class. Then I stuffed my stomach with beer and clouded myself with bouts of cigarette smoke, and yes, released more tears.

By late September of 1974, my fundraising efforts had proven futile. Like an ominous domino effect, the center began to lose adequate funding, leading to layoffs and ultimately a complete shutdown of the work site. Money disappeared like a drying well. Obinna struggled to find work, the work he needed to salvage the site. As a result, his banter ceased. His playful jabs at me dwindled. And even when I tried to engage him in idle banter just to bring him back to the good old days, his responses were feeble. He grew disheveled, started smoking cigarettes. Occasionally, he would return home smelling like *igbbo,* pot.

Then he stopped smelling like *igbbo*, but soon began spending more time outside, eventually staying out till two or three in the morning. At first, I decided not to speak about this. Perhaps he was somewhere in a bar drinking his sorrows away, that was the excuse I made for him. But after a few days of late-night aberrations, I could no longer suppress my staunch disapproval.

I chose to confront him on a Saturday afternoon. He was sitting at the dining table sipping coffee and smoking cigarettes. I sat across from him hoping something in my expression would induce him to admit his foolishness. I could have been a fly perched on the wall. His attention hovered elsewhere.

"Obi, *o gini*? What's going on?" I finally demanded.

He took a puff of his cigarette. Generous amounts of smoke escaped his nostrils. His borderline skeletal chest exposed, his white boxers dotted with coffee stains, his once flat stomach now pudgy due to excessive beer consumption.

"Obinna, I am talking to you!"

"Nothing."

"If it's nothing, why are you acting like a man who has lost everything? I also lost my job, remember? We have both suffered an injustice, but the world doesn't end, will not end. Life goes on. A way will be made," I said with hopeful sobriety.

He said nothing, only continued to smoke his cigarette flaccidly. Softening my tone, I said, "At least we have each other."

"Really, do I have you?"

"Yes," I said.

He stared at me for a few seconds. I thought I felt his gaze soften, but it was very brief.

"But what about the children Ada? Those children who need healing, who need therapy? Aren't Afrikan children with mental problems worth saving?"

My heart sunk. I could feel his pain. Even though the center was his idea, his brainchild, his womb birth, I understood the deeply personal feeling a cause could hold on someone. I had also helped with laying the foundation for this idea. This was personal to me as well.

"Our children are worth saving, and we will save them. But that doesn't give you an excuse to act irresponsibly," I said calmly.

"I can't have this discussion with you now," he replied flatly after a few moments.

"Is it another woman?" I blurted out.

There it was, my biggest fear, emerging out of the swamp of my mind like a long-hidden crocodile. Up until that point, I had this belief, or perhaps one might call it theory, that no lover of mine would ever be unfaithful especially if I gave him everything he needed, and by everything, I meant my trust, my surrender, a share in my inner sanctuary. And besides his flirtatious habit, Obinna had promised he would never stray. But could he?

"Maybe, maybe not," he said, shifting his gaze to the direction of his bare feet, hidden underneath the table.

"What do you mean?" My chest was rising, and not in a good way.

"Maybe there is someone else, maybe not. Does it matter in the larger scheme of things?"

I felt the mental explosions in my head. I felt blazing heat, like molten rock within me.

"Now I know I am with a boy, not a man!"

I stood up.

"Ada . . ."

I detected a tremor in his voice, but I was not in the mood to interpret it. I darted to the bedroom, quickly reaching for the Benson and Hedges pack on the dresser. I sat on the bed and lit a stick, permitting the nicotine to travel through my brain. As I sucked on my cigarette, all sorts of memories began flooding to the forefront of my mind like jigsaw puzzle pieces finally coming together. I recalled moving into the house that wet night in 1970 and how special he became to me over time.

And perhaps he had become special because the first time we made love after three months of living together it had been so easy, so effortless that I had wanted to repeat the act infinitely. Perhaps he was special because it did not matter to him personally that I was *osu*, even though it mattered to his ingrained beliefs and fears. It did not matter that my great grandfather had dedicated himself to a mysterious god, even though his very traditionalist mother almost fainted when he divulged this to her over the phone and his father remained firmly quiet on the subject. At least both of us, though dreamers, had limits to our expectations. At least we understood each other. At least we spoke the same language, on many different levels. At least we were both committed to the same cause for now. In this love affair, everything was out on the table, for the most part anyway. There were no pretenses.

During the day we were as close friends as we could be, and at night we knew how to satisfy the other in bed.

It was only after I lost my job and the center closed that things began to change like the appearance of an unwanted season. Physical affection and tenderness became less frequent. I considered it a side effect of his depression, but it never occurred to me even with all his flirtatious habits that he would have an affair.

My mind wandered to the object of his desire. For now, she had no name or face. It could have been Akudo, that fake "high yellow" back and front ballooned woman with little shame. It could have been that dull-faced, despondent assistant of his, Grace. It could have been Gloria, that disrespectful house girl of the Onyeagalis, or a combination of them, or someone else entirely I had never met or even suspected, I thought bitterly.

I felt my chest rising higher with each breath. I was now gripping the sheets, my knuckles protruding through my flesh. I had allowed myself to be fooled by a smooth-talking psychologist. Perhaps if I had been smart enough, I would have lingered in the United States instead of returning to Nabuka only to deal with the treacherous likes of Obinna. Perhaps I would have met a decent man in the United States. Perhaps even if I had remained single, I would have been more fulfilled living the American life with my old friends.

My thoughts drifted to less complex times, to college, to Nzingha and Anna, to high school, to Stacey and Sal, the two most important people to me back then. I pictured Stacey in San Francisco, trying to imagine her life without modern-day amenities. Would it be like life for millions of people in Nabuka? And how could she fulfill her dreams of becoming an actress in such a place? I didn't even know how to reach her.

My thoughts on Sal dwelt on all our times together and the not so idyllic way things had ended. Ma had insinuated what we had could not last. She was right. It didn't. A quiet knock on the door interrupted my mental sojourn. I blinked away the rising misery in my throat.

"Ada, I made some *moi-moi,* do you want some?"

"Ada!" The pounding persisted.

"Shove the *moi-moi* down your ass and while you're at it, go to hell!" I shouted, flinging a pillow at the door.

He hesitated for a moment and then I heard his footsteps disappear down the hallway. I felt my breathing grow tense just as I felt hot tears on the verge of trickling down. I had to leave the house as soon as possible.

"Where are you going?"

"Village," I replied grumpily, breezing past Obinna who was slouched on a sofa watching a news program on television—President Nixon's face plastered in the background as the newscaster gave an overview of the Watergate scandal and Nixon's resignation.

"Why?" I heard Obinna ask.

I stopped moving. I noticed a flicker of hope sweep across his face.

"To make a visit."

"Oh. To where?"

"My lover's house," I snapped.

"Ada, stop this nonsense," he said, sitting up.

"Nonsense?"

He let out a heavy sigh.

"You will understand everything, I promise . . ."

"Bye!"

I slammed the glass door and stepped out onto the veranda.

WHEN I ARRIVED AT NNE'S PLACE, I sat on the red sand, close to the mound of dirt and concrete that now housed her body. Ma and I had made plans to have the area cemented during her next visit. Crouched on the ground, I asked for

Nne's protection and guidance, confident and assured she was happy in the spirit world. Because she had lived a righteous life, under the laws of the land, the laws of life, she was now an elevated ancestor. With this thought in my head, I sang one of her favorite songs, the amazing grace.

The neighborhood was tranquil. No one was watching and even if they were, they made sure not to draw attention to themselves. After singing and kissing the foot of the grave, I entered the house. I moved through the empty spaces. It seemed like an anomaly not hearing Nne humming some Afa tune. It seemed like an anomaly not smelling something being cooked or roasted in the backyard, not hearing Ma calling out to me to end my daydreaming and help Nne with the dishes or to wash my clothes or do my homework. It seemed like an anomaly, realizing I would never see Nne again, at least not in this lifetime; that all the experiences I had had in this house with her could only be reawakened through memory.

I recalled sharing the same mattress with her during sleepless nights, and her gentle voice sending me off to sleep with stories about crafty tortoises, crafty foxes, and brave but foolish lions. Stories that started with *enwere otu mgbe, otu mgbe eriooo, once upon a time, a long time ago . . .* Stories that sought to explain why the tortoise had a cracked shell, and why the snake had no legs. Stories about wicked stepmothers and abused and lonely daughters. Stories set in simple times and simple scenarios. Moral stories with good endings. I wondered if it were possible to reverse the world so that what we referred to as the real world was the fairy tale and the fairy tale, the real world.

Gleaning no response from the spirits of the air, I meandered over to Nne's room. Her clothes were folded and placed in a box just the way I had left it before the burial. The mattresses and mats were gone, however, probably uprooted by a relative in need. For now, what was left, besides the luggage, was a painting of the Virgin Mary, her brown hair covered in a blue shawl, carrying the child Jesus, and a miniature wooden statue of Ani with a child on her lap. These symbols of motherhood were a needed consolation.

I explored Ma's former bedroom. A worn mattress, a cosmetic kit covered in dust, and vintage clothing. The clothes and cosmetics rested methodically and timelessly on a dusty square table. I accessed them for a while. I recalled Ma in some of the clothes. Ma, broom thin and towering over me back then. Now we were about the same height. And about the same weight too. I glanced at my watch. The day was still long. I needed something to do to distract me for a while. I decided to go for a long drive.

Minutes later, I was in the driver's seat listening to the monotonous hum of the engine combined with the radio sounds of Manu Dibango's "Soul Makossa." I was not headed in any particular direction. I was letting the road lead me, the music transport me to wherever it willed. Before me, red dirt stretched its way for miles. Thick vegetation appeared at various corners. I passed women with babes straddled on their backs and men, women, and children strolling in traditional and western attire. The glare of the sun formed a yellow streak on the window shield as beads of sweat congregated on my forehead and under my arms. A single application of deodorant never seemed to be enough these days, I groaned. I parked the car in front of a shop with a zinc rooftop held by four wooden poles. Inside, secondhand clothes, accessories, and shoes were on display. I got out of the car to ask the shop owner where I could buy something to eat. He pointed me two stalls away to a woman selling *agidi* wrapped delicately in banana leaves.

After the last bite of the cream-colored, rubbery textured, cayenne-infused *agidi*, I got back in my car and drove several miles until I arrived at a *go-slow*. Stretching my neck out the car window, I observed a cluster of police ahead. Police checkpoints. I had experienced them with Ma, with Ben, with Obinna, but never alone. I took a few deep breathes and mentally prepared myself for what was to come. Meanwhile, as the air thickened, I found myself on the verge of suffocation. As soon as I began to panic, the cars began to move one by one.

"Miss, where are your particulars?" one of the policemen asked me when I came up to the checkpoint.

"Good afternoon, sir," I said, wiping my face steadily with the handkerchief I had retrieved from the glove compartment.

The police officer, a stoic man with bulging reddish eyes, looked inside my car.

I reached into the glove compartment and handed him my "particulars." He looked through the documents, my driver's license and other paperwork, scrutinizing each document for an unnecessarily long time. I feared he would come up with something else to frustrate me with unless I complied and did what everyone was expected to do in these circumstances. I thought about Ma and how she handled these types of scenarios. Ma, being the practical realist she was, let money do the talking. No hassles. No small talk. Ben attempted small talk, cracked a few jokes. Still, he ended up having to lose something to gain something as well. As for Obinna, he philosophized, reminded them what they were doing was against the law. In response, they would tell him to shut up, that they were the law.

"Madam, where you dey go?" he asked.

"To a native priest, sir, to make offerings. You see my husband died. And I need to appease his soul because you see, he haunts me everywhere I go . . . *everywhere*," I said with pitiful eyes.

I spoke as if some wandering spirit had taken over my body, deciding to deal with this matter in its way. Lying was something I rarely did, if ever. *But wouldn't you rather lie than let them win each time?* A still voice said. So, I continued with the lie.

"He died during the war. A brave Afa soldier. And they say, those souls, still lurk. I want him to rest in peace . . ." I pretended to blink away tears.

The police officer's expression changed dramatically. He scratched his head, scrutinizing me with his eyes. It was clear he was very superstitious, like most Nabukans. He handed me my particulars, stepped away from the car, and waved for me to pass. I shoved the particulars back into the compartment and heard a fellow officer ask, "Why you let am pass, nah?"

"Believe me as I dey tell you, that woman na witch."

FEELING VICTORIOUS, I CHUCKLED THEN HUMMED an impromptu song about the nuisance of bribery as I breezed by small villages and forests until I arrived in an isolated area filled with trees and mud houses. I felt inspired to stop, so I did. I got out of the car. The sky held sparse clouds and the temperature was smoldering. Chickens and goats roamed the area, the chickens clacking irritably, the goats bleating in agreement, as they scattered, startled by my sudden appearance. I stood by the car and waited, perhaps for a sign on what to do next.

The sign came in the form of a melodious sound in the background. I listened closely. It sounded like a euphoric Pentecostal church service. Church. *I could use some praying*, I guess. For the first time, I analyzed my outfit; faded jean trousers and a sleeveless shirt. No scarf to cover my braided hair. Not appropriate church gear, but it was too late now. I sauntered towards the music, which came from a mud building. Using the back door, I entered to find a congregation singing to their God.

Then I saw a figure, a preacher, prancing on stage with a tree branch in his hand. He had charcoal skin and was of average height and build. His robe was a cream color with a red cloth draped around his neck. Suddenly, I could hear the thumping of my chest. How did I end up here? What had brought me here, of all places? I leaned against the back wall. I was only going to observe for a few minutes then leave . . .

The singing and dancing finally stopped with one motion from the preacher. Even from the distance I could see his patches of grey hair. I noticed some people beating the heat with handwoven fans with grass stems. Some wiped their faces continuously with handkerchiefs.

"It is time for why we are here."

His voice sounded like mellow thunder.

Again, it hit me, how did I end up here? What brought me here? What if this was a dangerous cult? What if I got kidnapped and my body parts used for money ritual purposes? I immediately canceled the thought but that didn't stop me from moving closer to the door, making a good assessment of the distance between me and my car.

I watched as people swept onto the altar on cue: cripples in wheelchairs, epileptics, victims of supposed witchcraft and possession. A mute girl attracted the preacher. She was barely five years old and frail. Her mother was holding her shoulders, kneeling behind her, lamenting that her daughter refused to speak for several months and that they had tried everything, including taking her to a native doctor, to no avail. The preacher approached the girl. He shut his eyes. If a cotton swab dropped, it would have resounded in the room. He opened his eyes. The little girl let out a piercing cry. Murmurs and gasps swept across the room. The girl's mother sprang to her feet and began shaking the girl.

"Can this be true? Thank you, God, oh!" She lunged at the preacher to embrace him. A male usher quickly dragged the woman and her bewildered daughter away from the stage. And then a woman, tall with loosely braided hair, stood up from one of the pews in the front and began to "prophesy."

"You, sitting next to your best friend, when will you tell her you are sleeping with her husband?!"

The accused wilted under her friend's glare.

"You over there, you are a witch. You should be in front not hiding back there."

The supposed witch cowered among the curious stares aimed at her as the congregation gasped in horror.

The woman suddenly turned around. Our eyes made contact. Boom, boom, boom, my heart went, the pounding so loud, it muffled my eardrums. She pointed slowly at me.

"You reside in the world of humans and spirits; it is for this reason you can never be fully content in this world until you find the secret to your destiny!"

I felt the entire room assess and judge me. Trembling, I stumbled out of the premises.

"The prophet, he speaks to you, but you never listen!" her piercing words followed me.

I hopped into my waiting Audi and didn't look back.

LATER THAT EVENING, I DAWDLED MY way to the living room to find Obinna waiting anxiously.

"I was worried about you. I almost called the police, and you know I don't deal with them," Obinna said, lines of worry visible on his face.

Obinna considered the police to be innately and irreversibly corrupt, just like the Nabukan government that fathered them. He was still in the same spot, on the same couch, a plate of *moi-moi* crumbs inches away from his bare feet on the rug. I lingered by the door, moping at nothing in particular.

"You look like you've just seen a ghost, are you okay?" he asked, leaping from the couch, and heading towards me.

"Do you have any cigarettes?" I asked.

He handed me one from his back pocket and helped me light it. He had grown to accept my smoking habits.

"*O dikwa mma*? Is everything okay?" he asked again.

I let the buzz from the inhalation fill my head. It created the desired woozy effect.

"This woman . . ." I began until I felt an inner nudge to stop. "Never mind," I concluded.

He continued to study me as if I was high on some experimental drug.

"I am going to bed," I said, finally.

He motioned as if to follow. With one glare from me, he retreated.

"That long war has ended finally!" It was Obinna. He had just burst into the bathroom with a newspaper while I lay soaking in the tub. It was early May of 1975. By this time, the water element had become my new best friend, clearing my mind and soul, like a recurrent baptism. Soaking in the tub was also a great way to have some alone time, away from Obinna with his newly acquired mood swings and bizarre conduct. If not for concerns of water scarcity, I would have performed this ritual every night instead of the usual bucket of water—a mixture of boiling hot water from the kitchen and tap water plus a sponge and soap. Moments like this felt like a luxury, and I wasn't too keen on Obinna hovering over me with a newspaper in his hand.

"The Vietnam War! It is officially over now!"

"Good!" I said as flashbacks of Stacey and I protesting on 44th Street in New York City rushed through my mind.

"In my days at Harvard, I considered joining the anti-war movement on campus until my father warned me against it. He said he didn't want people thinking I was a communist."

"I see." It wasn't his first time telling me this.

"I am glad foreigners and students were exempt from that draft. Imagine me escaping the war in Nabuka only to fight another war elsewhere."

"Uh, huh."

Awkward silence.

"Going out." Obinna said finally.

His movements, over time, ceased to become a major source of concern. In response to his statement, I simply waved my hand.

Alone once more, I immersed myself fully in the soapy water. The war in Nabuka had ended in 1970. It was 1975, and the war was just ending in Vietnam after all the sacrifices made to end it—the protests, the arrests, the lives lost. Still, the increasing global interconnectedness meant that news travelled faster, that awareness was increasing, that the veil of illusion was lifting. It gave me hope.

Moments later, I heard the telephone ring. I didn't get a lot of calls and considered ignoring it. But the shrill of it, the annoyance it released in the otherwise peaceful environment, forced me to tumble out of the tub, grab a towel, and dash to the living room.

"Hello?"

"Ada, *kedu*?"

"Ma . . .I am well. And you?"

Ma and I had gradually warmed up to each other again after our last explosive argument on the day of Nne's burial. Yet, there were still gaps in the relationship where there should have been closure. I didn't know if those gaps would ever completely close.

"I am well. I just wanted you to know that I thought long and hard about everything you said concerning selling Nne's house. You were right. She wouldn't have wanted that."

"We will come up with something together, to make sure it remains in the family," I quickly replied.

To myself, I thought maybe I might move in there permanently. Especially with the way things were going with Obinna.

"I might also be selling the house in Greensberg. I am ready for a change."

I thought about our house; my old bedroom with the green curtains, the tortured garden outside that bedroom window, the eerie painting of the teary-eyed girl on the living room wall and felt nothing but indifference.

“Ma, where will you move to?”

“I don’t know. I will figure things out, like I always do.”

After wrapping up the conversation, I sat on the nearest couch and drifted mentally about my future career prospects, my future with Obinna, the house in Ogu. What were my options? What could I do to escape this rut?

Hope is the pillar that holds up the world. Hope is the dream of a waking man. It was a quote I had recently discovered from a Roman historian, Pliny the Elder, credited with writing the first encyclopedia.

“Hope is the pillar of life,” I whispered with determination and made my way back to the tub.

Chapter Twenty-Two

June 1975

OBINNA WAS THE FIRST TO SEE the brown envelope addressed to me, tucked inside the mailbox. He brought it home and rested it on the table where minutes later I stumbled upon it. I tore at its edges carefully to reveal its contents.

Dear Ada,

This is Sal. How are you? Hope all is well. I am in Nabuka for work which I hope to tell you all about later. Besides that, I've been at Afa Ukwu for the past month to explore the Afa Ukwu excavation site. The discoveries of ancient bronze art are truly fascinating, and the locals have been very helpful. I made a brief stop at Ogu (I remembered it is your hometown) and I said to myself, why not search for Ada Ekene? To make a long story short, I encountered Miss Oluchi (after hours of roaming aimlessly) who claims to be an old friend. She gave me your address and phone number. I was tempted to ring you, but I thought you would prefer if I wrote first. I am staying at The Concorde. I would love for you to give me a call after you receive this.

Sal.

I remained motionless for several minutes. His phone number was written there at the bottom of the letter, but I didn't telephone Sal until a few days later. I needed time to figure out what this meant, if this was mere coincidence or fate and, if so, for what purpose. I was tempted to postpone the telephone call indefinitely until it dawned on me that the few days or weeks that he had left might be the only and final opportunity for me to see an old friend again. Obinna was away when I finally decided to contact him. With moist palms and a racing heartbeat, I set my suddenly dry lips against the telephone mouthpiece and dialed. After two rings, the receptionist answered then transferred the call. Moments later . . .

"Ada, long time no hear. I thought you would never call," he said half accusingly.

"Hi Sal, I can't . . . I can't believe you are in Nabuka!"

"Well, I figured if I had to wait for you to bring me over, it may never happen," he teased.

I remembered the words I had said to him many years ago on the night we spent by the lake: "I will take you all over Afrika."

I guess I had neglected to keep my side of the promise.

He was filled with excitement at the sound of my voice and thought "fate" was reconnecting us in this way. We arranged for a meeting the following weekend.

The next Saturday, while Obinna was still catching up on sleep from an overnight stay in an unknown locale, I drove to The Concorde. With sprawling, fancy swimming pools and exotic-looking palm trees, The Concorde was one of the state's burgeoning five-star hotels where tourists and the crème of society stopped by on business or personal or clandestine trips. At the main entrance, I noticed a cluster of people: a young Indian couple dressed in traditional Indian clothes chatting with a white man with a British accent and a Nabukan man who turned around every few minutes as if checking to see if anyone was noticing how affiliated he was with the foreigners. In Nabuka, this was a sign that he had "arrived." In other words, that he was now of elevated social status. Not every Nabukan was excited to encounter foreigners though—especially not foreigners of Indian origin. The common complaint among such Nabukans was that Indians were slowly taking over the country, owning restaurant chains and retail stores that could otherwise be owned by Afrikans. Obinna was one of those who complained.

"They come here, they take over our shops and eateries and yet have the nerve to look down on our culture. Some of them treat us worse than the white man does, and on average they are only a few inches lighter than us. It's astounding how far *colo* mentality has gone!" But today wasn't about Obinna and his philosophies, and I was determined to keep it that way as I made my way inside the hotel.

In the bustling lobby, I zeroed in on Sal sitting cross-legged on a black leather couch. He was clothed in a white traditional shirt with cultural symbols and a pair of cream-colored bell-bottom pants. His hair was cropped, his skin deeply coppered from long exposure to the sun. He moved forward to embrace me before settling back on the couch.

"Wow, Ada, you have become such a woman," he said and smiled, his brown eyes filled with sparks of light.

It had been a few years and, being somewhat of a late bloomer, those few years had added more curves to my hips and more rise to my breasts. By his response, I was certain he had noticed. I sat beside him.

"You look good," I said out loud. I lied. He looked more than good. He looked like a modern adaptation of a Roman god in Afrikan attire.

"You know, my biggest fear was that you would be five hundred pounds and ugly. Phew! I am relieved it isn't so," he teased.

I burst out laughing, punching him on the shoulder. He had broken the ice.

He told me he was traveling around the world, his roaming feet leading him to the shores of Europe, South America(a trip saddened by the conflict in Colombia between far-left guerilla groups, drug cartels and the government over control of the country), Asia, and now Afrika. What did he do for a living? He was a sociologist and, only two years prior, had begun working as a managing editor for a popular sociology-related journal in Italy. His position required him to travel and explore diverse cultures, then report back to the magazine with insightful articles. My heart leaped with excitement for him and descended almost immediately with slight jealousy for the liberal lifestyle he was living.

"Fascinating," I said after he was finished. "How about Afa Ukwu?"

"It's been great. Besides the bronze sculptures, locals told me stories about digging up coral beads, necklaces, and other accessories. Throughout history, they have even sold some to Northern merchants for some good change."

"Really?"

"Oh, yeah, and then there are the pyramids. Imagine that; pyramids in Afaland mysteriously gone. I wonder where those pyramids went or if they ever really existed. Either way, Afa Ukwu is something you need to explore."

I nodded thoughtfully. Too bad I couldn't teach this to my children at school.

"Any other adventures?" I said, not too eager to divulge on my personal life yet.

He smiled, eager to share more. "I just got back from India, where I visited an Ashram."

"What is that?"

"A spiritual community. The place I went to was owned by a woman who claims to be a reincarnation of the goddess of love. She has thousands of followers. People from all over the world come annually around summertime to pray and meditate."

"So, you've become a believer, huh?" I teased.

"I've always been a believer."

"Of what exactly?" I asked, with a playful smile.

"Of love."

Of love. The way he said it, with such pure frankness. The look he gave me, made me quiver and look away. I rapidly moved the conversation along, asking him about his current assignment. His current assignment, he replied, was ancient West Afrikan art. That was what had led him to Afa land. But was that the only reason he had come all the way to Afa land? I did not dare ask and he did not dare say more on that.

The spotlight was now on me. I couldn't escape it. I had to speak. So, I shared with him the details of my activities over the years. I mentioned Obinna briefly, said we were living together. He interjected almost too quickly that he too had a girlfriend. A nice girl from Colombia, a family friend, he met on his South American motorcycle adventures and whom his mother felt was the right one because she was a homemaker and did not "cause much trouble." He cared about her because she was highly educated and accepted him the way he was. She never complained about his nomadic lifestyle, unlike his past girlfriends. Whenever he made stops in Colombia, he spent time with the girl whom he referred to as Maria. Though he was still young, his mother was pushing him to marry and give her grandchildren. Maria might be the one.

To steer away from the topic of marriage, I divulged my latest teaching adventures and how that had failed.

"You were doing great work, Ada. Don't feel discouraged."

"It was great work done carelessly."

"Sometimes we make questionable decisions when stirred by passion."

"I don't think I have any passion," I said.

"You of all people? I doubt it. Passion is what wakes you up every morning. What keeps you going. With all the ideas you have, perhaps you should consider writing."

My heart stopped.

"You mean as a career?"

"Why not? It's who you are."

Many university graduates that I knew were lawyers, doctors, engineers, practical people climbing the socioeconomic ladder like lizards on concrete walls, and here was Sal encouraging me to write, one of the most belittled crafts in the elitist society that I was a part of—unless one made a lot of money from it, of course, which didn't happen often. But that was the thing about Sal. Around him, anything felt possible.

He glanced at his watch and said it was getting late.

"I don't want your boyfriend coming for me," he chuckled.

But I wasn't listening. My thoughts were elsewhere.

"This may seem unnecessary now, but I do want to apologize for the way things ended between us," I said, lowering my gaze.

"No worries," he said, waving his hand. "We were younger back then, weren't we?"

I became aware of myself, a few pounds heavier, dressed in a simple traditional gown. My braids begged to be taken out. My hair begged to be washed, conditioned, and restyled. When exactly did I stop caring how I looked? The sun would soon go to sleep, and even though Obinna and I were immersed in a grudge, I knew I still had a home and a man to go to.

We bid each other farewell, kissing the other on the cheeks. Once out of sight, I observed him walk up the stairs to his room, fixated by his casual stride, which held me in a tumultuous wave of acute nostalgia.

Chapter Twenty-Three

July 1975

Sal and I maintained our relationship over the telephone—in bits and pieces. I informed him of Nne's death. He said he was sorry he didn't get to meet her. Then during the second week of July, he invited me and Obinna to a seminar being held by a friend of his, a Nabukan scholar and Oxford-educated man. The seminar was taking place at a nearby university lecture hall and was going to be about the role the indigenous worldview had on modern society. He was going to be speaking with a small group of colleagues from Nabuka and England. I did not pass Sal's message on to Obinna. Instead, I told Sal over the telephone that Obinna could not make it. I felt a pinch of guilt for the lie but buried my conscience with the mental image of Obinna venturing to his mistress's bed. Even though he had not fully admitted to this, the idea of him being intimate with other women made me squirm.

Determined not to be visually surpassed this time by my teenage love, I went to a neighborhood hair braider and had my hair plaited in my favorite shuku style a couple of hours before the seminar. Then I went home and quickly donned my favorite white silk shirt and black crepe chiffon pants.

THE SEMINAR OCCURRED AS PLANNED IN a freshly painted lecture hall, with the Nabukan scholar, a Doctor Ndubuisi, hosting the discussion. Doctor Ndubuisi had that classic scholarly look, uncombed hair, a vintage suit and tie and thick rimmed glasses held by a string. We sat in a half-circle like the Ogu elder's council meetings I had sometimes encountered during my younger days on my way to school.

First, the presenters introduced themselves, then discussed the war, hailing the Afa indigenes in the room for their bravery and tenacity. Then they attended to the topic at hand. Some in the room argued that the old ways could only survive and thrive in the modern world through adaptation and evolution. Others argued that it was the modern world that needed to evolve by looking to the old ways. They said that the indigenous worldview saw everything as sacred and therefore was less inclined to be destructive towards nature, unlike the present technological age.

Someone mentioned *osu* as an example of an indigenous worldview and how the beliefs around it needed to be abolished, setting families free from unnecessary guilt, shame, and confusion. Doctor Ndubuisi countered, saying *osu* was not purely indigenous, but cultural, that it was something that had been created over time and therefore could be uncreated.

"So for the people in the room who are unaware of what *osu* is can someone kindly break it down for us?" A professor from the University interjected from the middle of the circle. With his salt pepper hair, youthful face, and round spectacles, he appeared prematurely distinguished and introspective.

Doctor Ndubuisi leaned forward, resting his elbows on his knees and cleared his throat. "The *osu* system is quite complicated," he began, searching the room with his eyes for approval. His Afa peers gave him the approval he needed with nods.

"But in a nutshell," he continued, "an *osu* is a person who has dedicated themselves to the service of a deity either by choice or necessity. In doing so, they have dedicated their bloodline to the service of this deity and can no longer mix freely with the freeborns of the land. Meaning, no intermarriage and in some extreme cases, no sharing of food, drinks, and so on."

"It has now become classicism disguised as culture!" A middle-aged albinoid looking woman with tight braids and crystalized rosary beads hanging from her neck interrupted. "How can one be forever ostracized for something their ancestors did a long time ago?"

"Exactly!" Doctor Ndubuisi agreed. "The rules created around *osu* existed for many reasons. It was seen as a badge of honor at some point in time. Now it is a stigma; as with anything adjustments must be made. *Osu* has no place in today's world, especially when you consider that many of the gods that people served back then no longer exist anyway."

"Plus, many of us are now Christians and therefore should no longer be worrying about *osu*!" The woman asserted.

The discussion went back and forth for a while. It was clear. On the topic of *osu* there was a consensus in the room that the stigma around it needed to be eradicated. It made the day dawn even brighter for me. After Sal had introduced me to a few people at the gathering, hailing me as a talented writer and poet while I bashfully dismissed his praises, we stood outside on the side street watching cars go by. The sun welcomed us in a very blatant and pure way. I could feel his eyes on me.

"How was it?"

"Entertaining. I mean, you don't need a seminar to debate what is obvious. The indigenous worldview, our last hope, is in danger of extinction."

Surprised by my tone, he fell silent.

"Actually, it was interesting, I enjoyed it very much. Especially the *osu* part," I said, recanting my earlier brashness. I didn't go any further. There was no need to share my *osu* status with Sal, in whose worldview, thankfully, it had no consequence.

"Me too," Sal said, jolting me out of my mental sojourn. He moved closer to me. "Mmmm, major question though. Whatever happened to that sweet, innocent girl from high school? How did she become so snappy?"

I smacked his arm playfully. He winced and chuckled.

"Look at you, Mr. God-forbid-I-stay-in-one-place talking about how I have changed. What about you, huh?" I said with a fake American accent.

"Hey, I wasn't aware you wanted me in one place," he said with a curious smile.

"Oh, shut up!" I said, playfully.

"Hey, what can I say? I am living my life, I guess."

I nodded. He was right. He was indeed living his life while I couldn't say exactly what I was doing with mine.

"Wow, it gets hot here," he said, putting on his sunglasses.

"That's Nabuka for you."

"Yes, indeed. By the way, I hear there's been an oil boom."

"Yes, there's oil," I said dryly. "But you know how these things work here, the wealth is shared with the powerful, and very little, if anything, is allowed to trickle to the bottom."

In the new regime we were under, media stories circulated about exploitation by multinational oil corporations, government corruption, and mismanagement, and how the general's foreign investment account was overflowing with looted money.

"Also hear the Delta region has been suffering from environmental pollution due to oil drilling for decades," Sal continued, interrupting my thoughts.

I nodded.

"Shameful," he replied, "A perfect example of the destructive aspect of our age."

I said nothing to this as my mind drifted to our times in Greensberg, how we used to sit still in the school backyard to listen to the coos of various bird species. We had both expressed our love for birds. Then my elemental friends had frolicked in the grass and the bases of trees. The ability to see things like that had lately ceased. I had become increasingly ingrained in the world now. I barely even made time for the sunset, which I had accidentally noticed the day before resembled a dome-shaped furnace from the kitchen window at home.

I had become one of them. I had failed.

"How do you get all the money to travel?" I asked suddenly.

"Oh, the magazine pays for it."

I stood there, unable to move.

"Well, I will be heading to my hotel," Sal said, suddenly. "Send my regards to your. . . er. . . boyfriend."

I jolted out of my stupor as he set off to hail a taxi.

"I will follow you," I blurted out.

"Pardon?"

Gulp. "I mean, I don't know when I will see you again. You will be leaving soon, right?"

"Well, I still have a couple of weeks left."

"And they are going to be busy, that's what you said. For all we know this may be the last time we spend together."

It was as if another Ada was speaking, not the one I was familiar with.

"Well, it's still pretty early. How about dinner at the hotel?" he said after a few minutes.

"Perfect!" I said. "And you don't have to hail a taxi, I have a car."

"I didn't want to be presumptuous," he replied with a wry smile.

After filling our bellies with *fufu* and *egusi* soup and emptying a bottle of palm wine at the restaurant, I sat on a chair in his hotel room while he lounged on the bed. Let loose by the palm wine, we laughed so much during dinner that we were naturally inspired to continue our discussion upstairs.

"Nabukan food is superb."

"That's what you say of every food you eat," I teased.

It was no secret to anyone who knew Sal that he had a large appetite. Once while we were in Italy, I watched him gobble down three large whole pizzas in one sitting. He was fortunate the amount of food he consumed did not show up on his bones.

He laughed heartily at what I said. "So what, I appreciate all food."

"As a traveler, it is necessary," I added, smiling.

"I discovered some incredible people, scenery and food in Colombia, Peru, Brazil . . . "

"I hear there are some similarities with the food here, example plantain and rice and beans," I said, thinking back to a documentary I had watched on Latin culture recently.

"Oh yeah. I discovered okra stew in Brazil. It's called, Quiabo . . . and smoked fish. Very popular dishes here as well. So tasty! By the way, do you know how to cook?"

His gaze dimmed. A harmless flirtation, I thought. It doesn't matter if a man has a woman, there will always be other women at least of curiosity to him.

"I can, but he is the one that does most of the cooking," I said, referring to Obinna. Mentioning Obinna may have been a way of suppressing the thrill that unexpectedly surged through me when Sal dimmed his eyes. Yet the sudden thought of Obinna upset me after all he had done.

"I see," Sal said.

Silence. To break it he asked how Ma was doing. It was the third time he asked, twice during dinner. Perhaps it was because he had suddenly grown nervous with the mention of Obinna and needed to deflect. Perhaps he was worried. I told him Ma was fine, really. Then my mind wandered to the last time I had seen her, during Nne's burial. For Ma, the end of Afa had meant the end of everything to do with Nabuka. Maybe Sal was trying to tell me something, that it was perhaps time I see Ma again to make sure she was fine, alone.

During dinner he had told me his family was also doing well, Sophia was aging gracefully. One of her granddaughters had moved into the house with her to care for her. In that moment, I came to admire the close way he held everyone he loved so dear to him—his mother, his sister, his godmother Sophia, his colleagues. No matter how far his feet wandered, he never lost sight of the ones he loved. It differentiated him from his father.

After a considerably long silence, I brought up the topic of Stacey. She was constantly on my mind, especially with Sal around. I wondered about her, longed to hear her squeal, hear her talk dirty and say shocking and politically incorrect things. I longed to hear her say "chick" at least one more time. Longed to redo our very last conversation, this time being more supportive of her decision, even promising to visit and spend hot San Francisco nights sucking on a pipe or something.

"It would have been perfect if Stacey were with us now, wouldn't it?" I said dreamily. "I have a feeling she would have loved it here."

Sal lowered his gaze, "Yes, she would have. Here people are real. What you see is what you get."

"You are right about that. I wonder how she is faring in San Francisco. She is probably married with kids. Or maybe not, since . . ." I half said and scratched my head.

Sal looked up, a fresh wave of concern moving across his face.

"I guess no one told you."

"Told me what?"

I watched him slowly sit up from the bed. I watched him unable to maintain eye contact. I watched him fidget.

"Told me what?" I asked again. I could feel myself getting weaker, my senses growing duller, my heartbeat intensifying, the air being sucked out of my stomach.

It was happening again, this feeling, this very familiar feeling . . .

"Stacey never made it to San Francisco."

Please Lord, tell me it's because she decided to relocate elsewhere . . .

"Her bus, it . . . it . . . crashed."

"What?" I mouthed out loud.

I watched his face grow pale and squeeze up. He shook his head.

"I thought you knew. It was years ago that this happened, I thought you knew."

"But how was I supposed to know? Who would tell me? I have been away all this time."

"I'm sorry."

"My God!" I whispered, burying my head in my hands. Then sharply, I looked up at him. I searched for details, thinking perhaps some sense could be made of the horror of what I had just heard. He said Stacey had been the one driving the bus with four passengers in it. The bus was yellow, with green flowers, and a blue lake painted on both sides, and the words *Aquarian Dawn* inscribed on it. They were rammed into by a drunken trailer truck driver just outside San Francisco. Matt, Stacey's brother, had relayed this to him on his last trip to Greensberg, when he decided at the last minute to check on Stacey's family out of courtesy.

I searched his face for any signs I was either dreaming or he was playing some sick, twisted prank on me. But there was no such sign. Instead, he stood up, dragged me to the bed, and made me sit next to him. Then he held me. I hadn't been aware of how much I was trembling until I experienced his steady grip. I hadn't been aware of the tears that fell from my eyes either until I felt his fingers tenderly wipe them away.

In Sal's arms I pictured her panicking as the truck drew closer at an increasing speed towards their bus, the cries, the loudness of the impact, the way her body must have twisted up due to the impact, the pain afterward, the deep red color of life oozing out of her without mercy until she was forced to exit her body. My mind went back to our accident together when Ted's car had swerved and hit a tree on our way back from the Dope Fiend concert back in high school.

How did fate decide it was her turn to go now but not then?

She had invited me to go along with her to San Francisco. *I could have easily been on that bus.* And the passengers, I had met them before. They had shown up at the hospital the night of the ankle injury. A little frightened by the fragility of it all my heart bled for a soul whose life had only just begun. I was tempted to fold within myself and feel sorry for her, for me, for human life, but I would not weaken her image or memory. I would choose instead to hold the concept of her as the perfectly formed radiant spirit that she was.

Sal remained quiet until the sun retrieved most of its light. In the shadowy room, he rested his back on the bed, facing the ceiling, buried in his thoughts. I was now crouched on the floor, the upper part of my body leaning against the bed, close to his knee. We remained that way until I became aware of time closing in.

"I have to go," I said, rising from the floor.

He sprang from the bed and embraced me.

"It was nice seeing you," he whispered.

We remained that way for what seemed like an exceptionally long time, rubbing each other's backs. Perhaps it was Stacey's puckish spirit influencing the both of us, for the familiar nature scent and his body heat suddenly saturated my being, filling my senses in a way it hadn't done before. I felt his soft lips on my left cheek and then the right one. We faced each other, nose to nose, peering into each other's eyes. The expression in Afa is *Ahurum gi na anya.* I see you in the eye, I see you.

With Sal and I staring at each other, everything seemed to melt into one: past, present, future. My knees wobbled, my chest rose, and descended rapidly. I felt my eyes close, then his lips on mine, quivering at first, then confident and seeking. I felt so feeble, so weak, so caught up in his sweetness and strength that I finally surrendered to his hunger for me. He reached for my left breast and squeezed, the sensation producing sweet fire between my thighs. Then the telephone rang. It kept ringing, loud and insistent. I pulled away from him with all the strength I could muster.

"What are we doing?" I whispered.

"I don't know."

Finally, he got to the telephone to answer it, but by the time his fingers made contact with the receiver, the ringing had stopped.

"It was probably Maria," he said ruefully.

I quickly adjusted my shirt, picked up my purse from the ground, and told him I was headed home. He picked up a book from his bed and handed it to me. Khalil Gibran's *The Prophet.* I had returned his copy to him while in Italy. Now he was giving it back.

"I thought you should have it, this time for keeps," he said.

When I strolled into the living room twenty minutes later, I met Obinna slouched on the couch in a singlet and boxers. He appeared agitated. The smell of *iggbo* reigned once again in the living room, but I could tell he was no longer high by the clearness in his eyes.

"Where have you been? You won't believe it, but I saw a ghost moments ago."

"Huh?"

"That's right. A ghost, spirit, *mmuo* . . ."

"Where?" I asked, feigning interest.

"By the bedroom window. I saw a man. He had gunshot wounds all over his body. He kept muttering something about how the sun failed to rise. Even though I was smoking at the time, I know what I saw!"

I said nothing.

"Ada, do you think this area is haunted?"

"Obinna, I think you are just tired. You should get some rest," I replied.

My head was starting to throb, still reeling from the news of Stacey's death, and from Sal. I needed a good rest myself. Obinna rose up, standing inches away from me, his face growing hot with suspicion. He glared at me for a few moments.

"You never answered my question."

"I went out to see a friend."

"And you are just coming back now? How come you didn't tell me?"

It emerged, that unfailing companion, my temper.

"Look, you have no business asking me where I have been or who I have been with!"

"Someone told me they saw you with a white man. It had better not be that ex-lover of yours who sent you that letter you never shared with me!"

I scoffed and headed towards the bedroom.

"Ada, answer me!"

"Don't you dare talk to me that way, I have put up with your nonsense for so long, don't even dare it!"

"But you are living in my house!"

"As of today, I am not!"

Subdued, he wiped his face and stared at the floor. I retraced my steps to the front door.

"Where are you going?"

I slammed the door behind me.

How disrespectful, who does he think he is? I thought, fuming. I roamed the street like a woman with no purpose, made a left to another street, and made another right. It was dark, the streets empty. After a while of aimless walking, my knees grew weary. Dark clouds formed in the sky. The air grew pregnant with moisture. I scurried back home, thinking about the many ways I would tell Obinna that it was time for us to perhaps split ways and move on with our lives. As I rehearsed the speech in my head, I made out the outline of a lorry parked in front of the house. I heard strange gruff voices emanating through the white, peeled gate. The gate was slightly ajar. My stride suddenly weakened as I went through it and headed for the front door—the open front door. Three policemen stood brazenly inside the living room. Obinna was handcuffed in the corner and standing next to the burliest of the policemen. My heart leaped to my mouth. The words came out, barely a whisper.

"What's going on?"

"She no get anything to do with am, abeg leave am," Obinna responded automatically.

The burly policeman glared at me.

"What's going on?" I asked again.

"Your husband here . . ." It was the same burly man with bumpy skin, who I now discovered had a stale mouth odor that reminded me of sewage. ". . .is being arrested for conspiracy against the government and for trespassing."

My lips flung open, hoping for the part where everyone would roll on the floor and say it was an April Fool's joke, even though it wasn't April, and no one seemed to be laughing.

"We are not married!" Obinna shouted.

"So who is she to you?" the officer demanded.

Obinna looked at me, his eyes pleading.

"Ada, why don't you go to your house, eh . . . go," he said. His eyes motioned for me to move, but my legs couldn't move. All I could feel was the rising sound beneath my chest.

"What are you going to do to him?" I asked in a shaky voice.

"Woman you better go, or else you will be carried off with him!" the burly policeman shouted as the two others arranged themselves in a position where they could easily latch on to me.

"Okay, I will go," I finally said.

With my gaze, I communicated with Obinna as best as I could that I would be there for him.

I left the house that night with my body and spirit feeling heavy with something strange and ominous, something unrecognizable. Once outside, the clouds pushed and gave birth to rain. I was immediately convinced that this day was, as written in the stars, destined to be one of the most wretched days of my life.

I thought about returning inside to retrieve the Audi but was afraid the policemen would see me. I thought of a few people I could stay with for the night. The Onyeagalis, who occasionally supplied Obinna and me with oranges and mangoes from their bountiful garden. But at this time of the night, they had to be asleep. A couple of other people came to mind, but I wasn't sure I could trust them to remain discreet after everything had settled. It was fair to say that I had significant trust issues.

My clothes latched on rapidly to my flesh. How and why would Obinna do this to me? What was I supposed to do now? And then I thought about him being roughed up by the police and felt guilty for my selfish thoughts. I hoped they weren't hurting him. I hoped he wasn't talking back to them. I was tempted to go back again but decided against it. Then I thought of Sal. In the pouring rain, I rummaged through my purse for his hotel room telephone number when *The Prophet* went crashing to the ground. Groaning, I picked up the soaking book when from within its scattered pages, a hotel key fell out. Shocked, I made sure to insert the key carefully into my bag.

Shivering from the growing cold, I stomped on the rising waters for several miles in search of a taxi until I spotted an *okada* speeding by. I waved at him to stop. Grudgingly he stopped his motorcycle, agreeing to drop me at my destination. I had only soggy cash to give him after we arrived at the hotel.

"Sorry sir, today has been a rough day,"

He gave me a disgruntled look and rode off without saying a word.

I rushed in, noticing the male receptionist respond with a seedy grin at my nipples protruding from my soaked shirt. I hissed under my breath, heading to Sal's room without stopping by the desk. I knocked on his door a few times, no answer. I felt my head reeling. I needed to sit down and think. Ignoring protocol, I swiped the key through the lock and entered the room.

"Sal! Sal!" I called, encircling the room, then to the balcony. But there was no sign of him except for a used towel on a rumpled bed. I was about to give up my luck when I heard a groan in the direction of the bathroom. I walked towards it, my heart rising to my mouth. He was crouched on the floor, behind the open door, staring at me in a befuddled state. I stooped to face him. His breath reeked of red wine. Imagine that. My mate and my lover both broken. *What did that say of me?*

Sal continued to stare at me as if in a lucid dream. Finally, he said, "You had my key, huh?"

"You left it in the book," I said.

"Oh, I see. I need to get up from here."

I helped him rise from the tiled floor and led him to the bed.

"I can't marry her. I don't love her," he slurred and paused. "I love you."

My heart stopped. "You need to sleep," I finally replied. I didn't want to deal with his confession, especially now that Obinna needed me.

"Stay."

"I will be here, I promise."

He studied my face in a drunken haze. I took off his shoes, unbuttoned the top part of his shirt, and moved the blanket up to his chest. He stared at me like a puppy not wishing to part from its mother.

"I will be here," I whispered in his ear to reassure him. I flicked off the light switch. I dashed straight for the balcony, glad for the recliners which appeared cozy and inviting. They felt a little damp from the splatter of rain, which at this point had ceased. I quickly plopped myself on one of the cushioned seats. As I unzipped my damp purse, my hands shaky and clammy. I motioned my palms against my pants before releasing a pack buried in the pile of keys, stuffed napkins, pens, business cards, and other going-through-life collectables. It still smelled fresh, tingly, herbal, like smoked dried leaves. The lighter had been tucked in its usual spot, in the box, cornered, beside its companions. With urgency, I placed the orange end of a stick between my eager lips. I sparked the other end with the rushing yellow flame induced by my fingers on the lighter. I took a long drag. I felt it, the smoke travel through my head, clearing the murmur. I fully adjusted my back against the chair.

I WOKE UP TO THE SOUND of my name. I had slept off on the recliner on the balcony. The sun had risen, placid and soothing as if apologizing for what the rain had caused earlier. Sal was standing by the drapes, dressed in fresh clothes, a vintage soccer shirt and knickers, his hair still wet from an apparent shower. He avoided eye contact.

"Sorry about last night."

I gave myself a moment to recall the events of the previous night before responding.

"I didn't know you drank like *that.*"

His face turned red. "I don't."

He continued to face the floor. I got up and headed for the bathroom. He trailed behind.

"What brought you here last night?"

I sighed as I lathered my face over the sink with the hotel soap.

"It's a long story."

He studied me for a while.

"Does it have to do with your . . . boyfriend?"

I dried my face with one of the fresh white towels hanging by the rail and faced him.

"I promise to tell you about it later, right now . . . I just . . . I don't know." My voice quivered.

"Hey . . ." he rushed forward and embraced me. "We can always talk about it later."

In his arms, I experienced a feeling of security that I hadn't felt in quite some time.

"Why do I treat you badly?" I asked.

"Maybe it's just you attempting to treat yourself well."

"You are too good to me . . ."

"Perhaps it's me just being good to myself."

My lips touched his, tasting the lingering Colgate in his mouth. We stayed kissing for several minutes, his gentle palm cupping my face. I could feel the fiery beat of his heart against my raging pulse. I needed to feel full, to feel whole, at least for a little while.

"Make love to me," I whispered.

He didn't hesitate this time around. Acting like a man on the verge of a desperate odyssey, he lifted me and placed me on the bed. Then he released me of my shirt and pants while feverishly planting my body with wet kisses. He kissed my stomach, kissed me between my slender thighs until I thought I would melt, and then one we became. The sweetest sensation swept through me.

Drunk with this sweetness, I flipped him over. Panting heavily, we made love repeatedly, each time bringing more ecstasy than the one before. All the years of desiring each other culminated into that moment. Compared to Obinna, making love to Sal felt like a sacred journey to each other's souls. With Obinna, it was a fulfilling passionate ritual. With Sal, it felt like the most important event of our lives.

Finally, we lay side by side, exhausted. For a moment, I forgot everything else. I was flying across the sky with a man who made me want to unravel the gift I was to the planet. But then he ruined the moment.

Acting as a man possessed, he blurted, "Sometimes I swear I am under a spell because every time I try to forget you, I can't, I just can't."

His words brought me back to our past, to the present predicament, to Obinna.

Purely naked, he rose from the bed and headed for the bathroom. With trepidation, I scooped out a cigarette from my purse, placed it between my lips, lit up, and began to inhale and exhale. It did nothing. Instead, tears trickled down my cheeks, free flowing with no intention to be stifled. Tears at the type of person I had become—reckless, desperate—and at the words just spoken, "I try to forget you . . ."

It played repeatedly in my head. What had I done? He had gotten to that point. I let him get to that point. I heard the trickle of his piss as it went into the toilet bowl. I heard the toilet flush, the faucet come on then off, before he emerged from the bathroom with a towel wrapped around his waist. He paused after noticing the cigarette then sat on the edge of the bed.

"So, what are your plans?" he said stiffly.

I covered my breasts with my left arm. What the hell was I doing in this hotel room? Obinna had just been arrested, and it took me less than a day to make love to another man?

More tears fell. He didn't notice. He usually noticed everything, and he didn't even notice this.

"Going home," I replied, my voice low and shaky.

"Cool. It was nice seeing you, Ada."

I threw a pillow at him. "Go to hell!"

I got up, flung the cigarette to the side, swiftly put on my clothes, and dashed towards the door. But I wasn't fast enough. He stomped the cigarette with his barefoot like a superhero, rushed forward, and grabbed me by the arm.

"*Hapurum aka*! Let me go!"

"Are you okay?"

"I have never needed anyone, and it is not now I will start doing so!"

I opened the door. He closed and then locked it. With his thumb, he wiped the tears from my cheeks. He kissed my forehead, my nose, and my lips. He leaned his forehead against mine.

"Would it be wrong if I said I didn't want you with him?"

"But you have someone yourself."

"There's no comparison, there can never be. All you have to do is say the word and she's gone."

I said nothing, only sniffed.

"Remember we talked about passion."

I nodded.

"My passion is you."

I gulped, tasting more of the salty tears in my mouth. I wanted to say something similarly sweet but didn't know what. So many conflicting thoughts darted through my head.

"Marry me."

"Don't be silly," I chuckled sadly.

"Why?" he asked, pushing his head back.

I wanted to tell him the truth about the true nature of my relationship with Obinna but instead uttered a quasi-truth. "I'm not sure I believe in marriage." I watched him ponder before adding, "You are not ready to get married either. You are just trying to keep me close by."

"Whatever it takes," he admitted. "But I also believe marriage goes beyond the institution. That at this moment, here and now, we can be married and are already married," he said softly.

I knew his mind had wandered to that night, that special night, in Tuscany. I looked to the side and shook my head.

"This is a bad time to be having this type of conversation," I said and sighed.

"Why?"

"Obinna has been arrested."

He took a step away from me.

"Why?"

"For conspiring against the government."

"What?"

"It doesn't even make sense. I need to get the details myself. I don't know if he is safe. I am afraid for him."

He held me to his chest. "Above all things, I am your friend. I will be there for you because I understand where you've been, where you are."

I wasn't sure what he meant, but I said nothing as I rested my head on his shoulder. He too said nothing for a while.

I found the ebbing movement of his breaths to be like oceanic waves beneath the moonlight. It reminded me of the mother I never had, the mother I should have had, or a mother that I had but I wasn't aware of. Finally, when he spoke again, his voice was low, so low I had to truly listen.

"Ever since I was a child, I have been looking for something . . . I am forever searching for something I can believe in, something I can hold on to, a world I can claim is mine. You know you can travel places to escape, but you can never escape your own shadow." He paused for a moment. Then even more slowly, he continued, "I have never felt I belonged, never felt understood, never felt I was seen, until I met you . . ."

I looked into his eyes and noticed fluid darkness I had never seen before.

"Sal . . ."

His eyes grew even more watery. He was more fragile than I realized.

I pressed my nose against his. "It's okay," I said. "You are not alone in this. Truly."

He smiled solemnly, almost tragically.

Hours later, we lounged on the balcony, the nocturnal sky draped in an infinite number of stars, the evening breeze creating a sacred ambiance around us. He was going to be leaving for Italy in a matter of days. Our time together was valuable.

"Sal . . ."

"Yes?"

"Do you believe in destiny?"

"I believe that everything happens for a reason. I believe that the universe is that precise. Why do you ask?"

"A strange woman told me some time ago that I couldn't be fully happy in this world because I straddled two worlds and . . ." I recalled what she had said specifically about the prophet and my refusal to listen to him.

"Sal, what page was your key in *The Prophet*?" I asked abruptly.

"Guess?"

I smiled faintly and quickly wrapped up the story.

Later, when Sal was resting in bed, I escaped to the bathroom with *The Prophet.* Under the bathroom light, I read softly, out loud, the passage on love he had wobbly underlined with red ink, the lines I had scanned numerous times but obstinately refused to ponder upon because I felt it required too much.

Love gives naught but itself and takes
Naught but from itself
Love possesses not nor would it be possessed
For love is sufficient unto love

When you love you should not say, "God is in my heart," but rather, "I am in the heart of God."

And think not you can direct the course of love, for love, if it finds you worthy,

Directs your course . . .

SHUFFLED SOUNDS. I DROPPED THE BOOK and turned around, surprised to see him up close, a half-smile and a fiery glow in his eyes. From behind he shoved his hand under my shirt and grabbed my bra strap. I felt the moisture between my legs, felt myself dissolving. I thought I was going to die. It was all too much.

"Sal . . . please . . . not now," I pleaded.

He kissed me tenderly on the lips, let go of my strap, and returned to bed.

Facing the bathroom sink, I hunched over and sighed.

THAT NIGHT WE MOSTLY STAYED UP, restless in bed, each of us tormented by our thoughts, our ravaging demons. I kept replaying our passionate encounter, the desperation, and hunger that came with it, the feeling that we had both needed it to keep living. Even though destiny seemed to be pointing us towards each other, I felt guilty for the act and that I was still in his bed. The guilt was strong enough to keep me at bay. I was an adulteress, like one of those lonely, unscrupulous housewives you find in soap operas. This was no longer about what Obinna had or hadn't done. It was now about me, what I had done, what I had become. Ma was right, I was better than this.

By the following morning, I had decided on my next course of action. I was going to return home, retrieve my car and visit Obinna at the federal prison. I had hand-washed my muggy clothes from the day before and left them to dry in the bathroom rail. In the meantime, Sal had let me wear one of his shirts and ordered room service for us when the hunger pangs came. That morning after breakfast I dialed Ma. We hadn't spoken in several weeks though I suspected she might have tried calling me more than a few times. For the first time in a long time, I perceived slight tremors in her voice.

"How are you, eh?"

"I am fine."

"And how is Obinna?" she asked, rather reluctantly.

"He's fine," I lied. I couldn't bring myself to tell her what had transpired even though that was the initial reason for the call. I was afraid the response would be *I told you that man was a waste of time.*

"I was just calling to check on you Ma. I promise to visit soon."

She sighed with relief.

"Yes, it is about time."

"Ma . . . em, are you okay?"

"Well, I did get engaged," she said.

In an instant, something fell away, something that enabled me to breathe easier. Later I would realize it was guilt—this stuffed feeling I had carried for leaving her behind in the United States despite Ben's instructions.

"Congrats, Ma!"

"His name is Doctor Iheanyi Iroegbu. I met him at a medical conference in New Jersey and we will be moving to California once I sell the house. Hopefully, you will meet him," she said cheerfully.

"Yes, Ma," I said and smiled softly.

"How is Ogu?"

"Changing like everything else but still managing to be the same."

I had recently heard from Oluchi that there were now talks of building a hotel near the town square to the resistance of some of the elders who feared the possibility of strange visitors polluting their way of life. While others argued that it would create more jobs, and encourage more roads and, potentially skyscrapers, as Ogu with its endless red sands and forestry was fast becoming a reflection of an outdated era.

I added, "Perhaps one day you will change your mind later and retire there, live in Nne's house."

She was quiet for a long time, so long that I wondered if she was still on the line.

Finally, she said, "Ada, even though your life did not go in the direction I had planned, I still think you should finish university or college and Lord knows, do so many other things differently . . . I have to say you have proven to be strong and independent, which is what Ekene women are known for."

"Thanks, Ma," I replied meekly.

If she only knew about Sal hunting me down in Nabuka, about my current love troubles. If she only knew how truly an Ekene woman I was.

After our goodbyes, I called out to Sal, who had been awkwardly toying with the toiletries in the bathroom. He stepped out meekly. I told him it was time for me to go home and face things.

"Ada, I'm sorry if you feel like I am pressuring you. I should be more understanding of your relationship . . ."

"I love you," I said.

His face brightened like a sudden burst of sunlight.

"However," I continued before he could get too excited, "I also love someone else, and I have to make sure he is okay."

He responded with a single, heavy nod.

Chapter Twenty-Four

July 1975

I WOULDN'T LET SAL ESCORT ME home, out of respect for Obinna. However, I let him order a car service to drop me off at my destination. Once home, one of the first things I did was dial Obinna's family to deliver the news to them. His mother lamented. His father gnashed his teeth.

"My boy is going to be released. I will do everything in my power!" his father bellowed in my eardrums.

That afternoon, I drove to the federal prison, but the authorities were very resistant about providing information in the absence of a bribe.

"But that is crazy!" I shouted to the police officer who stood above me in a gritty, small, office space.

"Madam, at least fifty pounds and you can see him."

"I am not going to give you fifty pounds to visit an inmate. That is not constitutional," I said.

I heard an officer chuckle in the background at the word, "constitutional."

The heavyset officer's cheeks began to puff up.

"He is a criminal and a trespasser. He doesn't deserve to be visited!"

"Criminal? What did he steal? Whose land did he trespass?" I shouted. "Tell me!"

The chuckling officer showed up behind me. He was about the same size as the first one.

"Madam, you have to leave. You are disturbing the peace!"

I turned around and glared at him, and then at the first officer, before storming off.

My fingers trembled on the steering wheel as I drove back home. I thought about Obinna, and how he was being treated. I wondered if he was eating enough, if his rights were being respected. In my worried state I did not notice right away the pile of garbage on a side street. It took a few moments for what resembled the stench of rotten eggs combined with urine to hit me. I quickly geared the car away from the garbage, holding my breath. Thinking of Obinna, I stopped the car on the side of the street, broke down, and wept.

IN A PERIOD THAT STRETCHED INTO days, I contacted friends, colleagues, and former co-workers to inquire about Obinna's underground activities. They had no answer. I ended up having to reassure the ones who had become worried. I scanned through the phone book that he kept underneath the telephone. Dead ends.

I was about to give up when a number I had accidentally omitted suddenly piqued my interest. I dialed it. A man answered. I narrated the ordeal, proceeding immediately to the follow-up inquiry. He revealed to me in hushed tones that Obinna had been involved in an underground group that advocated the actualization of a separate Afa nation. This was what Obinna had told him and that was all he knew. Shocked, I thanked him profusely before ending the call. So that was what Obinna's covert behavior had been all about? But why hadn't he shared this with me? It suddenly hit me. Of course, he could not. In many ways, my nationalism represented everything he stood against.

As I ransacked my brain for solutions, I recalled the last words Obinna's father had said. He mentioned he would do everything in his power to release his son. By power, I now understood he meant, in part, money.

I was beginning to have a better understanding of money, why people like Ma believed in it, spent their entire existence in pursuit of it. Why many sold their souls for it, died for it, killed for it. Money was a powerful force. It paved the way, opened doors, made things happen. It was the secret and open ruler of the world.

That night, I put aside fifty pounds. I had no choice but to give the prison officials what they wanted. Initially, I had considered not giving them the money as a way of rebelling against the system, but I needed to see Obinna. In the end, Obinna's wellbeing was worth more than my scruples and activism.

The following afternoon, after paying the required amount to the seedy policeman, I finally got to see Obinna, problem solved. We met in a small room, a grubby table between us. A warden stood in the distance as we talked. Obinna looked noticeably emaciated in the few days he had been held. But his spirit was unbroken, in fact, contrary to my expectations, he appeared more resolute than ever. He was glad to see me, said I looked beautiful. I watched him devour very quickly the rice and chicken stew I had brought for him in a flask. After eating, I gave him a hard curious stare.

"I know you are wondering why I am here."

"I know why you are here. I just don't know why you are here."

He stared at me for a while before nodding. He understood what I meant.

"I was caught canvassing for our people's right to self-governance. Someone whose compound I had supposedly trespassed and who did not agree with what I was doing called the police. A robbery had occurred a few days earlier in that area. They used that as a perfect opportunity to indict me."

I wanted to say something in the line of, "Our people's right to self-governance? Get over it Obinna, we already lost, and we lost big."

Instead I said, "But that's not fair especially since there is no evidence."

"Ada, there is no fairness for the common man in this country."

Perhaps he was right. But wasn't that the case in every other place in the world?

"How are the conditions?" I asked.

"I share a tiny room with several other men. We share a bucket where we take care of our business. I eat one slimy meal a day."

It took a lot of strength not to break down in tears, not to pull my hair out and condemn the prison officials for their disregard of human life. He wanted to be strong, needed to be strong, and it was my duty to be strong with him.

I let him know his family was aware of his situation.

"Thank you," he said somberly.

"When is your trial?" I asked.

"I don't know."

We both shuffled in our seats. Our time together was nearing its end. He grabbed my right hand and stroked it. He peered into my eyes. "Ada," he quivered, "do you still love me?"

I flinched and quickly averted my gaze. When I heard a faint groan from him, I wished to replay my reaction to something more amicable. It was too late. I felt like Judas.

"Obinna, I . . ."

"Please," he said tenderly. "Let me speak. Allow me to apologize for all the pain I caused you."

I stared into his eyes, wishing I had done that much sooner.

"Obinna, you have nothing to be sorry about. You've always been yourself with me. I should be sorry. I did something wrong. I . . ."

"Our marriage. Was it real?"

With shock I whispered, "What do you mean?"

"You know what I mean. There was no family. No witnesses. No gift giving. Plus, we did everything in our power to make sure we had no children."

I looked away and reflected on what he said before speaking.

"But Obinna, it still doesn't excuse . . ."

"As long as you are happy, as long as you promise me to always be honest with yourself, to always be the person you were meant to be, that is all that matters," he said, his voice strong and defensive.

I had wanted to tell him about Sal, about everything that had transpired. But he seemed to be in denial about what he already knew. To hear it from me would have forced him to confront that denial, and that, I realized, was the worst thing I could do at that moment.

The warden's footsteps got louder. Our session was over.

When I walked into the living room, the telephone was ringing. It was Sal. He said he had called a few times earlier to inform me that he was leaving for Italy then the United States to visit his family, and to make sure that I was okay. I told him I would remain in Nabuka until Obinna was out of prison. There was a long pause. Then he confessed in a trembling voice that he wanted to stay behind and be with me and love me with every part of himself. I wanted him to stay too, to hold me in his tender way during these trying times, and to love him back the way he deserved. Instead, I told him that I needed to be single and alone for a while. I felt his heart drop. Quickly, I reminded him that if distance had not managed to erode our bond in the past, why would it do so now? He paused for a while before promising to visit again soon—after a trip to South America for some work-related assignment.

After the call, I burst into tears. The house felt so empty of life, of meaning, with Obinna absent. My heart was shattered, abandoned, with Sal gone. Loneliness attached itself to me like a newly acquired shadow. On the sofa, letters from the landlady requesting rent. We were falling short. Maybe I should have asked Obinna's father for money. Surely, he would have given it to me, I thought. However, I couldn't bring myself to do so. It would hurt Obinna's pride deeply.

I needed some relief, something quick and timely. But I had no more cigarettes. I had exhausted the last one two nights prior when I couldn't sleep, swearing it would be my last. Filled with renewed grief, I lay across the carpeted floor and closed my eyes.

Nne's words hit me then. I had known for a long time—I was not alone. I felt so helpless that I was willing to try anything, including praying in a way that I had never done before.

There comes a time when one must let go and surrender to the will of forces beyond their control. I did just that.

"Show me a sign that I am still a part of you. Show me a sign that I am not forgotten, that nothing takes place without your awareness, that I am your child," I whispered to the night air from the depths of despair. I remained in a fetal position until, like a much-needed blanket covering, I was enveloped in darkness.

DEEP IN THE NIGHT, I SLID out from what ended up being a sleep state and dragged myself to the bathroom to wash my face as was my custom before going to bed. The tap running as I washed my hands in the cool, moonlit space, I was inspired to look out the window when I saw her—a woman with a timeless face and a serene countenance. Nne? Could it be? She was by a palm tree and yet seemed to be the tree and the space surrounding it—the branches, the trunks, and the fronds were interwoven with the reddish hue of her skin. It was only for a moment, the vision, but it was enough for me to know. Suddenly, I felt compelled, powerfully compelled to reach for my notebook.

Abandoning my face, I rushed to the bedroom and retrieved the book from the bedside drawer, the ethereal feel in the air still with me. I could hear the words from deep within me: Write what you see . . .

I wrote.

I see an age where the noblest of dreams become reality, where equality is fully realized regardless of caste, race, gender, or sexual orientation, where true escapism becomes the window to opportunity, where light is the only thing we acknowledge, and the truth is allowed to redeem us.

Dare to believe what you see . . .

I dared to believe Obinna would be released soon because he had power on his side, that I would be free to love, and that this time I would fully pursue my destiny, adding to the highest destiny of the world.

Then, exhaling, I ceased all thought and released all concept of time to the nothingness that had remained.

A few moments later, a slight wind brushed against my cheeks, and I heard giggles seep through the pores of the air . . .

I exhaled with the spirits of dreams.

In my dreams, the kiss of morning breath met my eyes, followed by three desperate and urgent knocks on the gate. I got up from the floor. The hardness of the floor had created soreness in my spine. But it did not matter, for in my heart was a sweet feeling, a feeling of something familiar, something special being near. I opened the gate, and there he was standing, the streetlight mingled with morning light illuminating his brown hair, his beige skin, his old soccer shirt, that same one from Coral High. Stuck and stuffed with too many words, my mouth barely opened and closed.

In my waking he remained standing. His eyes on fire, aimed at mine. His face hardened like a stone settled in time. I knew then that he wasn't going anywhere, nowhere where I wasn't in sight anyway. And no words or prodding of mine could move this pillar of flesh off my driveway. And in all the ways imaginable, secretly, and deeply, I was grateful.

About the Author

Ebele Chizea was born in Nigeria and moved to the United States at age sixteen. Since graduating with honors in 2004 from Thiel Colege in Greenville, PA, she has published fiction, poetry, and essays in various publications including *The African, The Sentinel, The Nigerian Punch, Sahara Reporter,* as well as her own online publication, *Drumtide Magazine,* which featured interviews with prominent figures in the entertainment and literary fields including Afro-punk pioneer Lunden DeLeon, afrobeat musician Seun Kuti, and award-winning Nigerian Belgian novelist, Chika Unigwe. She is the author of *How to Slay in Life: A Book of Proverbial Wisdom. Aquarian Dawn* is her debut novel. She currently lives in Santa Monica, CA.

RECENT AND FORTHCOMING BOOKS FROM THREE ROOMS PRESS

FICTION

Lucy Jane Bledsoe
No Stopping Us Now

Rishab Borah
The Door to Inferna

Meagan Brothers
Weird Girl and What's His Name

Christopher Chambers
Scavenger
Standalone

Ebele Chizea
Aquarian Dawn

Ron Dakron
Hello Devilfish!

Robert Duncan
Loudmouth

Michael T. Fournier
Hidden Wheel
Swing State

Aaron Hamburger
Nirvana Is Here

William Least Heat-Moon
Celestial Mechanics

Aimee Herman
Everything Grows

Kelly Ann Jacobson
Tink and Wendy
Robin and Her Misfits

Jethro K. Lieberman
Everything Is Jake

Eamon Loingsigh
Light of the Diddicoy
Exile on Bridge Street

John Marshall
The Greenfather

Aram Saroyan
Still Night in L.A.

Robert Silverberg
The Face of the Waters

Stephen Spotte
Animal Wrongs

Richard Vetere
The Writers Afterlife
Champagne and Cocaine

Jessamyn Violet
Secret Rules to Being a Rockstar

Julia Watts
Quiver
Needlework

Gina Yates
Narcissus Nobody

MEMOIR & BIOGRAPHY

Nassrine Azimi and Michel Wasserman
Last Boat to Yokohama: The Life and Legacy of Beate Sirota Gordon

William S. Burroughs & Allen Ginsberg
Don't Hide the Madness: William S. Burroughs in Conversation with Allen Ginsberg edited by Steven Taylor

James Carr
BAD: The Autobiography of James Carr

Judy Gumbo
Yippie Girl: Exploits in Protest and Defeating the FBI

Judith Malina
Full Moon Stages: Personal Notes from 50 Years of The Living Theatre

Phil Marcade
Punk Avenue: Inside the New York City Underground, 1972–1982

Jililian Marshall
Japanthem: Counter-Cultural Experiences; Cross-Cultural Remixes

Alvin Orloff
Disasterama! Adventures in the Queer Underground 1977–1997

Nicca Ray
Ray by Ray: A Daughter's Take on the Legend of Nicholas Ray

Stephen Spotte
My Watery Self: Memoirs of a Marine Scientist

PHOTOGRAPHY-MEMOIR

Mike Watt
On & Off Bass

SHORT STORY ANTHOLOGIES

SINGLE AUTHOR

The Alien Archives: Stories
by Robert Silverberg

First-Person Singularities: Stories
by Robert Silverberg
with an introduction by John Scalzi

Tales from the Eternal Café: Stories
by Janet Hamill, with an introduction by Patti Smith

Time and Time Again: Sixteen Trips in Time
by Robert Silverberg

Voyagers: Twelve Journeys in Space and Time
by Robert Silverberg

MULTI-AUTHOR

Crime + Music: Twenty Stories of Music-Themed Noir
edited by Jim Fusilli

Dark City Lights: New York Stories
edited by Lawrence Block

The Faking of the President: Twenty Stories of White House Noir
edited by Peter Carlaftes

Florida Happens: Bouchercon 2018 Anthology
edited by Greg Herren

Have a NYC I, II & III: New York Short Stories;
edited by Peter Carlaftes & Kat Georges

No Body No Crime: 22 Stories of Taylor Swift-Inspired Noir
edited by Alex Segura and Joe Clifford

Songs of My Selfie: An Anthology of Millennial Stories
edited by Constance Renfrow

The Obama Inheritance: 15 Stories of Conspiracy Noir
edited by Gary Phillips

This Way to the End Times: Classic and New Stories of the Apocalypse
edited by Robert Silverberg

MIXED MEDIA

John S. Paul
Sign Language: A Painter's Notebook (photography, poetry and prose)

HUMOR

Peter Carlaftes
A Year on Facebook

DADA

Maintenant: A Journal of Contemporary Dada Writing & Art (Annual, since 2008)

FILM & PLAYS

Israel Horovitz
My Old Lady: Complete Stage Play and Screenplay with an Essay on Adaptation

Peter Carlaftes
Triumph For Rent (3 Plays)
Teatrophy (3 More Plays)

Kat Georges
Three Somebodies: Plays about Notorious Dissidents

TRANSLATIONS

Thomas Bernhard
On Earth and in Hell
(poems of Thomas Bernhard with English translations by Peter Waugh)

Patrizia Gattaceca
Isula d'Anima / Soul Island
(poems by the author in Corsican with English translations)

César Vallejo | Gerard Malanga
Malanga Chasing Vallejo
(selected poems of César Vallejo with English translations and additional notes by Gerard Malanga)

George Wallace
EOS: Abductor of Men
(selected poems in Greek & English)

ESSAYS

Richard Katrovas
Raising Girls in Bohemia: Meditations of an American Father

Far Away From Close to Home
Vanessa Baden Kelly

Womentality: Thirteen Empowering Stories by Everyday Women Who Said Goodbye to the Workplace and Hello to Their Lives
edited by Erin Wildermuth

POETRY COLLECTIONS

Hala Alyan
Atrium

Peter Carlaftes
DrunkYard Dog
I Fold with the Hand I Was Dealt

Thomas Fucaloro
It Starts from the Belly and Blooms

Kat Georges
Our Lady of the Hunger

Robert Gibbons
Close to the Tree

Israel Horovitz
Heaven and Other Poems

David Lawton
Sharp Blue Stream

Jane LeCroy
Signature Play

Philip Meersman
This Is Belgian Chocolate

Jane Ormerod
Recreational Vehicles on Fire
Welcome to the Museum of Cattle

Lisa Panepinto
On This Borrowed Bike

George Wallace
Poppin' Johnny

Three Rooms Press | New York, NY | Current Catalog: www.threeroomspress.com

Three Rooms Press books are distributed by Publishers Group West: www.pgw.com

CPSIA information can be obtained
at www.ICGtesting.com
Printed in the USA
BVHW081508260422
635314BV00004B/13